LOSS OF MEMORY
IS ONLY TEMPORARY

ALSO BY JOHANNA KAPLAN

Other People's Lives (1975)

O My America! (1980)

ECCO ART OF THE STORY

LOSS OF MEMORY
IS ONLY TEMPORARY

STORIES

JOHANNA KAPLAN

LOSS OF MEMORY IS ONLY TEMPORARY. Copyright © 2022 by Johanna Kaplan. All rights reserved. Printed in the United States of America. No part of this book may be used or reproduced in any manner whatsoever without written permission except in the case of brief quotations embodied in critical articles and reviews. For information, address HarperCollins Publishers, 195 Broadway, New York, NY 10007.

HarperCollins books may be purchased for educational, business, or sales promotional use. For information, please email the Special Markets Department at SPsales@harpercollins.com.

Ecco® and HarperCollins® are trademarks of HarperCollins Publishers.

FIRST EDITION

Designed by Angela Boutin

Library of Congress Cataloging-in-Publication Data has been applied for.

ISBN 978-0-06-306163-7

22 23 24 25 26   LSC   10 9 8 7 6 5 4 3 2 1

CONTENTS

PREFACE

BY FRANCINE PROSE

Since its initial publication, in 1975, the hardbound first edition of Johanna Kaplan's *Other People's Lives* has accompanied me through several cross-country moves and has easily survived any number of bookshelf culls: those pyrrhic victories in the struggle for space between the books and the humans. Because I have so frequently reread it for pleasure and inspiration, *Other People's Lives* has become a book that I cannot imagine living without.

These beautifully written stories—with the addition of "Tales of My Great-Grandfathers" and "Family Obligations" now included in this volume—have retained all their freshness, depth, and humor, their paradoxically scathing and compassionate insight into character and behavior. They continue to surprise me, on this most recent rereading with intimations of what I was too young to understand or imagine, the first or second or even the third time I read them: the magic trick that time can perform within a single life span, turning the known world into a lost world, transforming a city and its people into a new city full of strangers whose lives continue to be shaped by many—if not all—of the same desires, dreams, hopes, and fears.

At once precisely specific to a particular period, place, and milieu—New York in the decades after World War II, among Jews who have themselves fled Hitler's Europe or who live among refugee relatives or neighbors—these stories also describe the all-too-common (perhaps universal) discovery that the world doesn't warmly embrace the kind of girl who sees more than the people around her would prefer her to notice. Kaplan's smart, uneasy, cranky heroines remind me of Jane Eyre, but even more of myself as a child: listening to the grown-ups' conversation and to its simultaneous translation, the commentary inaudible to anyone but myself, the background chatter that combined a know-it-all, eye-rolling superiority with existential dread.

The hissing of the radiators that Miriam—home from school with the measles—hears in "Sickness" is my Proustian madeleine. These high school girls in these stories dress (or are expected to dress) the way girls dressed in my high school: "long hair, dangling earrings, Mexican serapes, and chunky leather sandals." ("Babysitting")

The experience of these characters, their language and their interior voices, so closely resemble what I remember that reading these stories is, for me, like looking at a family photo album with all the transfixed fascination and none (or almost none) of the nostalgia and grief. They remind me, all too clearly, of what it was like to be young: to feel that I existed on sufferance, that clear-sightedness was not a gift but a burden, that the people around me were more or less untrustworthy and hopelessly benighted; I remember how it felt to wish, as does one of Kaplan's characters, that I could follow a family glimpsed on a city bus—and exchange my life for theirs.

When these quiet, deceptively complicit young women speak their minds, the result can be deflating, hilarious, and thrilling.

Here, for example, is one of the barbed, satisfying exchanges between the adolescent heroine of "Babysitting" and Ted Marshak, the famous, self-important, self-infatuated poet whose children—Sascha and Pietro—the babysitter has been hired to mind. Returning from a trip to Milwaukee, Ted tells his kids,

> "Daddy saw Grandma, and Daddy saw Aunt Marilyn, and Daddy brought you two presents." He unzipped the duffel bag and took out two matching sailor-style playsuits with the price tags still attached, and several large wrapped packages.
>
> "Guess which is from Grandma and which is from Aunt Marilyn." His voice had become very cocky; he was not talking to his children, but to me.
>
> "And look what Grandma sent for Mommy! Another present!" Out of the duffel bag came a two-pound box of chocolate mint creams and a small bottle of dietetic French dressing. "My mother," he said. "Jesus Christ. My mother."
>
> "I guess I'll go," I said. "As long as you're home, they don't need a babysitter."
>
> "Wait a minute, I'll walk you to the subway. I have to get cigarettes."
>
> "Are you going to leave them alone?"
>
> "For five minutes? To get cigarettes? Are you my mother?"
>
> "No," I said. "I'm your Aunt Marilyn."

Like "Babysitting," the novella-length "Other People's Lives" transpires mostly in one of the rambling, going-to-seed apartments of the pregentrified Upper West Side, steps away from Broadway, where the benches on the median island were, in those days, the domain of old ladies who looked just like my grandmother except for the numbers tattooed on their forearms. In those postwar years, the catastrophe in Europe was intensely present for us, as it is for the characters in these fictions; history informs everything, in complex, unpredictable ways. In the nerdy Zionist summer camp where "Sour or Suntanned, It Makes No Difference" is set, the young campers celebrate Parents Day by staging a musical production about the destruction of the Warsaw ghetto. "When I write fiction," writes Kaplan, "I think of history as an implicit presence—in a way akin to the world of dreams: perhaps not always clearly recognized, yet undeniable, a ground bass in people's ordinary, surprising day-to-day lives." ("Tales")

These stories offer the useful reminder that Jewish history—"The mystery of Jewish destiny"—extends way back past Hitler, beyond the early twentieth-century Odessa of Isaac Babel, whose spirit informs "Family Obligations," past the great rabbis and the *shtetls* in "Tales of My Great-Grandfathers," all the way to the biblical legends and the poetry of the Song of Songs, the fantasies and quotations that fade in and out of Miriam's consciousness, in "Sickness." In her fever dream, Joseph, the Jewish prince who is also (like any Jewish prince worth his royal rank) a Jewish doctor, is called upon to diagnose an imaginary Sultan—a story that spins out in wry counterpoint to the mutterings of Miriam's mother. "What's a doctor? He sits and sits studying long enough so that finally in one place his bathrobe wears out. . . . In medical school the big expense is in bathrobes."

Louise Weil, the sympathetic and ferociously observant heroine of "Other People's Lives," comes from a family that fled Vienna for the Dominican Republic. Now she has arrived on the Upper West Side, via Washington Heights, a short stint at Oberlin and two longer ones in a private mental hospital. She's found a temporary haven (of sorts) as a boarder in the home of another refugee,

Maria Tobey, this one from Germany, as we are repeatedly reminded by a neighbor who, in a brilliant touch, can't let Maria's
German background go—because, for him, the unrelenting Nazi
jokes have been weaponized into unfunny, obnoxious flirtation.

Here, as in all the stories, the dialogue has the literary equiva-
lent of perfect pitch: we can always identify the note and key in
which a character is speaking, especially when that speech repre-
sents an outpouring of undiluted, semi-addled emotion unmedi-
ated by any censoring notion of audience or decorum. Kaplan has
an almost uncanny ear for the way the language is fractured by
those whose command of English is imperfect, and for the speech
rhythms of people who don't know the difference between log-
orrheic monologue and conversation. The strain with which her
young characters work to decipher what's being said is exacerbated
by how rarely these monologists care about who (or if anyone) is
listening.

One striking aspect of these stories is the way in which the
sheer control—of language, of observation and reflection—creates
a kind of still center amid the rattling cacophony that the narrative
describes. "It sometimes seemed to Miriam that if a person from
a foreign country—or even a miniature green man from Mars—
ever landed, by accident, in her building and by mistake walked
up the six flights of stairs, all he would hear was screaming and
crying: mothers screaming and children crying, fathers screaming
and mothers crying, televisions screaming and vacuum cleaners
crying; he could very easily get the idea that in this place there was
no language, and that with all the noise there were no lives."

ONE OF THE REASONS I'M SO GLAD THAT ECCO IS REISSUING THIS COLLEC-
tion of Johanna Kaplan's stories and essays is that (I know it's
wrong, sorry!) I'm a compulsive marker-up of books, an underliner,

a scribbler of exclamation points in the margins. But my first edition of *Other People's Lives* is pristine. It's lasted all these years without one dog-ear or pencil dot, perhaps because I feared I might not readily find another copy. Now, with the new edition in hand, I can go nuts, highlighting the phrases and sentences that delight me, that I want to be able to find when I'm quoting from the book, when I'm telling friends why they should read it. I'll no longer have to search so hard for this description of a drive through a rural landscape in a certain light, a certain weather: "Trees, paths, houses; houses, paths, trees—although it was probably noon by now, the grayness of the day had not abated, and the lights of the occasional lamps from the windows filled up the narrow road with the mistaken intimacy of twilight." Or this passage about the sound of another language: "In Poland, my mother said, it rained constantly from Rosh Hashanah straight to Simchas Torah and rained again from Purim all the way to Pesach, and that's why when people speak Polish it sounds like a rainstorm. Not that Eva the Refugee thinks so. She comes up to see my mother when she gets the feeling that she had to speak Polish. As far as I'm concerned, if she opened up an umbrella and used a little imagination it would be just as good." Or this account of what it's like to be a city girl, awake at night, at summer camp: "Miriam played with the dark like a blind person in a foreign country: in the chilly, quiet strangeness, her bed was as black as a packed-up trunk, and her body, separate in all its sunburned parts, was suddenly as unfamiliar as someone else's toothpaste." Or this portrait of the camp's Yemenite folk dance teacher: "With her tiny, tight, dark features and black, curly hair, she flew around the room like a strange but very beautiful insect, the kind of insect a crazy scientist would let loose in a room and sit up watching till he no longer knew whether it was beautiful or ugly, human or a bug."

Just open this book at random is not always the most sage and useful advice, but in this case, trust me. Everywhere you'll find passages and plots that amuse and surprise and move you, as the book, like all great writing, transforms the past into the eternal present and reminds us of how rapidly time moves by, so that all that remains in its wake is memory—and the relative permanence of art, of eloquent and precisely chosen words on the page.

LOSS OF MEMORY
IS ONLY TEMPORARY

OTHER PEOPLE'S LIVES

———

I

WHAT STRUCK YOU FIRST ABOUT THE TOBEYS' APARTMENT, NOT COUNTING the zany clutter of half-together furniture and piled-up arts-and-crafts materials, were the very long halls and huge white walls, empty of anything but the photographs of Dennis Tobey in what had to be called his former life. Caught in the heightened, unusual, and possibly excruciating lighting of theatrical shots, he did not at all stare out at you personally, but there in his various peculiar and austere dance costumes, his mind and body engaged elsewhere, he was clearly reflecting the famous agony and ardor of his art. It seemed embarrassing and arrogant at the same time. Also, he looked very thin.

Louise Weil, who was standing by herself in this empty strangers' apartment in her new blue boots—bought for new health and new life—was concentrating very hard on being struck with what she knew she was supposed to be struck with. What if she couldn't even do that much? Her coat was dripping so that she was afraid to sit down, her boots—high, shiny, and fashionable—were uncomfortable and hard to take off. What if she were found out struggling over them like a child or a cripple? She stood there sweating and staring: she had brought ill-health with her in the pools on the floor and the sour wet smell of her clothing. Naturally. Probably, when Maria Tobey came home, she would ask Louise if she wanted to take a shower—a normal question. But by that time her medication would have worn off, she would say no, the sweat, dampness, oily hair, and sourness of her body would stay with her, invade Maria Tobey's sheets and furniture, and it would be totally clear to everyone around exactly the kind of burden Maria had been stuck with. What if the phone rang now? Who would she say she was? How would she explain what she was doing there? What if the phone rang now? She would have to stumble her way through the apartment, leaving the marks of her streaky disorder everywhere. Still holding on to her suitcase, she looked up again at the pictures of Dennis. The acute pain in his expression, whether contrived or genuine, was repellent, familiar, and catching.

"What's *that*? What are you doing?" said the voice of an invisible questioner, having found her out taking her medication publicly.

"I'm just taking a pill."

"Why are you taking it? What is it for?"

"It's for my health," said Louise, finishing off this smug, naggy spy, and towed along by the brief, dependable euphoria that came with waiting for the pill to take effect, she counted up, in wonder, these things: that she had found her way out of Grand Central with a suitcase, gotten a taxi in the freezing rain, that she had paid, tipped, and arrived at the right building and—despite the confusion of elevators, lobbies, and unmarked doors—at the right apartment. And not only that: since there was nobody home (a possibility she had been told about), she had been able to find the key where Maria Tobey had left it—not under the mat as in all books and movies, but, for safety, covered by the sand and stubs in the metal ashtray near the back elevator.

"For my health," Louise said aloud, meaning "to my health," not a wish, but a dare. That she was no longer in Birch Hill, where right now, at five o'clock, she would ordinarily be getting ready for supper and the doctors' cars would be pulling out to their homes and their families. It was just the time of day when the trains beside the Hudson were rushing past, carrying all the passengers away to their far-off towns, their lit-up houses, and their normal lives. It was possible, of course, that they would crash.

"Matthew? I know you took your schoolbag, but this time you forgot your lunch. I did not find the turtle and if you can't even be responsible for a turtle—a little *turtle*—what the hell are we going to do with a dog? Matthew!"

"Hello?" Louise said. "Nobody's here. I'm Louise Weil."

"Oh!" the woman said. Her arms were full of packages, she, too, was wet from the rain, her thick blond hair was slipping out of a bun. "My God, it's terrible out there. Do you think he could be *outside* in this weather? Because if he is anywhere *near* Riverside Park, I'll kill him. Both Andrew *and* Jonny Axelrod were mugged there on Friday and Jonny is a strong kid. Hefty. Heavy? Hefty? Whichever one you say, *I* don't know. My God, do you know that you can't even take a shower in this house? That damned boiler is broken again and some idiot has torn down the notice. He won't ever have it fixed, the bastard, he only wants it to go co-op and I'm *not* going to another tenants' meeting to-night, I don't care who rings the bell. Do you know what they love? Petitions. I'll tell them they can forge my signature, I don't care. I know it's unmoral—amoral? Immoral? It's not moral, but they have so many lawyers. What do you think?"

Louise stared at her: she had put down the groceries, taken off her coat, and fallen into a chair—all in one movement. As she closed her eyes now briefly, it was like a mistaken wind-down in an old-time movie. So this was Dennis Tobey's wife: a little slovenly, a little plump, but on the whole she had the healthy, unselfconscious prettiness of hardworking peasant girls who did not worry over themselves in mirrors or anywhere else, and who, though they sweated profusely, smelled of hay.

"Have you been here long? Did Matthew telephone? Did you see somewhere a turtle?"

"No," Louise said, and picked something out among all her confusions. Maria Tobey, the defected Russian dancer, had a very strong German accent. No one had told her.

DIAGNOSIS WAS, IN EVERYONE'S OPINION, A TRICKY THING. THE FIRST TIME Louise came to Birch Hill, at fifteen, she had not been able to eat, sleep, or go to school for a long time, but had gone on practicing her cello, which consistently, and regardless of the time she spent struggling over the pegboard and her fingering, remained to her ear out of tune. She practiced and practiced, but her intonation did not improve. Neither did anyone else's: listening to records or the radio, it was amazing to realize how many respected performers and famous orchestras allowed themselves to be sharp or flat. Was it possible that they didn't know it?

"This is absolutely typical—but *typical*—American musicianship," her mother said. "In Vienna such a thing was not possible. In Vienna a concert was a concert. Viennese concerts have for me ruined anything else." Which was a line stolen entirely from Stefan Zweig's autobiography, though it was possible her mother honestly believed it to be her own thought. Stefan Zweig had committed suicide in Brazil; he left a note.

Pablo Casals, living in Puerto Rico, did not have faulty intonation, but hummed, audibly hummed on all of his records. It did not matter; he was a very old man. He got up early every morning and practiced for hours every day till the sun became too hot. Years before, on a mountain-climbing expedition in the U.S., he had fallen and injured his arm. "Thank God," his first reaction was supposed to have been, "now I'll never have to play the cello again." He did not mean it: he got up early every morning and practiced for hours every day. Louise, living in Washington Heights with her mother, did not get up early most days; could not. She clung to the whiteness of the sheets, which were pure in themselves and which banished the babble of melodies which she could not control, and of intonation which she could not perfect—though her birthday was the same as Pablo Casals's. He had not always lived in Puerto Rico.

Louise had not always lived in Washington Heights, but had been born in the Dominican Republic, a country she did not remember. Her mother remembered it all too well: a country whose climate had ruined the fairness of her skin, forcing it into unnatural splotches, a country which had ruined her marriage and forced her to keep company with all kinds of other Jews who had been able to buy their way in. These people were grateful to the Dominican Republic, even Trujillo, for saving them from death and hiding, and for putting an end to the endlessness of waiting for visas. Louise's mother was not grateful to the Dominican Republic: it had ruined her idea of herself—a lovely, young, promising voice student. In Washington Heights she went on giving piano lessons and writing letters to a friend of her young days who now lived in London.

The first time Louise went to Birch Hill, her mother moved

to England for good. Her father, who was paying for her, remained in the Dominican Republic, where he dealt in the import and sale of American agricultural equipment, and where he had had for years another family: actual Dominicans. Her sister Elisabeth went on living in Sweden, where she was married to a Swedish architect, and was also an architect herself.

"You look like a little Dutch girl," said a beautiful, dark-haired girl who lived on her floor.

"I'm *from* the Dominican Republic," Louise said to shut her up, but knew in a way what she meant. The Dutch-girl strain ran all through her family, allowing her mother in youthful, rosy, clear-featured vivacity to have had an affair with a highly placed, unsuspecting Nazi official. He had called her *"ma petite,"* been unwilling to give her up, and even wanted to adopt Elisabeth. "He *adored* Elisabeth," her mother said. "For him, Elisabeth was as precious as she was for me." In the end, it was this Nazi officer who had personally helped arranged for the visas, and personally stolen all the family belongings.

The Dutch-girl strain in adored and precious Elisabeth, despite the climate of the Dominican Republic, had left her fair-skinned and nearly towheaded; it had allowed her to make herself Swedish, so that as the wife of Anders Bjelding and mother of Per and Arne—two tiny towheaded boys living in Stockholm—she could easily never have *heard* of Elisabeth Weil, let alone been her.

The Dutch-girl strain in Louise herself had left her chunky, full-cheeked, unclear in coloring and appearance, and, by mistake or mutation, clumsy, as if she were constantly clogging around in invisible wooden shoes. That such shoes had once actually sat by the doors of Birch Hill was, in fact, very likely. An estate built high above the Hudson, it was exactly in the country of the old Dutch patroons. In the rooms upstairs, young girls had practiced the virginal, their eyes elsewhere, their fingering perfect.

Against half-open casement windows, they mulled over letters, surrounded by fruit bowls and cool white jugs. They had lived, all of them, in the perfect light and order of unending Vermeers.

There were no birches in Birch Hill. Skinny, scrawny Russian trees, silly in their tiny, pathetic intimacy, what would they be doing there?

The second time Louise went to Birch Hill, at nineteen, her mother was still living with her old school friend Trude in London. The neighborhood was called Swiss Cottage, a name which offered the suggestion of abandoned, rosy-cheeked schoolgirl holidays in cuckoo-clock, flower-filled Alpine meadows. Her father was still living in the Dominican Republic with his delicate-looking, black-haired wife and four delicate-looking, black-haired daughters. Their eyes were shy, their faces were Indian, they seemed absolutely beautiful; they came in pictures.

What also came in pictures was Elisabeth. On one of the back pages of the Entertainment section of the Sunday *Times* there was a short article about a new, unusual building in Stockholm designed by Anders and Elisabeth Bjelding. Above the article was a photograph that was very hard to make out. It looked like a blueprint photographed so as to give you an idea of what the building would one day look like, but was in fact a picture of the actual building photographed to look like a blueprint. In the foreground was the figure of a girl with grainy, wind-blown hair and cameras (also grainy) slung over her shoulders. The girl, though it didn't say so, was Elisabeth; the photographer, in discreet small print, was A. Bjelding.

Louise herself had gone to Oberlin College, where she took an overdose of various pills when she was alone in her practice room. She did not blame her cello or even the college, where she had managed to last less than a month. She had spoken to very few people and nobody made any sense. She was furious at her doctor, who had left Birch Hill and moved, for his wife's sake, to California. The climate of wintry New York State was ruining her, she had told people. She was *from* California, this whiny bitch, and, in Louise's opinion, looked it.

When Louise finally left Birch Hill two years later, it was because her father could no longer afford it. His business was being badly affected by the Recession. In the meantime, Birch Hill had become much more expensive and Louise was not the first patient who had had to leave in such a peremptory way. Either you went back to your family or you went to a state hospital.

In open conferences, through which Louise sat dumb and purposely slightly overmedicated, it was clear that no one could see sending her to a state hospital. She was not, they said, "state-hospital material," despite her suicide attempt, which no one remembered as well as she did. By this time she had gone through so many changes of doctors that her attachment was not to a particular person, but to the place itself. She felt at home in Birch Hill in a way she could not imagine feeling anywhere else.

"*Ma petite*," her mother's brief and occasional letters to her had begun. Only one person, a doctor freshly back from Vietnam, suggested that she go to London. He was accustomed to dispatching people, helicoptering them here and there; he did not know Louise at all and spoke in a cold, dismissive, patronizing voice, as if she were not in the room. Up to then he had been doodling on a lined medical form, and when he surprisingly raised his donkey's face to say "London," his brayed contribution ended in a yawn.

"Why don't *you* go there?" Louise said. "Or even better, go back to Vietnam."

Stockholm was out of the question, though everyone was very impressed with Elisabeth's reputation. Louise had, on her own, written to Elisabeth several times, but the only time she ever got an answer was one year at Christmas: a picture of Elisabeth's two small, handsome, towheaded boys—naked, absorbed, and agile, playing at the seashore. Serious and European, their smiles bent the sun. "These are my *nephews*," Louise had said, marveling over and over again. And it was true, but so what?

The Dominican Republic *was* mentioned, though Louise's father had never at any point in her life suggested that she come and live with him. He had often invited her to visit—for a month, for a summer, and before she was sick, might even have meant it.

In the end, Louise's social worker came up with a solution. She knew a family in New York who had a very large, old apartment and only one child. For various reasons which she did not go into, they could no longer keep up the rent and were now seriously looking for a boarder.

"The Tobeys," Mrs. Zeitlin said with great accomplishment in her voice. "Dennis and Maria Tobey." She stared around the room, squintily raising her tinted prescription glasses, as if removing them altogether would allow her to see what she was looking for.

"They live in Manhattan, these people?" the director asked her. *"Dennis Tobey."*

They lived in Manhattan, on the West Side, not much more than a crosstown bus ride away from any analyst Louise would be referred to. She would have the advantage of living with a family, and the assurance that though her father could no longer afford Birch Hill, he would still be able to take care of her living expenses in New York.

"Dennis Tobey!" Mrs. Zeitlin said excitedly, rushing up to Louise as soon as the meeting was over. "I'm so glad I *thought* of them. It'll be marvelous for you, Louise. Absolutely marvelous."

Still in the slowed dullness of her medication, Louise said, "I don't know who that is. Who they are."

"Louise," Mrs. Zeitlin said overgently, taking her hand and speaking in that particular social worker's voice, "Dennis Tobey, the dancer." And then gripping and shaking her so it seemed to Louise that Mrs. Zeitlin had suddenly become a ridiculous carousel of her long red hair and her whirling long peasant dress, "Louise! Dennis Tobey! The dancer! Dennis Tobey."

Dennis Tobey, it turned out, was a dancer whom Mrs. Zeitlin had once studied with. Very early in his career he developed some kind of revolutionary and idiosyncratic combination of modern dance and ballet, and whenever he performed, there was no newspaper or magazine issue that came out without acclaiming him. He was an ordinary small-town boy; he was a phenomenon. He worked day and night and, through singlemindedness, turned himself into a revered, living genius and a figure of glamour. People trailed after him constantly, but Dennis—pale, taut, ascetic, idiosyncratic Dennis—lived only inside his mind through his feet.

"You could always tell how far away he was," Mrs. Zeitlin said. "And I don't mean detached. I mean committed. *Completely* committed. You could see the ideas rushing through his head and his body so that he couldn't stand still long enough to listen to you."

On a cultural-exchange tour with his company through the Soviet Union, Dennis met a Russian dancer—Maria. The faraway, committed Dennis fell in love, and Maria, the Soviet ballerina, defected. Later, in New York, they married; it was a very romantic story, and Dennis's career was in no way changed. Every new dance he created was acclaimed as before. People still trailed after them constantly—pale, taut, idiosyncratic Dennis and beautiful, energetic, high-spirited Maria. Much later, even, they had a child, a son. Only recently, within the past two years, Dennis had become very sick—Hodgkin's disease—and was frequently in the hospital. Without him, naturally, his company had fallen apart, and now that he could no longer dance and make a living, the Tobeys needed a boarder.

"Imagine it, Louise! You'll be living with the Tobeys. I envy you. Really. Aren't you excited?"

Louise had no interest in dance, and knew nothing about dancers. She was being carried off to the Tobeys' as other people were being carried off to state hospitals.

II

"I THINK MAYBE I'LL GO TO AUSTRALIA," MARIA WAS SAYING. "THE WEATHER is better. What do you think? Also the parking problems. Even also I think the schools."

"Australia? *You?* Before you knew it, you'd be starting up with a kangaroo. Where *you* should go is Pago Pago. One grass skirt and you'd be in business, a water buffalo would get you around. No meters, no tickets. Maria, *liebchen*, I've just solved all your problems."

The kitchen faucet burst out suddenly, but over the running water Louise heard Maria say, "It's not in my mentality, Arthur." Arthur and Joan Tepfer, Bert and Reba Axelrod: they were Maria's neighbors, these people, and were constantly in and out of her apartment as if it were an extension of their own. Their children played with Matthew, and the strange, unfinished arts-and-crafts projects that Louise had first seen strewn around the house mostly belonged to Joan Tepfer. She was always starting something new, and left what she could not finish with Maria, who usually could and did not seem to regard it as an imposition. She did not seem to regard it at all. "You're so inventive, Maria," Joan and Reba would say. "Isn't she marvelous?" They meant it, and would watch, fascinated, as Maria's hands rapidly pulled and shaped the various materials, calling out at the same time, "Matthew! You're slamming the God-damn refrigerator!" Or, "Damn it, I also forgot about the cheese."

Maria worked as a dance therapist in a community rehabilitation center for drug addicts, and since there had been a cutback in staff, also did much of the arts-and-crafts work, which she had picked up from watching. Creativity was something she connected solely with Dennis.

Louise remained standing in the hallway, listening. It meant she had to face the pictures of Dennis, but still she would not go into the kitchen: Arthur Tepfer made her nervous.

"No, Arthur, really. I am sick of that God-damn parking. I am sick of that God-damn car. I think maybe I'll sell it. What do you think? Only I love it to drive, it's a very good car, only it's always breaking. I am a *very* good driver, Arthur. Only I don't like the tickets."

Arthur Tepfer began whistling a German marching song. He said, "Who told you to get a foreign car? I told *you* not to, I told Dennis. If you had to have a foreign car, at least it should have been a Volkswagen—you'd feel at home in it, first of all, and as soon as you said *Achtung* it would have to listen."

"*One* time be serious, Arthur. Just today—now—I went to the hospital again, and I *found* a parking place. Legal. When I came out, no car. I can't find it. Some stupid bastard has just pushed it! It could have rolled down the hill, I don't know. Also, I don't even *like* the East Side. It's not in my mentality."

Joan said, "Oh, Maria. How is Dennis?" She said it in a very reverential voice, the same way all the people in the building always said it.

"How is Dennis? How is Dennis? How do *I* know how is Dennis? Dennis doesn't know *who* is Dennis. I am sick of the God-damn parking, it's a *terrible* hospital. Only parking for doctors."

"Are they giving him any new drugs? Is he still getting radiation?"

If Maria answered this, Louise did not hear it. She yelled out, "Matthew, please! Clean up the cat shit, we're having dinner. And afterward, baby, angel, no television until after all the homework. *Please.*"

"Why do you push him about *homework*, Maria?" Joan said. "If the material was interesting intrinsically—*you* know—*alive*, he would do it. It would be like play."

"Play!" Maria said. "Exactly! He's a good boy, Matthew, really. But that's what he does—play."

Louise already knew exactly how Matthew played: he sat over a large chessboard by himself and moved both sets of pieces, exclaiming to himself and crinkling his small, fair, freckled face in absorption and a kind of gleeful, separate happiness. It struck Louise as being strange, but all Maria ever said was, "Oh, chess. I don't know how it goes, the pieces. Dennis taught him, he was very little."

Matthew's other way of playing was drawing. He made very colorful, elaborate pictures and sang songs to go with them. Often they were about space and spaceships—a topic in which Louise had no interest. She tried to follow the melody line as he sang, but had trouble; in fact, had trouble with Matthew altogether. No matter how much Louise tried to talk to him or play with him, Matthew gave back the same short, fishy stare. Often he simply got up and walked away. Naturally. What did she expect?

Joan Tepfer said, "I really don't see why you took him out of private school. At his age! At seven! To be regimented so young. Everyone knows what public schools do, Maria, and you *care* so much about his education. It's obvious."

Early in the morning when Louise was in her still, strange bedroom, trying to get up, she heard children's voices calling up from the private-school cars, waiting outside. "Adam, Jonathan, Jennifer." It had a singsong quality, and in repetition had the far-off wonder of an echo. "Adam, Jonathan, Jennifer." They ran down then, bundled up and yelling greetings. "Have a good day, kids": mothers had come out with them, wrapped in coats and sleepily waving, on their way to walk the dog. Or "Bye, muffin": fathers hugging extravagantly, spruced for the morning, halfway into the *Times.*

"*Je suis desolée*"—it only meant "I'm sorry": Louise's new French course. "*Je suis desolée,*" an idiom she hung on to, it was part of her morning collection. "It was empty, forlorn, and apparently abandoned"—Rip Van Winkle (American Lit). And from a Katherine Anne Porter story, the two words "sour gloom."

"Adam, Jonathan, Jennifer"—it was from *Wozzeck,* that children's street song, when no one was left on the merry-go-round, which kept turning. Empty, forlorn, and abandoned. In the sour gloom.

The school cars blew their horns and zoomed away down Riverside Drive. "Matthew!" Maria would call brusquely from the kitchen, where she was making sandwiches. "Hurry up! I know you have only to walk, but it's late. Again. Also I'll be late. *Again.* I have for you Frosted Flakes and Red Cheek apple juice. Also Skippy peanut butter. Crunchy. Come *on,* Matthew, angel, hurry up!"

No one had ever asked Louise what were her favorite foods, and bought them. *Je suis desolée*: I'm sorry, merely, sorry. That's all.

Arthur said, "*Achtung,* Matthew! You heard your mother. A little heel-clicking would make her happy . . . What that kid needs, Maria, is a strong male image."

"Always no problem with *that,*" Maria said, giggling strangely.

"Maria, I mean it," Joan Tepfer said. "I can't *understand* why you changed his school, it's not good for him."

"It was show, only. Charity. I had to."

"*Charity?* For God's sake, he had a scholarship! Do you know how many people would donate whole buildings to get their kids in there? Let alone get them scholarships."

"It's the same thing for Black children. For show only. So they can say, we have these many children from Harlem and these many children of famous persons. So they can think always, here is the son of Dennis Tobey, so sad, so wonderful. Not just Matthew, a little boy in the school. Like other children. He is *not* like the other children there, Joan. It was *not* good for him. They are too rich."

"I can't see what that has to do with it. You're just creating phony issues."

"With maids and country houses and sailboats and horses? Always they were treating him, the parents, the maids. And taking him places. I can't take *them*. Too many God-damn birthday parties. With magicians. Too many presents, I can't afford so much those God-damn birthday presents . . . Matthew!"

Matthew came bounding through the hallway to the kitchen. "Louise is here," he said, and ran straight for Arthur's lap. "Do jellyfish have hearts?"

"How the hell do I know?" Maria said. "I think I never saw even a jellyfish. Hi, Louise, sit down. Did you wash your hands, Matthew?"

"There was a terrible epidemic of jellyfish on the Sound last summer," Joan said. "We finally actually felt lucky that we're nowhere near the beach. Except for that constant pool-cleaning. Christ! I feel like Madame Curie, walking around with those idiot test tubes."

"Country houses!" Maria said. "Swimming pools!"

"Well, we have to, Maria. Connecticut's for tax purposes. *Which* I don't understand. We might be bought out for the highway, though. Did I tell you?"

Arthur began whistling again and said, "She remembers when she built the Autobahn. By herself. Otherwise, highways don't interest her."

"Tax purposes! Country houses! Sailboats! There is something wrong with this country, I'm completely serious."

"Mmm, Matthew." Arthur widened his eyes and rubbed his hands together. "Look what your mother made for dinner— the Führer Special. Sauerbraten, sauerkraut, *und* a little *kartoffel salat.*"

"I *used* to, Arthur. I am a very good cook, I'm completely serious. I made sometimes fantastic sauerbraten. For Dennis. I marinate it overnight, it's very simple. Also, dumplings." She moved very quickly from the stove to the sink, pouring the spaghetti into the colander. The steam from the boiling water rose to her face, a burst from the cold-water faucet came down like a hurricane, strands of her hair flew out of her bun. "If you mix up the sauce with the salad, too bad, Matthew. No separate plates. Too many God-damn dishes. He is *so* particular, I don't know where he learned that from. Not me. It's not in my mentality. I don't need so much dishes and dishes, I hate them dirty."

"I'll do the dishes," Louise said uneasily. Her mother, cooking, had done this: locked the kitchen door, filling the small room entirely with her own cigarette smoke. If the food had had a smell of its own, there was no way of telling. She should not have had to do any cooking; naturally, her own mother had not had to; there were maids for such things: it was not in her mentality.

"Where's the Parmesan cheese?" Matthew asked, rubbing his eyes beneath his glasses and sliding off Arthur's lap.

"*Exactly* what I mean," Maria said. She banged down the cheese bottle with one hand, and with the other, wildly ladled out more meat sauce. "I make you a bet tonight there's no hot water!"

"We're eating out," Joan said. "Jennifer has a recorder recital."

"Toot-toot." Arthur cupped his hands and blew through an imaginary recorder, making Matthew giggle uncontrollably.

"Eating out! Do you know when was the last time I ate out? All that money for the God-damn hospital. And the parking tickets. And for what reason? Anyway, soon it will all be over."

"Maria!" Joan said.

"What? He can't know that his father will be dead? My father was also dead. Only we didn't even know it. We thought only he was missing. Nobody knew anything, it's not better. A rumor came from his register—regiment, a man from our town who heard it. That he was killed. So we knew finally it was true. Always rumors were true, it's not better."

Arthur said, "I've been meaning to ask you, Louise. I hear you were in Birch Hill. What was it like there?"

"What do you mean—what was it like?" That she was crazy.

"I think I saw a movie about a place like that—a lot of birches, a lot of bushes. What went on there behind all the birches?"

Stiffly Louise said, "There was a convent next door."

"See that, Maria? *That's* what you should have become—a nun. Who knows what you could have found between all those bushes?"

"Mushrooms," Maria said, laughing giddily, oddly. "I am very good at finding mushrooms. I *always* used to, Arthur. I'm completely serious. I lived on them. In the war."

The three of them were standing now, Joan at the door, and Arthur with his arm around Maria, who laughed even more, saying, "When I was *very* skinny."

Joan said, "You know my Indian cooking lessons? I think I should have an Indian tablecloth for when I make the meals. The thing is—I don't want to *buy* it. Could you show me how to make one?"

"No problem," Maria said, "it's very simple. Just bring me the material."

"That's what she said when she was turning out lampshades. Exact same words."

Maria began to laugh again.

"Arthur, we have to *go*. Excuse me, Maria, he's impossible. The jacket he's supposed to wear tonight is completely wrinkled. He forgot to bring it to the cleaner's. I don't know what we're going to do."

"You only hang it up in the shower, it's very simple. Turn on very hot water and let it stand in the steam. The wrinkles are steamed out, no problem. I did it always. For Dennis."

"Dennis," Joan said, suddenly resuming her holy voice. "Tell him we love him, we *all* love him. Give him my love."

Maria nodded; Matthew, his mouth red from spaghetti sauce, shrieked out "Toot-toot" and giggled; the door closed.

"They are very nice people, the Tepfers," Maria said very slowly. "Joan cannot do one fucking thing, she is very lucky."

Louise said, "Do you ever miss Russia? Do you think about it?"

"*Russia?* How can I miss it? I was there only once for one week. With the folk-dance troupe from my factory. Matthew! Take out the garbage! And I don't want to hear yet the television. We made steel parts, pieces, I don't know. I drove a giant something—a crane? It was very noisy. Also my family was terrible. Asking me always for money, especially my brothers. Families are shit. Then I was very skinny, but before even skinnier. Do you smell still the cat shit? Matthew! Cat shit is also garbage. I miss sometimes *mushrooms*. They're different in this country. You open them and if in a few minutes, seconds, they turn purple, then they're bad. It's how I could tell. Always."

"Mrs. Zeitlin told me that you—"

"What did she tell you? She cannot forgive me that I married

Dennis. She was in love with him. Why, I don't know. He was good for a dancer, but terrible for a husband. Terrible in bed and terrible for responsibilities."

"She said you were a ballerina, that you gave up your career and left Russia because you fell in love with Dennis."

"You see how she makes it up so glamorous so she can feel better? She would *feel* better maybe, I think, if she did something different. Or had a baby. She had once a baby, but it died. It's a disease only for Jewish people. Tay-Sachs. She could have probably another baby, but it might also die."

"She wanted to be a dancer, she said."

"That's because of Dennis. It's why she says *I* am a dancer. She's crazy, really. Not crazy, *I* don't know. Matthew! *Still* I'm calling you! Did you take out the garbage? Did you do your homework? Why am I hearing only TV?"

Matthew came running in on very light feet—lithe, they seemed suddenly, like dancers'. "Mommy, can I get a hamster?"

"A *hamster*? No dog and no hamster. It's enough that cat and the turtle. You *must* do your homework, Matthew, angel. Hamsters! It's what we did in the war—you know, for getting food. For saving it. You stuff it up in the cheeks, like hamster faces, we called it hamstering. I was *very* good at it. I got caught only one time, I was running. In the country. I don't know who shot. A farmer, maybe, I think there weren't soldiers there yet. Later, farmers were always very nice to me. When I was crossing to the West . . . Matthew! Out! Homework! *Please,* angel. It was then very easy because of haying season. Always I could sleep in the fields, they were very nice. I didn't like the forests. You know, people said always they were safer, but I didn't like them. A farmer pointed for me a small little I don't know—stream? brook? And I went across. There *were* soldiers near then, only not for that brook. Russians, I think. Maybe East Germans."

"That's how you got away with Dennis?"

"Dennis? I never even heard then of Dennis. It's not anyway what people told you. I was the first woman Dennis was with. Before that, only men. Not many. I was working then in I don't know, dancing clubs? nightclubs? In West Berlin. To dance with the men. Dancing only. Not a prostitute. Sometimes. For food mostly. I didn't care so much about clothes. Sometimes, for exchange mostly, but, you know, I was tired of that. Fed up. I did always exchanges from when I was very little, better than my sister and brothers. *Much* better than my mother. You know how I spent my first twenty marks? Chocolate. I was very skinny then, but not so skinny as before. It was *terrible* chocolate."

"And Dennis was on tour with his company when you met him?"

"He was very good to me, Dennis. Always. Except for later with responsibilities, then not so good. In Berlin then, he helped me for the abortion. *Not* his child. You know, nobody believed that. But he was very good. And I was tired, really tired. Fed up. With the war, with the peace, with Hitler, with not-Hitler. With Communism, with not-Communism. With East Germany, with West Germany. I thought probably America will be better. My *God*! I forgot again to wash up my underwear. And Matthew's shirts! What will he have tomorrow for school? Matthew! Do you have left your blue jersey? Look in your drawer. Now, baby, angel, did you hear me?"

"A *green* one, Mommy."

"That's too small, I think. I don't remember. Does it fit you still? Did you try it?"

Matthew came into the kitchen holding up the green shirt. "Does Arthur know about jellyfish? If they have hearts? Can I call him?"

"He's not home now. It *is* small, Matthew—look! What else is in the drawer?"

"Then can I call him later?"

"Later you have to be in bed. Already it's later. Look in the drawer. Hurry up!"

Louise said, "Why does Arthur tease you about lampshades?"

"Oh," Maria said, smiling, "you know—I was in Hitler Youth. In school. Also, after the war, in the factory I was in Communist Youth." She stood up, indiscriminately banging around the dishes, pots, and pans. "Damn it, it's already rusty this pot and I think I only just bought it. Two years ago. Made in Japan. Also, I was first Protestant and then, after, when we went to my cousin in Bavaria, I was Catholic. My cousin was terrible, but I liked very much the country, especially the cows. Really he was terrible, Klaus. So old and so, I don't know, crankly? cranky? Only my sister and brothers were worse. Also my mother. They were shit, all of them. I'm completely serious. Families are shit."

The day before, walking on Broadway, Louise had seen an older man walking slowly, his hands clasped behind his back. He reminded her of her father, but that was not possible. "My mother lives in London, my father lives in the Dominican Republic, and my sister lives in Sweden."

"I don't know *where* is anyone in my family and I don't give a damn. They could be dead for what I care. My mother probably is. She was a stupid Romantic. To name *me* Maria!"

"My mother named me Louise for a Schubert song that she liked, and she named my sister Elisabeth for Elisabeth Schumann."

"Schumann's wife? That one he got crazy over?"

"Elisabeth Schumann. She was a Viennese *lieder* singer."

"Oh," Maria said. "Vienna. I was never there. I didn't know any Jewish people till I came here. Oh my *God*! I forgot again that stupid hand cream. Damn it! My hands are cracking, also my face. I should go down now very fast and buy it. *If* there is a drugstore open. I should go down now. What do you think?"

III

ON THE MORNING OF THE BLOCK PARTY, A SUNDAY, LOUISE WAS AWAK-ened very early. It was Maria banging around in the kitchen. Throughout the whole building, in the wintry darkness, only this one kitchen window had a light.

"They can have these pots and also these ones. Joan, I think, is making *cassoulet*. Why, I don't know, it's only beans mostly. It's only farmer's foods, peasant's foods—she thinks it's fancy, but what does she think farmers eat? It will give her diarrhea probably, she's not used to it, just like that *foul mudammas*. Also, I forgot who, is making *felafel*, they need a big ceramic bowl and I promised the forty-cup coffeepot. Electric—they'll have to put up wires in the street. What I have so many pots for, I don't know. I'll leave the door open, they can come in and take what they want, it's better than leaving the keys, probably they'll only lose them. What do you think?"

Still sleepy and in her bathrobe, Louise watched Maria reach up from an unsteady stepladder and grab recklessly at enormous pots and pans. A lid fell into the sink, just missing Matthew's thin blue nighttime water glass.

"*Damn* it!" Maria said. "I can't find that stupid coffeepot and I promised it definitely. Also, everything is absolutely filthy, I must first wash them now, it's not right, I think, to lend out dirty pots. They'll say anyway I'm hostile, I don't care, but it's not right . . . *Here* maybe is the coffeepot, the cord is coming. Oh, shit! A whole cockroach nest, babies only, because of the hot-water pipes probably, but I have now to spray the whole God-damn shelves and change the paper, and I have already my hand lotion on, it will stick to everything. Also, I should put out now the powder, it's only boric acid, very simple, but they don't get ammunized?— immunized?—to it, I'm completely serious." She wiped her forehead with a dish towel, marking it with black grease, and said, "Absolutely I can't do it now myself. Maybe Matthew will do it, he likes to always, only I'm not sure now about the spray. It's bad for ecology maybe, he bothers me from school . . . Matthew! Get up, baby, angel. I have for you a special job. I *know* it's Sunday, Matthew, but if you hurry up quickly, you can watch still those stupid cartoons and I can make breakfast. Matthew!"

Maria climbed down from the stepladder, and on her way out of the room said, "Breakfast! How can I make anything with so much dirt and these many pots? Even when I wash them! Also, I think I should make lunch for us to take along. In the car. I don't believe to stop on the highway, it's not in my mentality— too much money and the car maybe won't start again, I make you a bet. I could *make* it start again probably, but I'm insecure of it. What do you think? Insecure is a good word, they like it, but it's for people only, not for cars . . . Damn it! Look at my blouse! Already I have to change my clothes and I only just got up. A half hour! What I have so many pots for, I don't know. I think maybe I didn't ever use them, even. Sometimes."

Louise knew what pots of this size could be used for: they had lined the shelves and ranges in the enormous, chilly kitchen at Birch Hill. In Maria's house, though, these pots meant something entirely different. Enormous pots for enormous parties: people had trailed after the Tobeys constantly—brilliant, pale, revered Dennis and beautiful, high-spirited, energetic Maria. The elevator nearly burst from the numbers of people who rode up in it, neighbors peered in to see who was there and what they were wearing, the long halls of the apartment were filled with the separate smells of perfume, liquor, cigarette smoke, and excitement, which did not abate. The crowds became so thick that occasionally people stepped on each other's feet, but they were careful always of Dennis's. He stood there surrounded, but remote. In the kitchen Maria's hair slipped out of her bun, she looked glamorous anyway; the trailing guests pleaded with her to let them help out. "He was brilliant," they said to her hopefully, or possibly, "Darling, it was a triumph." The elevator brought up a new crowd of people; even though it was past two in the morning, no one complained.

"Didn't you used to have big parties?" Louise said. "For Dennis, after his recitals?"

"Too many cigarette-hole burnings. I liked usually the cooking, but I couldn't stand the holes. Nobody watches. I *gave* them out ashtrays. Always. Matthew! Please, baby, angel—*up*! Once even almost there was a bad fire—a girl's hair. She was bending to light her cigarette from a candle flick. Candle wick? Her hair caught fire, she didn't know it. I *put* out matches. Somebody saw it in her hair, *he* was an idiot. He poured on her what he had in his glass. Liquor, naturally, so it got only worse. I threw at her ice water. From the bucket. I put out so many matches, I don't know. People don't teach themselves to be careful."

On the whole, Louise was glad they were not going to the Block Party. She imagined herself hanging back on the windy, crowded street: balloons and streamers would blow all around her and she would not know how to get them back up; she would say "May I help?" five times before somebody heard her, and then when they did she would knock over a gallon ceramic pot of *cassoulet*. She would smile at the children who whizzed past on their bicycles or shrieked with their Frisbees. Naturally. She would smile till the corners of her mouth hurt: it was the same sickly, stranded smile.

Other people were not glad about Maria's decision. Joan said, "I know it's painful for you to be there without Dennis. Everyone understands that—but you're *wrong*, Maria. It's not that kind of thing. It's *group* participation, that's very different."

"You're crazy for this weather," Maria said. "For outside you should make it in the spring. It's what I already told you."

"That's exactly why we're doing it now. We'll be the first ones! *All* the Block Parties are in the spring. By that time there's such an overload that people don't even absorb the notices."

"You think you can make more money when you have only wind from the river and people standing with their teeth shattering? Chattering. Between West End and the Drive is always the coldest street in the city."

Arthur said, "Come on, Maria. With something like this you'll be able to remember the good old days. The worst winds, the highest number of shattered teeth. You can't pass it up—it'll be just like the Russian front!"

"I am going for a drive to the country, I promised it already to Matthew. For a treat. You know how I thought about it? I was going across town through the park from Dennis in the hospital. It was already dark and I thought suddenly: I am fed up looking only at buildings and people. It's time to see something else. So I told it to Matthew and to Louise and then when Julie Dresner called me up, I invited her also. Only I hope that God-damn car is all right, it won't sometimes start when I stop it."

Joan said, "Julie Dresner. She used to be your babysitter, didn't she? Why don't you tell her to come to the Block Party? She'll love it."

"Why you think it's better so much to make a special day for looking at the same people and standing in the same dog shit, I don't know. Also the cold weather. Already I promised it to Matthew, I made out the arrangement with Julie, it's what I decided for my plans. It's not right, I think, to change plans like that. I hate the confusions. You'll say probably I'm rigid, I don't care, I hope only the *car* isn't rigid."

"Maria, why don't you sell the car?" Joan said. "We'd get rid of both of ours if we didn't need them for the house. For the country."

"It's what I think sometimes, Joan, I'm completely serious. Only while I have it still I should use it for something nice. It's why I'm going now to the country—just quickly. For getting away."

Joan said, "Oh, I wish you'd change your mind and come. I showed Paula Kopell my Indian tablecloth that you helped me make and she said it would be fantastic if you would share what you know and give a demonstration."

"Paula Kopell? That one who—"

"Who's captain of the Block Association, and her husband's going to be on television again, did I tell you? He's doing this series on alternate forms of city subcultures. It'll be on next week, I'll remind you."

"Paula Kopell—that one who let in the muggers and then got so upset when people called the police."

"Well, Maria, how was she supposed to know? She *asked* them what they wanted and they said they had a doctor's appointment."

"In all the years I am living in this building there has been only one doctor. Gruenfeld. And he's dead."

"Notice how she still keeps up that body count on dead Yids," Arthur said.

"What about that psychologist on the fourth floor? *You* know—that Israeli woman? Rina Gershuny? She has a private practice. Paula didn't want to pry."

"Two junky muggers would look definitely that they're going to a psychologist! This is the demonstration I would share to Paula Kopell."

"Anyway, they might have been speed freaks," Joan said. "How am I going to make *cassoulet* for so many people? Maybe I should just tell them I'll do the Greek salad . . . Which one, Arthur? You're going to have to eat it and help me make it. What should I do?"

"Come on, Maria. *You* help her out. Tell her which one goes over better with speed freaks."

"Too bad, Arthur. I told it already to everyone: I'm going to the country."

The long-legged girl just starting down the windy hill in dungarees and an unzipped fatigue jacket was Julie Dresner. Her shiny black hair blew out of a turned-up tan wool cap—the kind that lumberjacks wear. She looked exactly like the students in the college town near Birch Hill: Louise had seen them on the days she had town privileges.

"Julie!" Matthew screamed, and ran up to hug her.

"I think again maybe she dropped out of Bennington," Maria said. "It's probably why she called me. I hope not. It's very good there for dance, it's why she went. Dennis suggested her to do it. Only I can't give her advice, I'm not Dennis."

Julie's arm was around Matthew as she finally turned the corner. "Oh, wow," she said, "you still have the Saab. I love it."

The car was a dull, bluish gray; it matched the day exactly. Perhaps it had once been another color—a kind of snowy, pearly blue, like the mountain lakes in Sweden where it came from, and where Elisabeth, her eyes coldly narrowed against the glare, was accustomed to sleekly plunging in.

"I think definitely, Julie, I'll sell it. Why I need now a station wagon I don't know. Be careful for the back door, it doesn't close. The handle gets jams."

"I'll go through the back window, Maria. Remember? I always used to. It's so weird, really. I *hate* cars now, but I still love this one. It doesn't matter if things are broken in it—it's a happy car. Like someone's old attic. When you find your old teddy bear and it's completely wrecked but you still love it—I mean, that's *why* you love it . . . I don't even know if I ever *had* a teddy bear, I don't remember. My mother is such a crazy compulsive bitch, she throws out everything. Sometimes I think I don't remember anything, but how can I remember things if she throws everything out?"

In dreams, Louise thought of answering, but didn't. Sitting in the front seat next to Maria, bundled in layers for the cold of the country, she knew she could not have moved to reach out for a tissue, yet Julie slipped in through the half-opened window with the unthinking ease of a child on a sliding pond. Naturally.

"Matthew had once a teddy bear, he was a baby. Do you remember, angel? He had then so many things, presents. People sent them. For Dennis, really. Or me. *I* don't know. I was in the hospital still, he couldn't even see them. We put them away and later he played only with the boxes. It's what everyone always says, I know, but it's true. Damn it! Look how this green Japanese idiot has cut me off! Toyotas are worse cars even than mine."

"When I'm stoned sometimes I remember things," Julie said. "Like I'll remember my bedspread from the apartment where we lived when I was in kindergarten. From before my father moved his office."

"*Damn* it, Matthew, *that's* what I forgot! Again! To wash your bedspread. I asked you now all week please, please to put it out with the washing. It's what I hate—filthy bedclothes! And also the basement *completely* filthy, roaches and roaches!"

"God," Julie said, "I used to be so scared of the basement when I was little. I mean *terrified,* it was incredible. Even the elevator man looked different to me when he let us out there. It's funny—I never told my father. He should have asked *me,* though. I mean, he should have *sensed* it." Julie leaned forward; her arms, long and easy, were spread out across the front seat like a sun-blind, resting swimmer's. She was speaking to Maria, who any minute now, Louise knew, would say, "Families are shit, I'm completely serious."

"Again the green Japanese," Maria said. "Probably he bribed up the driving tester, I make you a bet. It's only touching thighs they care about. For a man, bribing. What do you think?"

"Mommy, I'm hungry," Matthew said.

"You had already breakfast, Matthew. Soon, later, we'll have lunch. Sandwiches. Shit! See what I have now? This stupid yellow Flashback. Fastback. The highway, I hope, will be better. Only not also if I still have that *green* idiot . . . I think maybe children get hungry always immediately inside a car."

Julie said, "That's exactly what always happened to me! I used to *love* all those plastic places. Howard Johnson's. When you stop on the highway. Let's stop now, Maria, before we get to the highway. I didn't have breakfast."

"I don't believe to stop on the way, it's too much money. It's why I made us up sandwiches. For lunch. I think Matthew is maybe only bored. He knows how it looks here, all the streets and the stores. It's the way he walks to school, he makes pictures of it all the time—*that's* what to do, baby, angel. Draw some pictures. I put in the glove compartment Magic Markers. Fine-pointed ones, your favorite."

"Oh, Maria, let's stop *here*! In the city, in a *real* store—not plastic. Right *here,* that little luncheonette place. With that big sign. *Los Primos.*"

"*Los Primos! Definitely* no! It's milkshakes only. Very, very sweet—for throwing up, it's not in my mentality. I have trouble still with chocolate, and Matthew already has too much for the dentist."

"*Tropical* fruit shakes?" Julie said. "Is that the one? It's famous, I've been dying to go there! Maria, I'll meet you inside. Come on, Matthew! I'll race you!"

Hanging on to Julie and totally disregarding Louise, Matthew giggled and leaped out of the car.

"From your allowance, Matthew!" Maria screamed. "*I* can't get out of the car. Again they'll only push it. And he's already so pale, he's getting sick, maybe. And then he can't go to school, probably. How can I stay with him? Look how they beep and beep, I don't blame them. It's what I can't stand—double-parking. Only I think—shit!—I forgot to bring with me Tampax. And here now are no drugstores, I know it. It *says* only Farmacia, but it's income-taxing place. Or else community storefront, *I* don't know."

"I'll look for a drugstore," Louise said, overwhelmed suddenly by the closed-in, cloying sweetness of Maria's hand lotion.

Across the street, she watched people coming out of church. Dressed specially for Sunday, they crowded the steps and the sidewalk: little boys in suits and brilliant ties like their mustachioed fathers; women, a bit puffy-faced from tears, solemnity, or maybe just the sudden brush with the wind, were carrying small black prayerbooks and their heads were covered by lacy, netted veils or shawls. Mantillas. The boys, awkward in their suits, began running and playing off the steps onto the streets so that their mothers yelled out to them in Spanish, but the little girls, their shining, springy holiday dresses blowing out through their coats in the wind, hung together still on the steps, telling secrets and giggling. *Productos Tropicales*—it was on all the store signs. In the tropics, girls menstruated early.

And all over the rest of the neighborhood, normal for Sunday mornings, people in pairs huddled into each other's coats and scarves. These were their weekend clothes and were not unlike Julie's. Against the wind, they balanced the heavy Sunday *Times* and bags smelling of the bakery. The day, in its pleasant laziness, stretched before them, so they walked even more quickly to their apartments, where the smell of the newspaper would remind them of the cold outside, and the taste of coffee cake and bagels would seam them again to the day's warm, sleepy order.

"Here it is! I *found* it! It was buried only, I didn't forget. So much junk now, shit!" Maria waved the Tampax box through the window and said, "Again all that God-damn beeping! Tell them please quickly hurry up because I'm holding up traffic and it's beeping."

In *Los Primos* there were bright orange café curtains covering the windows. Between them you could see the tables, which were not yet set up: chairs were stacked upside down on them, like the end of the day in an elementary-school classroom. Someone, arriving early and alone because it was Sunday, would have to unlock all the locks, push up the grating, turn off the burglar alarm, and wash the floor. Thinking of his family, whom he had left dreaming and turning in sleep, he would finally take down the chairs and, through the smell of disinfectant, start the day.

Julie, her elbow on the counter and all her hair way over it, turned when Louise came in. She said, "Matthew's so incredible! He knew exactly what he wanted! I feel like I've been here a half hour and I still can't decide. I asked the chick what all the flavors are, but they all sounded so fabulous, now I forgot. I think I should've taken Spanish."

The woman behind the counter, chunky and Indian-featured, was looking at them strangely. Why shouldn't she? Perhaps she was the one who had had to leave sleeping children. If Louise were one of her half-sisters in the Dominican Republic, she could have spoken to the woman, explained everything, straightened out the silliness, belonged in *Los Primos*. As she did not.

Matthew said, "*Los Primos* means cousins. Hector told me. He speaks Spanish in his house."

"But you got papaya, Matthew. You could get that anyplace, it's boring. I think I'd get pina-pineapple, but it sounds like a drink. *You* know—like my parents, when they come back from Mexico or the Caribbean. Mango's probably just mango, and I *hate* bananas. What about *guan*banana? Or trigo? Except I forgot what she said that they were. Where is she?"

Toward the back, two men on counter stools sat over coffee cups, drinking and stirring as the steam rose up. Every now and then they looked up at the three of them with a distant, smiling curiosity, but it seemed to Louise that their interest had by this time passed. They were tired of hearing Julie repeat, "Trigo, aanon, guanbanana, mamay, papaya, pina-pineapple, mango, banana." The woman behind the counter was tired of it, too. She was reading a letter, an aerogram in foreign script; she read it slowly, her cheeks flushing, and stopped only when parts of it made her smile. The smile was nostalgic and removed her entirely from the voices of the teasing men, the bursts of the espresso machine, and the ongoing whine of Julie's indecision.

"Maria's in a hurry," Louise said, and felt suddenly as if she were speaking Spanish. "Why don't you get mamay, it's probably delicious."

Julie began fishing in her knapsack and said, "Great! Mamay! Except I don't have any bread."

"I do," Louise said. "We better get out of here. Matthew, is yours paid for?"

"From my allowance," he said, and continued hanging on to Julie as if Louise were not there. From the back, one of the men drinking coffee looked up at Louise and smiled. He smiled at her as if she were any ordinary girl.

"All this time only beeping and beeping!" Maria greeted them. She threw her purse down and seemed to be looking wildly at the traffic through the windows and the mirror. "You'll throw up and it won't squench your thirst! *Quench* your thirst. Where you'll throw it I don't know. Take-out! Wonderful American inventing, to take it out so you have no place to throw it and then on the highway you can have a fine!"

Sipping her tropical fruit shake, Julie leaned forward. "I just remembered this really weird thing!" she said happily. "This song we always used to sing in the car. When I was a little girl. 'George Washington Bridge, Ge-orge Washington, Washington Bridge.' You know: 'Stars twinkle above, it's the loveliest night of the year.' Except we used to sing, 'George Washington Bridge, Ge-orge Washington, Washington Bridge. George Washington Bridge, Ge-orge Washington, Washington Bridge.'"

"For New Jersey only," Maria said. "And that's not where we're going. Except Jesus Christ! Look how I made a mistake! I am going on the *East* Side Highway and we need the West Side! To *pass* the George Washington Bridge only, not cross it. How I did this I don't know!"

"You should see my mother when she has to drive! My father has this theory that she's brain-injured. She's OK when she knows exactly where she's going, and if she's done it the same way a million times before, but if there's ever a detour like for construction or something—shit! She gets *so* hassled, she *lets* it hassle her. That's why she hardly ever drives. She just sits there reading the *Times* and bugging me. That there's a sale in Bonwit's and all I have to do is walk in and use her charge. That there's this terrific pantsuit in Bergdorf's and if I don't like shopping, I could order it in a couple of different colors and have it sent. She once sent me five suede skirts from Bloomingdale's that were *exactly* the same! Except for the colors. And the pockets. She is such a compulsive bitch I can't believe it."

"I know someplace there *is* a linking-up," Maria said. "A turn-off. Someplace in Bronx. But where? For Major Deegan, I think. If I watch the signs I'll find it, no problem. I hope only I don't have a blowout. So I'll have Major Deegan in Bronx, then Saw Mill comes and then Taconic. Saw Mill is what I love, not the traffic lights, *they* are a pain, but the trees. They make in one place an arc. An arch? It reminds me always of roads in French movies. Only *there* they are famous for too many accidents, I'm completely serious."

"You know what's weird, Maria? That I took French for so many years and I still have to read the subtitles. I can never understand *anything*. Even when I was in France that time in July. *Nothing*. I couldn't believe it. I got so pissed that I always had such rotten teachers."

"French," Maria said. "I never had to know it. First, Russian. A little only, at the end of the war. For the soldiers mostly. To feel more safe for what they were saying. Even usually I pretended not to. *You* know—to act stupid. Also, then later it was very good in that factory. For a better impression and not getting into troubles because I didn't like so much all the meetings for learning Marx. And then English, the same thing. Only English really for what happened later, I had to really *know*. So if people laugh sometimes still, too bad. You learn languages always when you have to. Matthew now learns Spanish a little, no problem. Mostly cursing words probably, *I* think, but other ones, too. I tell him only not to say them in front of his friends' parents. Yes, angel?"

"Angel is a *name*," Matthew said. "For a boy. If they're Spanish."

You learn languages always when you have to: once, years before, when their apartment was being painted, Louise had found, in a carton of her mother's old music papers, a hard-covered book. It had ruled lines like a notebook and handwritten daily entries, all of them in French. Sitting with it on the floor in the disarray of painters' cloths and dislodged furniture, Louise turned page after page and stared: it was an account book. "*Jeudi 14 Novembre: miel, beurre, pommes, tomates, oeufs. Lundi 23 Décembre: fromage, café, oignons, riz, fruits.*" It went on: days, dates, lists of foods, prices, totals—and that was all that there was. There was not even any indication from the numbers what the currency had been, so there was no way to tell the country. The handwriting, foreign, precise, and elegant, was probably her mother's, though Louise was not certain, and some entries looked as if they had been written by somebody else. Who? When would her mother have needed to keep such a careful account book? Why? And why, above all, had she written it in French?

"Soon, now, I think I turn," Maria said. "Except—*damn* it! Here comes a stupid red Gremlin too fast, he doesn't know *what* he does there. It's his tires, maybe. Also *I* don't have snow tires, they are only to cheat you. Especially for city driving—so they can have more money for what you don't need. Only for where we're going, maybe there *will* be snow. What do you think?"

Where *were* they going? "To the country" was all Maria had said, and had gotten up early and made sandwiches to prove it. To the country, Louise had repeated, testing it over and over again in her mind: it did not have anything to do with Birch Hill and out-trips—the awkward, overheated feeling of a special day out among ordinary people.

"Finally they fixed up that damned Hawthorn Cycle, great deal! For Rockefeller, *I* think. Now comes Saw Mill, and right after, Taconic. There is a little stream here sometimes. Only you can't maybe tell it."

Louise looked out for the stream, but saw only other cars:

suits and dresses dangled on hangers over side windows, skis and suitcases shifted on roof racks, children and dogs pressed against back windows, fathers at steering wheels peered nervously at mirrors, mothers with tinted glasses folded over maps. Families, families. "Families are shit," Maria had said.

"Here comes soon now the exit, Matthew! So far, I'm definitely OK and the little roads I think I remember. The house with the waterwheel! Mill wheel? Fake, naturally, and probably very expensive. You used to love it, baby, remember?"

Matthew looked up from his drawing. "The windmill house, Mommy? The one with the big pond?"

"Also fake, I think probably. Silly, whoever they are, they must only throw out their money. But anyway still pretty."

Julie had unzipped her fatigue jacket and kept rubbing at a small spot on her wrist. "Does that sound plastic!" she said. "Maria, why don't we go up to Woodstock? It's not that far and there's always a lot going on."

"Woodstock? For what reason? For a lot going on you can stay in New York. Besides, we're already here. It's very nice, very quiet. Only in summer *not* so quiet. We used to come here always with Dennis. For people he knows who have summerhouses, also weekend houses."

"Dennis?" Julie said, turning newly to the houses and the lawns. "I never knew there were people around here who're into dance. Who?"

"Jamie Laufer, Mommy! We can visit him!"

"Laufer," Maria said. "Laufer . . . Oh! Who was in your old school? With the big red Irish dog and the two little twin sisters? I don't know if they're here today, Matthew, and it's anyway too cold for going in his boat. There will be *some* people. Definitely. I make you a bet. Who, I don't know. Just watch now for our exit. Yes, angel?"

Matthew screamed, "*Here*, Mommy!" Maria, no longer muttering over tires or highways, made the turn and Louise realized that the safety of being inside, merely riding, would soon be over. Trees, paths, houses; houses, paths, trees—although it was probably noon by now, the grayness of the day had not abated, and the lights of occasional lamps from the windows filled up the narrow road with the mistaken intimacy of twilight.

"You can't see from here the lake," Maria said. "It's what's very nice in summer."

"Summer," Julie said, falling back again to her swimmer's position. "Sometimes I think that was the only time I was ever really happy. In our summer place. Which they sold—naturally! Did I tell you, Maria? My mother said it was too far, she has to have a place for weekends. So *now,* I can't believe it, they're renting this absolute, total monstrosity near Amagansett, and the only thing that bitch can think of is how she can *get* me to go there."

"Here comes now motorcycles, God damn it! I could anyway without them have trouble going up this hill—with the snow. From my gear-shiftings."

Louise looked out at the motorcycles as they roared through this small, unlikely road in the snow, speeding on to an invisible lake. What could they want here?

"There's my ice cream store! Look, Mommy! It's still here— the same one!"

"Oh." Maria smiled. "Marzano's. It's a store for everything, baby. *They'll* know who's here today probably. If they're open. They could be maybe in church. What do you think?" She pulled the car closer to a low white shack that in no way resembled a store. Outside it was a rack for newspapers, and nearby a hand-lettered sign and arrow that said ANTIQUES—R. RELKIN. "*That's* who's here today definitely! Rebecca! It's who we'll go and see.

Never mind Marzano, closed or open, it's no time now for ice cream, Matthew, and she is too sour anyway, Marzano. She won't even give you ever the night of day."

Julie said, "Who's Rebecca? Is she a dancer?"

"Rebecca has always here an antique store. Not exactly a store. She sells sometimes antiques. It used to be for summer only and sometimes weekends. *Not* for making a living. Only now I think she lives here all year round."

"Is she the old lady with the fat hands? And she *touches* you with them?" Matthew's small face crinkled in distaste, increasing its resemblance to the pictures of Dennis; but he bounded out the back window with Julie, whose long, lithe legs slid out now as easily, trickily as before. Naturally.

"God damn these gravels for my tires! But here anyway I won't be towed away or have pushings."

The same sign, ANTIQUES—R. RELKIN, hung on a post at the beginning of the driveway. A small, plump, gray-haired woman came rushing down it before Maria had even parked.

"Maria!" she screamed. "Maria, darling! I thought it was your Saab that I saw, but I couldn't believe it and you won't believe why I couldn't believe it. Because naturally I don't believe in ESP, not that everything is always so rational and I absolutely agree with all the wonderful young people who are showing us what false gods we've been worshiping, not that I eat organic food, I love eating too much and don't tell me it doesn't show, but I was thinking of you and Dennis this morning! In fact, I almost called you, but you don't know what the phones are like up here, it's the one thing that drives me crazy and there's nothing you can do about it, don't think I haven't tried—you know my mouth when I get going. Even though I pride myself—I'm always careful to be a lady about it, it's what I always taught my daughters: by example. Because otherwise you're only taking it out on workingmen! Although around here, find me one—*one*—who isn't a Fascist, you should see their faces when they look at you, and I'm always *very* nice. I offer them coffee, beer, anything. Leon always tells me I'm *too* nice, but I can't help it, that's the way I am. And you should see their children! Who do you think breaks all the windows around here? And not just windows! You heard what happened with the Dorfmans' house, and with all their other troubles that's just what they needed! Although Sybil Dorfman—I've always said it and I've said it to *her*: You can't spend your life with your eyes closed. He's a pig, though, there's no question about it, a brilliant pig, but still—! And the pity is the children, especially the little one. How she'll pay them back I don't even want to guess! But what am I telling *you* for, Maria? You know them much better than I do." Louise thought that Rebecca had stopped, but it was only to rub her hands together and stamp her feet; it made her look like Rumpelstiltskin.

"Dorfman I never even heard of," Maria said, and, slamming the door of the car, reached in through the back window for the bag of sandwiches.

"Of *course* you did, darling," Rebecca said, and, with her arm around Maria, propelled her up the gravel path. "But what are we talking out here for? In the cold? Let's go inside. Not that it's so warm in there—the boiler's broken and I'm *aching*. Why do you think I'm dressed like this?"

It was exactly what Louise had been wondering about. No matter what your eye hit—her Laplander's boots, wool Scottish plaid slacks, long Mexican serape pushed over a turtleneck Irish fisherman's sweater, a child's bright red furry earmuffs half covered by a multicolored, flower-filled East European peasant kerchief, Rebecca looked, as Louise stared, like a package that had been sent on from one wrong foreign address to another, receiving at each mistaken customs office its country's distinctive stamp.

"You'll have to forgive me, Maria—I *know* you'll forgive me, with you I don't even have to say it—but everything is in such disorder. I'm half here, I'm half still in the city, sometimes I don't even know *where* I am. Everyone always says to me, I don't know how you can bury yourself in the country like that—you of all people. But I don't *feel* buried. And that's what's important! Here, it's beautiful, the air is beautiful, I can take walks wherever I want to—and I don't have to be afraid. Of course it's true, I loved the city, for me the city was everything. I *loved* my neighborhood, I taught in a *wonderful* school—for thirty-five years, Maria. Did you know that? Thirty-five years! *Everyone* cried when I retired— the janitor, the principal, the elevator man. Cried? Wept! They used up more Board of Education tissue boxes because of me that last week—*I* got back at that God-damn Bureau of Supplies! And the letters—you should have seen the letters I got! From students. From alumni. Begging me, pleading with me not to leave. Young people are wonderful."

Turning toward Matthew, Julie, and Louise, Maria said, "Rebecca was a history teacher."

"History? Maria! Darling! I was a *French* teacher—you know that! Of course you have so much on your mind now, don't think I don't understand. Although *lots* of people think I was a history teacher, it's because I *know* so much about it, I've always been so involved. And I've lived through so much of it, I'm practically a part of history myself. Leon's always teasing me about it, he says that's why I'm so interested in antiques, I'm practically an antique myself. Although I'll tell you something, Maria, I'm not so old that I can't be flexible. And that's why young people always gravitate to me, they *feel* it, I'm on their wavelength. I'm like a mother to them, but a mother they can actually *talk* to. That brilliant little Carla Saltzman, she's a hematologist, *she* calls me long-distance from *Denver*. She's working on an Indian reservation,

I'm *so* proud of her. And when I walk outside here, I don't have to worry about being mugged; I don't know how you stand it, still living on the West Side! With all the druggies and the junkies and with what went on at Columbia. And the way they *look*! Not that I disagree with them—they're brave and they're wonderful and I could never stand to sit in school myself. But they don't *know* anything. They think they *invented* everything. Everything! What do they think *we* did in the thirties? Do they think we didn't also have bodies? Or beds? And sometimes *not* beds, because, believe me, then parents didn't just hand over money and apartments and houses. I'll never forget—right in the middle of the woods in that broken-down camp, Leon thought I looked so innocent, was *he* in for a surprise! . . . *We* called it free love, it *had* to be free. It was still the Depression. And politics, too—the Spanish Civil War! They weren't even *born* yet."

Rebecca's arm was still around Maria; they had reached the house, but continued standing outside it. In her cold and discomfort, Louise concentrated on the odd quality of Rebecca's voice: she had quacked French verbs at students for so many years that now, without knowing it, she could not stop the quacking. Worse, she plowed down on words and consonants with lingering lopsided lips and with her tongue emphasized the sounds that students, in a dictation, might have forgotten to underline.

Maria said, "It's all, I think, different here now, Rebecca. You had always on the left side your studio."

"*Studio! Please,* Maria! You think I didn't know what I had there? It was a shed! A shed is a shed. And it was all right for the summers, but as soon as I decided that I would really be *up* here I knew I had to have something different. And Leon wouldn't let me sit all day in what was practically an outhouse, so I'm building a marvelous showroom that's an addition to the house, and it was designed by a *brilliant* boy from Yale Architecture School.

You probably know him—Jesse Sandweiss. He's young and marvelous and full of wonderful, creative ideas and he comes from a wonderful family, I always loved him and told them to have faith in him, no matter what! And I did, and I was right, and there's nothing he won't do for me. But there's nothing he can do about the builder! Who's a crook and a reactionary, you should see his pig eyes and his German wife and it frightens me to even *think* of their children someday in a ballot box. And that's why you have to forgive me—because most of my good stuff is still in the shed, and all because of that lousy builder the showroom is freezing and you won't have anything to see."

"I can't anyway afford things, Rebecca. It's not why I came."

"I know, darling. Who can? It's a terrible time and I saw it coming—I lived through one Depression and now I'm living through another! I *warned* Leon. We lost so much money, I saw all the signs and our broker feels *terrible*. He's a wonderful boy— Bobby Meltzer. We've known his father since God knows when and you can imagine how *he* feels! He gave him all his business— and after all that, Bobby lost everything. Everything! Of course it's not his fault—it's the times, it's economics. But he's a very sensitive boy, Bobby. Not that he's a boy anymore. He has a wife and three little babies. And his wife is marvelous. From a *very* wealthy family. And with her taste and her background she can't stay away from me and my beautiful things. She loves my attitude about life—you know, with that kind of money there isn't always a lot of warmth in the home—Ooh! Did you hear that? It's the phone! I can hear it through my earmuffs. Let me quick run and answer it! Come on!"

Inside, stamping her feet from the snow and the cold, Rebecca disappeared—even more like Rumpelstiltskin—through a swinging door, leaving them all in her large, chilly showroom. It was wood-beamed but mostly empty—two small antique chests and a highboy stood to one side, and several sets of andirons were laid out before an unfinished fireplace. Exactly in the center, like a stage set, were an old kitchen table, a few ordinary chairs, and a potbelly stove.

"A *Koche Ofen!*" Maria said. "It's what we had at my cousin Klaus's. You heat up the bricks and it makes you then very warm. Not, you know, *so* warm, but better."

Matthew said, "Mommy, Jamie *Lau*fer. When can we ask her?"

"As soon as she comes off the phone, angel, I promise. You can have now the sandwiches, yes, baby?"

Julie, who had zipped up her fatigue jacket and pulled her wool cap down so that it covered her face almost entirely, looked around the bare room and said, "Typical. Absolutely typical. Andirons and no fire! I can't believe it—it's exactly what my mother would do. Except that we did have a real fire and a fireplace. In the country."

"She would have, I think, a fire, Julie. Only she doesn't yet have the fireplace finished. If you stand near to the stove you'll be warmer."

Maria herself was not standing close to the stove but was sitting on a faded upholstered wing chair that she had pulled up to the table; to Louise she seemed suddenly faded, too. Her hair was disheveled, her shoulders were hunched, and the yellowish, lined raincoat that she always wore was half open, as if she were unaware of the cold. Her arms were spread out on the table, but the heavy canvas sandwich bag still hung from one of her wrists. She seemed caught in an odd, unconscious oblivion: her face and body drained, her eyes far away. Had she sat this way once at her cousin Klaus's? When she was *very* skinny? Sleet began hitting the wide, unshaded windows and one of Matthew's Magic Markers fell; the sounds were simultaneous.

"I love fireplaces," Julie said. "I really love them. I mean the real kind—with a fire in it, like the one we had in the country. It was *so* beautiful—I used to sit there in front of it, watching it for hours and hours. You know what I just flashed to? The pictures in children's books! I used to just stare and stare at the fire and sort of turn the pages in the books and get so high that I would really get into those pictures. I mean really *into* them, like I was *inside* of them. They were very stoned."

How do you like to go up in a swing,
Up in the air so blue?
Oh, I do think it the pleasantest thing
Ever a child can do!

It was what Louise's mother had read to her—and read very quickly, in obvious annoyance. Her accent had been more noticeable even to Louise, and seemed so especially now in remembering it: her fair-skinned, distant mother in a blue-green suit, sitting on a park bench in the playground, with one hand rapidly turning pages, with the other shielding her eyes—not from the sun, but from the sight of the sandbox, which offended her. The noises offended her, too: the gossiping women, the crying children, the planes overhead, the trains underneath.

"We had for children *terrible* books," Maria said. "Always ugly, always punishings. Struwwelpeter! Max and Moritz! Only bad children and only terrible things to happen to them. Fairy tales, too. *Not* like here—Grimm stories they make very different in America. I *know*—from reading them to Matthew. Do you remember, Matthew? When I read to you those witches stories? No? I think probably you're only hungry, *that's* maybe the trouble. Yes, baby? What do you think?"

"Maria, guess who that was! It was Leon!" said Rebecca, pushing through the swinging door with the force of her clothes and her voice. "I told him you were here and he sends his love and I told him how amazing it was that you're here because I was just thinking of calling you this morning because of Elliot. And I said, 'See! You can never tell what'll happen!' but he wasn't surprised at all because I can *always* tell. And we're so proud of Elliot! I said, 'Call up Elliot right now and tell him that Maria will be glad to tell him everything that he needs to know.' Because I know you would, I don't even have to ask you, and anyway you're exactly the right person."

Maria was unwrapping the sandwiches. She raised her head and said, "Rebecca, this is Julie Dresner and this is Louise Weil. But I think I don't know who is Elliot."

"Maria! You know Elliot—my wonderful, brilliant nephew— really he's Leon's nephew, and we're so proud of him and we always were, even when his mother used to complain that he was too quiet and he wouldn't talk to her, and who could blame him! I wouldn't talk to her, either, she never shuts up, she's one of those really overprotective, *you* know what I mean—*smothering* mothers, so naturally he had to retreat into his books and his studies, and now even *she* has to admit that she's proud of him for what he got. But we're even more proud of him because not only did he get it but also now, finally, he'll really be able to get away from her. And you'll see how he'll flower! I told him never mind if she carries on before he goes, it'll be good for her."

"What did Elliot get?" Matthew said. His voice was high-pitched, his mouth was thick with peanut butter and jelly; he looked, Louise thought, like a little boy just checking up on someone else's special present.

"Look at him, Maria! Just look at that face—that adorable, precious face! He looks exactly like Dennis . . . But what are you feeding him, darling? *Peanut* butter? I feel *terrible*! You know me with my cooking, I *love* it, I would have made you *anything*. Never mind the limitations I have to put up with here and the broken boiler."

"It's all right, Rebecca," Maria said. "I didn't anyway know where we would be coming and I don't believe ever to stop in the highway places."

"Darling, I know it. The food is inedible, it's American Bland—that's what *I* call it, and who knows what crap they put into it! I *always* took along my own wonderful things. Breads and meats and cheeses and pâtés! Of course, now everyone does it, but they buy them from Zabar's and they think they're being so original. And they don't even *believe* me when I say that *I* made everything myself. Because I wasn't afraid to experiment, and as far as foods go, in my opinion, all they are is Nouveau Gourmet."

"An apple, Matthew, baby? Or a tangerine? Which?"

"Tangerines, tangerines—that's the one thing I have plenty of," Rebecca said, hopping again through the swinging door. "That's the least I can do for you, and don't think I forgot about Matthew and his peanut butter. Remember when he was little? How I always kept a jar of peanut butter waiting specially for him? Because who else do I know who would touch it?"

"Rebecca," Maria called out. "Your nephew Elliot. What do you want him to ask me about?"

"Oh, Elliot? I *told* you, Maria. He's going on a very special scientific exchange program to the Soviet Union, and he's going to be in Leningrad and he was practically handpicked. And it's absolutely marvelous and exciting and I knew you'd be able to tell him everything."

"Leningrad I think is very cold," Maria said. "I wasn't ever there. Where it's warm, I think, is the Crim? Crimea? I don't know how you say it—they took us only to Moscow, also very cold, but people said always where it's nice, pleasant, is the Black Sea."

"Oh, it's *all* wonderful, I knew you'd think so. You're exactly the right person to ask and I'm so glad I thought of it." Rebecca returned with a cellophane bag of tangerines which she cradled under her layers of clothing.

"Tits," Matthew whispered to Julie, giggling. "Look at all her titties."

"Aren't children wonderful, Maria? Even in times like these they can find things to laugh and be happy about. And *we're* the ones who take it away from them. I don't know why and I don't know how, but it's something I was always very careful about and people can say I have a childlike nature, I don't care. Because it keeps me young in my attitudes and that's what everyone always appreciates about me."

Rebecca put the bag of tangerines out on the table and said, "I know this isn't very fancy, I didn't put it in a bowl or anything, but I never believed in being bourgeois. Come on, girls, aren't you eating?" It was the first time she seemed to realize that Louise and Julie were there. But it was not Louise whom she was looking at. Naturally. "Darling," she said, turning to Julie, "you look very familiar to me. Tell me your name again. How do I know you?"

Pulling her wool cap down as far as it would go, Julie stared straight at the andirons. She looked extremely sullen, but clearly didn't worry that other people might think so. Why should she? It wouldn't make them wonder about *her* mental health. . . .

IV

LOUISE'S NEW DOCTOR, WHO WAS TWO BUS RIDES AWAY, WAS NAMED Dr. Vinograd. On the New York City buses, which she had forgotten, his name chuffed toward her like a Russian train station—Vino*grad* Vino*grad* (whistles blew in the icy expanse)—and when he came out into the waiting room to greet her—balding and heavyset—he seemed to be chuffing, too: last train out, the barrier down, the stationmaster swaying with his lantern in regret and stamping his feet in the cold. His size surprised her: so large and broad-shouldered amid the exact neatness of scaled-down, precise waiting-room furniture, how did he not bump into things? Intent on keeping her thoughts in one line, she looked up into the roundness of his face—expanding, creasing forehead and unending, puffed-out cheeks—and tried to find in it a map of Russia. Other than a vague idea of vast and lonely endlessness, she did not know what the map of Russia looked like.

In fact, though she had been given very exact directions, Louise had missed her stop. In the late-afternoon January slush, she had been watching two sets of children coming home from school, carrying notebooks and art projects, each with their mothers. Louise noticed the first set as soon as they got on the bus: a small, dark-haired, small-featured mother and her two daughters. One of the girls had short, dark, curly hair like her mother's and the other's long, straight hair, clasped back in a ponytail, came out in child's runny strands beneath her rain hat. The mother, to Louise's eye, was obviously European. She spoke very quietly, with a trace of a British accent, and smiled at her two little girls in a kind of wonder as they chattered together, unaware of the bus or the rain. The girls' voices, excited but indistinct, rose occasionally in the bell-like shrillness of childhood.

"Rachel! Evie!" their mother said as she half raised a finger to shush them. She smiled as she said it, and seeing that Louise had taken it in, she looked up directly and smiled at her, too.

Because of this smile, Louise could not look at them any longer and finally, having passed her stop, she stood up to pull the cord and saw that Rachel, Evie, and their mother were no longer there. They had secretly climbed out of the bus before she could climb into their lives.

AS FAR AS LOUISE COULD SEE, THE MOST IMPORTANT THING TO TELL DR. Vinograd first was the faces she kept seeing everywhere. Literally, they would not let her rest. In her room in Maria's apartment, creases in the sheets and the pillows, cracks in the ceiling and the walls, each of them, all of them gave back strange, changing faces. First they were vague and cloudlike, but they changed immediately as she looked at them into odd, distorted, devouring shapes. They were not animals, not people, but freak-like pieces of features: a round, growing, man-woman's cheek stretching into a smirk or a howl. It would dissolve into a small, sharp, barking dog's single sharp, triangular ear. Or the curtain would stir and there would be a certain monkey's lean, vicious face—leering, ridiculous—till the leer itself turned into a curling, switching, bodiless tail smelling of a zoo.

"Don't be afraid of the noises," Maria had said the first evening. "He's only crazy." She did not mean the awful clang of the plumbing which went on constantly, vibrating through all the apartments on that line whenever it was used, but the nightly noises of the man in the next-door apartment, whose bedroom wall was on the other side of Louise's. Every night he yelled the same wild karate commands and apparently knocked over large pieces of furniture. He kept it up for a long time and when the throwing and yelling part was over, he laughed in a loud, stupid, braying voice; beside it you could hear a girl's voice giggling and shrieking, high-pitched and equally stupid.

"It's only foreplay," Maria said. "I don't know how he pays the rent. His father, maybe. He used to be in advertising, advertisement—*I* don't know. Now he doesn't have a job. He has a motorcycle. This girl has been for a long time, I think maybe she has a job. He has always the same maid—*she* has a job, the laundry also. From his parents, probably. *I* think."

At the bathroom sink, Louise did not arrange her toothbrush and face soap, but stared at the drops of water as they gurgled into the drain. They clung to the basin in groups, separating singly, dismally, as they were forced, without control, toward the drain.

It was all this, Louise knew, that she had to tell Dr. Vinograd, but though she began to, he did not ask her to go on, nor did he ask her about dreams. He talked to her instead about registering for courses.

"I *can't* go to school," Louise said. "I'm not ready. You know what happened before."

Dr. Vinograd pulled at his tie, it seemed to be a characteristic gesture. "It wouldn't have to be for credit, you could do it nonmatric. Take two or three courses and see what you like. You're testing *them,* you know."

"I'm not taking cello *anyplace.*"

"You don't have to," he said, and smiling boyishly, pleasantly, seemed to mean it. The smile was inward; it fogged his glasses and gave his large, round face a momentary nostalgic look. "You could take history."

"I *hate* history," Louise said, surprised at her own vehemence, and knew that what she meant was she hated her own. That was the other thing she had to tell him about, get it over with now, but Dr. Vinograd was on the phone. It seemed to go on ringing incessantly, and at each new call he scrupulously said, "I'm sorry," or shook his head in what might have been genuine dismay.

Louise was not sorry: she turned to look at the one wall lined entirely with bookshelves. It was the same wall of bookshelves she had been looking at since her early teens. What did familiarity breed? Dr. Vinograd's voice went on at the telephone: a woman's nightmare, maybe, had burst out into the middle of the day, a boy had flunked out of school and was going to be drafted, a girl's father had died suddenly and she had run out of medication. Maybe. Maybe. Dr. Vinograd turned through the pages of his appointment book. Maybe they were just all canceling their appointments because something better had come up. It was more likely; in other people's lives, it was always more likely.

"About ten?" Dr. Vinograd said. "I thought you said about two. I know, I know, it's only my own wishful thinking."

About. About. A-boat, was what he said. He had a Canadian accent.

The Collected Papers of Sigmund Freud, the Ernest Jones biography, the *Physicians' Desk Reference*, *Psychosomatic Medicine*, *Childhood and Society*, *The Origins of Psychoanalysis*, *Organization and Pathology of Thought*, *Disturbed Communication*, *A History of Medical Psychology*, *Schizophrenia as a Human Process*, *Psychoanalysis of the Neuroses*, *Psychoanalytic Education in the United States*, *Community Programs for Mental Health* . . . What familiarity bred was a dazed, dumb sense of safety and the giddiness of something slightly ludicrous.

To Louise, Dr. Vinograd said very seriously, "I'm terribly sorry we've had so many interruptions." He pulled at his tie; any minute now, he would certainly say "What are you thinking about?" It was not foreknowledge, it was not déjà vu, it was simply familiarity.

"What were you thinking about all that time?"

A-boat. A-boat. To stop herself from laughing, Louise said very quickly, "I know why my sister wouldn't write to me."

Elisabeth walked around the streets of Stockholm, her blondness the same as the city's pure white light, her cold, even features the same as its architecture. Cameras were slung over her shoulders and her small eyes squinted into the distance, envisioning in it a building which did not yet exist. Her clothing also seemed blond, which in these streets appeared unremarkable like everything else about Elisabeth, but, exactly like the photograph in the *Times*, was the purposeful opposite of what was true. She stopped now and then to buy things; she smiled though she did not mean it, she spoke in perfect Swedish, she counted up her change and left. At an outdoor stand she bought flowers, and in her stark, blond, grainy apartment, placed them in a dark red cut-glass vase. The vase did not exactly belong with the apartment, but stood out in its own old-fashioned vivid beauty just for that reason. It had belonged to her husband's family for generations, and had been given to Elisabeth as a wedding present. She walked with it carefully, nimbly, quietly to the kitchen, where she filled it with water and, still carrying it, managing it easily, went past her sons' bedroom. It was neat and colorful, this room, filled with unusual, ingenious European toys. The two little boys, Per and Arne, tiny and towheaded, were playing together, rolling on the floor, giggling and shrieking. Elisabeth smiled and raised one finger to shush them; it was possible, even, that she might have hugged them, but she was carrying the flower-filled vase, which she did not return to the living room. She walked on with it farther back into the apartment and put it down finally on a small white ledge in the study. In this room, wide-windowed and curtainless, the light was ice-cold and the stillness absolute: it was exactly what Elisabeth liked. Two high, slanted drafting tables and raised high-backed chairs were facing opposite walls. On one of the chairs sat Elisabeth's husband, his body straight, long, and lean, his hair very fair but slightly curly. Only the back of him was visible, he was concentrating on a blueprint on the slanted drafting table. The phone rang—the short several buzzing rings of European phones. Elisabeth's husband got up to answer it. He did not say hello, but said, "Bjelding," and after a brief conversation consisting mainly of Swedish monosyllables, hung up the phone and noticed the vase and flowers on the sill. He smiled at Elisabeth and more or less grasped her hand. They stood that way for a few minutes, and then sat down, both of them, on their high-backed chairs, which faced opposite walls. Occasional Swedish monosyllables floated between them in the ice-cold light of the room which Elisabeth loved. She had climbed directly onto the screen of a Bergman movie, and had allowed nothing and no one to stop her.

"She's afraid I'll contaminate her and make her crazy."

"Explain to me how that—" Dr. Vinograd was beginning, but the phone rang.

The Ego and Mechanisms of Defense, Symposium on Suicide, Elementary Textbook of Psychoanalysis, Language and Thought in Schizophrenia, Psychoanalytic Concepts and the Structural Theory, Wayward Youth, Searchlights on Delinquency, Character Analysis, The Collected Papers of Otto Fenichel, The Psychoanalytic Study of the Child, Men Under Stress, Patterns of Mothering, Modern Clinical Psychiatry, Dreams and the Uses of Regression.

"We'll have to talk about that next time, Louise. It's very important. And next time, I promise you, I'll have the answering service pick up the phone. In the meantime, get ahold of some college catalogues and find out about registration. Anyway, you can register late, it doesn't matter."

He had not said "Our time is up." Standing up herself, Louise felt as if she would have to say it for him, but instead said, "Are you Canadian?"

Dr. Vinograd smiled. It was the same surprising, boyish smile that had come with his suggesting history. "I was brought up in Montreal."

Beyond the waiting room, a narrow hallway separated Dr. Vinograd's office (LAWRENCE VINOGRAD, M.D.) from his apartment:

against one wall, which was as far as Louise could see, was a pair of skis. They stood upright, ready, waiting. Rumpled, heavy Dr. Vinograd went skiing down mountains in the snow! His expression lightened from exhilaration and surprise; his wide Russian cheeks grew red and boyish from the cold. Wearing a ski jacket like everyone else, he did not pull at his tie, a gesture characteristic since boyhood; also, there were no phones to answer. It was possible, of course, that he would break his leg.

V

IN THE CHILLY ROOM, REBECCA REPEATED, "I'M ABSOLUTELY *POSITIVE*, DARling. Where did I meet you? Just give me a hint!"

Very quickly Maria said, "That's Louise Weil, Rebecca, and this is Julie Dresner."

"Dresner, Dresner . . . Of *course* I know you! Your father is that *marvelous,* brilliant lawyer."

"He's a psychiatrist."

"You have an uncle who's a violist. With that *wonderful* new chamber group—I remember them from Spoleto!"

"My cousin. He plays the oboe."

"Your sister was a camper at Bucks Rock when my younger daughter was a counselor there."

"I don't have a sister."

"Didn't your parents have a house on Fire Island? *Years* ago— you would have been a baby."

"Martha's Vineyard. They just sold it."

"Wait a minute, darling. Your father's a psychiatrist, the house is on Martha's Vineyard, you're an only child . . . Didn't your mother write a book about indoor plants? It was just reissued?"

"Yes," Julie said. "Her plants! It's the only thing that stupid bitch ever cared about."

"*Darling!* What a *terribly* unfair thing to say! Your mother always cared about so *many* things. Why do you think she wrote that book in the first place? *You* don't know! *You* don't remember! You don't know what those times were like! And I don't only mean McCarthy, though you probably don't know who *he* was either! A big blur on the television screen—that's all it was to you!" Rebecca's hands were shaking so hard that a section of tangerine fell to the floor. Her face, already puffy and red, became an even darker, more alarming color as she bent down, and a fringe of her choppy gray hair grazed the table. Matthew giggled. There was a smell of sawed wood, cold, and tangerines. It was not "like" anything, Louise thought, and realized that the uneasy, sleepy distance had left her.

Maria looked very surprised. She said, "What was this book?"

"Oh, *you* know," Julie said, fully raising her head, but still sneering. "My mother wrote that stupid, boring book for stupid, bored housewives. How to make your *plants* look beautiful. How to make your *house* look beautiful. It's all just a reflection—how to make your*self* look beautiful, that's really all it is. All ego. All self."

"*Julia.* Darling. I know I yelled at you and I'm sorry about it, but if you keep talking that way I'm going to have to yell at you again. And it does *terrible* things to my blood pressure."

Matthew said, "Her name isn't Jul*ya*, its Jul*ee*."

Louise looked at Rebecca: she had regained her balance, but the rosiness of her cheeks no longer looked like windburn.

"And you're another one, Matthew! Don't think I don't see it coming! Sitting there with your sandwich and your drawing paper—did I get one word? One hello? One kiss? One *any*thing? Go ahead and giggle, Matthew. Life is so funny."

Maria sneezed. "God *damn* it if I now get a cold. I can't afford it from my screwed-up sick leave. I would *have* the time, it's only from the stupid cutbacks, they are always hedging and hawing."

"Darling, I *know*. Sometimes I feel so discouraged about the future. We were all so *care*ful, we were all so *self*less. We were going to raise the best, the freest generation of children ever known in the history of mankind. And we did. They're *wonderful*. But sometimes I think: My God, after all, what are we? A few generations up from the monkeys, a few generations down from the trees. And monkeys! At least monkeys don't kill each other."

Maria began sneezing spasmodically and shaking things out of her purse. "Monkeys are I think the one animal Matthew didn't ask me for yet. Yes, angel? *Damn* it if I can't now find even tissues, I know I have some. And also histamines. It's maybe only sinus and not a cold. I *hope*."

"Maria, darling! Don't *take* anything," Rebecca said. "I'll make you some tea. My marvelous *Lapsang souchong,* you'll love it. It's from a wonderful couple who know *everything* about tea. They go all over the world looking for it and they've been to Ceylon and the Amazon and *every*where! Leon calls them the Teacups because their name is Kupperman and because *you* know Leon, I hate to say it, in some ways he's a very conventional person. And some people might think they're a little bit kooky or a little bit nutty, but as far as I'm concerned, I don't see what's wrong with having a special interest or with pursuing it! And that's something young people could learn—that you have to *pursue* things and social change doesn't come overnight."

"We had I think camomile tea, I don't know what," Maria called out as Rebecca went off through the door to the kitchen. "It was from some kind of roots, you can pick them. Not real tea. Also not real coffee, my cousin Klaus used always to complain that he missed his *bean* coffee. We made it from hickory. Chicory? I don't know what. Real coffee, *bean* coffee I had first when I went to West Berlin. It tasted to me, I don't know what, funny. I had first to get used to it."

"That's exactly what I've always said, Maria! You can get used to anything. And it has nothing to do with age! Some people, even if they're young, can get stuck—in a rut—and that's it! And other people can go on and on—changing. Exploring. Look at me! If I can adapt, at my age, to living in a freezing house, without any heat, with no one around and isolated in the country. Without even a stove working properly! And it isn't as if the builder didn't have time, God knows I *called* him enough times." Rebecca's voice suddenly got louder as she came in carrying a tray. She said, "Anyway, what can I do?"

"That's a beautiful teapot," Louise said. It was delicate handpainted china—pale flowers on a black background—and contrasted oddly with the heavy brown clay mugs.

"*Thank* you, darling." Rebecca beamed. "It's an antique, but I didn't have the heart to part with it, so I decided, What the hell! I'll call it a fringe benefit." She looked at Louise for the first time and, immediately turning to Maria, said, "Weil? You said her name is Weil? Is she related to the perfume people? Because we *met* them in Greece—in one of those *marvelous* ruins, it was in the middle of a downpour and there was no place to take shelter."

The Kuppermans, a slightly kooky, slightly nutty couple, were tramping through the tropical underbrush of an out-of-the-way Caribbean island. They were both wearing high boots and safari suits, having learned from long experience to be prepared for anything when they were pursuing their special interest. Still, the heat and the mosquitoes were getting to them, and out of all the plants and roots they had looked at and touched they hadn't found anything that could qualify as tea. The air was very heavy;

it felt as if it might rain. A bird screeched above them. Mr. Kupperman touched his head for droppings and said, "Do you think we could have made a mistake? That this place is better known for coffee? Or papayas?" Mrs. Kupperman, bent over with her special tea shovel, the same one she had taken along on every trip, said, "That's exactly what you said in the Amazon. Remember? I hate to say it, but in some ways you're a very conventional person." The bird screeched again and Mr. Kupperman said, "The last time we heard a bird screaming like that was in Ceylon and we got caught in a monsoon."

"If I only listened to you," Mrs. Kupperman said, "we'd just be stuck and in a rut. It's a good thing I'm open to change and flexible."

"But there isn't even anyplace to take shelter. Do you *hear* how that bird sounds?"

Just as Mrs. Kupperman was reluctantly getting up, still holding on to her tea shovel, they heard a slight rustling sound close by. There, in a tiny clearing which they hadn't even noticed, stood a delicate-looking, olive-skinned little girl who was staring at them and smiling. She had long black hair, her eyes were shy, and her features were Indian. Months later Mrs. Kupperman told her friends that the child had stepped out of the jungle like a vision, making it impossible for her to speak. At the time, though, what she did was grip her husband's shoulder and cry out, "My God! Did you see that? What an adorable child! Will you just look at that face? She's precious!"

"Here we go again," said Mr. Kupperman. "Starting in with natives! For all we know, right in back of that adorable, precious little face there's a bunch of adorable brothers, uncles, and cousins waiting around with their blowguns."

"You're being ridiculous," said Mrs. Kupperman, who for years before her retirement had been a high-school Spanish teacher.

"But I'll ask her where we can go just in case it *does* rain—for your sake."

Uneasily, Mr. Kupperman leaned against a tree. He was determined to look casual, friendly, and unafraid for the moment when the blowgun party would decide to make itself visible. Meanwhile Mrs. Kupperman began speaking to the child in Spanish, plying her with questions. She spoke overloudly, overslowly, pausing and enunciating each syllable as if it were a dictation. The little girl, who was not a vision, but might just as well have been, did not respond in any way. She remained standing there, continuing to stare at them politely and smile shyly. As Mrs. Kupperman repeated her questions even more slowly and with growing impatience, Mr. Kupperman, seeing how useless his wife's efforts were, decided that simply *looking* unafraid would not save them. He would step forward, turn out his pockets, open his hands, and call out with high-spirited, brotherly conviction, "*Productos Tropicales!*"

Finally, Mrs. Kupperman could no longer control herself. She stopped smiling at the girl, and with terrific disgust screamed into the comfortless jungle air, "*Casa! Casa!* Where's your *house,* darling? My God! Don't you even know *that?*" At this point the little girl stopped staring. She turned around and on her lithe brown legs began skipping away casually, agilely through the high, coarse grasses and the strange, spiny plants.

"Come on!" Mrs. Kupperman yelled to her husband. "Hurry up! She's trying to tell us to follow her. Young people are wonderful, and no matter where I go they always gravitate to me because of my attitudes."

The Kuppermans, in their high boots and safari suits, made their way through the dense and difficult ground, trailing after this beautiful, vision-like child who had in no way signaled or beckoned to them. Suddenly they lost sight of her.

"I knew I didn't like this," Mr. Kupperman said. "Running around with no maps in the middle of a jungle! With a monsoon coming up!"

"You're being rigid again," said Mrs. Kupperman, though she was worried herself, and because they were out of breath, they both stopped and for the first time looked directly around them. There, only a few yards ahead of them, was no jungle at all, but a large and beautiful house with a wall of greenery around it. Through the greenery, which was pleasant and not steamy or ominous, they could see "their" little girl and three others like her swinging through the air, high above the wall and the garden. Delicate-looking and black-haired, all of them, their eyes were shy and their faces were Indian. They swung higher and higher and were not afraid; occasionally their voices rang out through the tropics in the bell-like shrillness of childhood.

"*There* she is!" Mrs. Kupperman called out, pointing in triumph, though she could not actually tell which was the girl they had seen before. They crossed the road and, drawing closer to the house, noticed a neatly lettered name plate. "Weil," Mrs. Kupperman read aloud in surprise. "Weil . . . Weil . . . Do you think she's related to the perfume people?"

"I don't know who I'm related to," Louise began to say aloud, but Rebecca was no longer interested.

"Oh my God! Look at this! I almost forgot!" she said, beaming again and pointing with pudgy, outspread hands to the carefully arranged table. "I don't want you to think I'm dogmatic, and I wouldn't want you to get the idea, especially *you*, Julia darling, that I would ever interfere with anyone's free choice, but this is one thing—*one thing* that I absolutely have to insist on. Honey! With *Lapsang souchong*, if you put sugar in it, you might just as well pour it down the drain."

Still sneezy and sniffling, Maria began pouring out the tea, carefully holding and turning the strainer as if it were either a total novelty or else an object she hadn't seen for so long a time that it might be calling up memories.

"Yucch, Mommy," Matthew said, as the steam rose from the teapot and the cups. "It smells like bacon."

"Oh, Maria! He's so *sensitive*. It's not as if I believe in heredity, everybody *knows* the difference that environment and exposure makes—otherwise what would be the point of it all! But just look at him! Listen to him! He's just like Dennis. Even his *nose* is sensitive!"

Maria said, "My nose is stopped off. Stopped up? And I can't smell anything. How can it be like bacon?"

"Because it's *smoked*, Maria. That's what's so specially marvelous about *Lapsang souchong*. It has a wonderful distinct smoky aroma. And taste! So just don't anybody ask me for sugar because it's the honey that brings it out. Here!"

Rebecca put the jar of honey on the table. Louise saw no sunlight in the room, but a slow, golden, streamy, comfortable reverie: honey in a jar. There was no sunlight in the room but this leaden, brown, sticky syrup—a hot, sick, fevered, gluey ball. This sun was diseased and tropical, quarantined in a glass jar. "*Cordon sanitaire*"—a technique conceived and named by Marcel Proust's father, a neat, precise French doctor, efficient and disciplined for the public good. A small man, probably, with a beard or mustache which he curled or pulled at, a characteristic gesture left over from his student days. In his high-ceilinged, large, neat, official room—bureaucratic, but his—he pulled at his mustache and puzzled over methods to improve life for people he would never know. And possibly didn't care to. At home, his small son choked, sneezed, drank tea with lime-flavored cookies, and dreamed and dreamed constantly in his own private *cordon sanitaire*. He had no regard at all for the public good.

"I'll have it open for you in one minute, don't worry," Rebecca said as she struggled, banging and trying to turn the top of the sticky honey jar.

"You could run it under hot water," Matthew said.

"I know, darling. Isn't he sweet? I always said you were sweet, Matthew. But with the way that boiler is working in there, by the time the water gets hot your tea'll be cold. Just don't get impatient and don't go looking for sugar."

Julie said, "White sugar is very bad for you."

"Oh, darling!" Rebecca said, throwing out her arms and immediately ending all her efforts with the honey jar. "I knew we'd agree! You're a wonderful girl and you have a wonderful mother—you were a *baby* practically when she wrote that book! So how could you have understood? In fact, you were probably the baby she wrote it *for*. Not that I want you to get the idea that your mother could *ever* have been the kind of person who would do a thing like that! Who could limit her interests and concerns to her own uterus. That would have gone against the grain of everything she believed in and worked for for years!"

"That's I think *too* much honey, Matthew, angel," Maria said. She had, with almost no one noticing it, opened the honey jar, swiftly turning the top with the frayed end of her raincoat.

"Oh, Maria, thank you, dear. I don't know why I didn't think of asking you. You have the most marvelous hands. Just like Dennis. He has the most marvelous feet."

Louise waited for Maria to say: Not anymore, he doesn't. But instead she scratched some honey strands from the lining of her raincoat and said, "I teach him always hot water because I am afraid with banging there could be sometimes broken glass. Little pieces. It happened to me sometimes when I am too impatient."

Rebecca said, "Julia, darling, now I *know* you'll understand what I mean. All the things parents have to think about and take into consideration. That's why what your mother did was so brave and heroic and absolutely idealistic."

Julie spooned the honey into her tea and, examining the jar, said, "I don't know if it's natural."

"But, darling! Of *course* it's natural. What you just don't understand is the climate of those times. It's too far away for you. When your mother wrote that book, it was the Age of Conformity. And I'm not just talking about gray flannel suits! What I'm talking about is all those people who got caught up—they couldn't help themselves—in the whole trend and sway and spirit of the times. Not that *I* got trapped into it even then. Because it always seemed escapist and reactionary to me. And that's all that was going *on* then—flight into the suburbs! Your own *lawn*. Your own *house*. Your own *psyche*. Your own little *garden*—and for some people, not so little! And *that*, Julia darling, was what your mother was up against! Forget the city and live in the trees! And these were genuinely progressive people, not just ordinary *shtunks*! . . . So *your* mother got the idea that if she could only *show* people, *explain* to them that if what they wanted was greens and the gratification of making something grow, you could do it in your own apartment. In the city. And you didn't have to run and flee! Because it's nothing new, everybody knows: Since when is flight an answer?"

Rebecca stopped, took a long, resonating swallow of the tea, which was now cold, and, opening her mouth again, exuded an odor which seemed to Louise like fish gone rancid. "Of course they were all very foolish to give up their old rent-controlled apartments, even *with* the increases. Though that's something your mother didn't mention. Not that she could have known it *then*, especially with her emphasis on plants—as if anyone could make a life out of pots and leaves! Although you should see all the nurseries around here! And the way people are taken *in* by them!"

"It's the same I think with the new flower stores, planting stores in the city. Cheatings only for what you can do yourself."

"Of *course,* darling! Why do you think her mother's book was reissued? Capitalism! Consumption! And she *still* didn't mention a word about all those people who gave up their rent-controlled apartments. And believe me, are they jealous! I know! I'll *never* give up what we have, even *with* the increases—and of *course* landlords are bloodsuckers! They always were and they always will be. And everyone knows, especially the *young* people in my building who are wonderful and brave and forthright and out-spoken, and it's pathetic! Because they know absolutely zero. And they keep on expecting the whole world to just fall into their laps the way their parents did!"

Maria said, "Rebecca, I still don't understand. What book? What did Julie's mother do?"

Julie looked around at Louise and Maria. "You mean you haven't heard of it? You haven't even seen the ads? It's called *Green Thoughts and Other City Surprises,*" Julie said bitterly. "*That's* my mother's book!" and slumping back, she suddenly looked to Louise as sallow as her olive-drab jacket.

"*Well,* Julia, darling! I see at least you memorized the title! It must mean *some*thing to you. I don't know what else you ever memorized in your life! And it's obvious that you don't even know where the title came from!" Rebecca was standing up now and focusing on Julie, her face again purple and her eyes enlarged.

"I think I probably never had such tea, Rebecca," Maria said. "I wish only my God-damn nose wasn't stopped and I could smell it. It's definitely very good. I'm drinking more and more and still no aroma, God damn it!"

Julie said, "Me, too. I'm drinking too much, I have to pee. Elimination is right for your body."

Rebecca said nothing; her expression had not changed. In

the silence, which no one knew what to do with—only hailstones clapped against the windows in the useless, drugged safety of Ping-Pong balls in the lounge at Birch Hill—Rebecca continued to stare at Julie as if she could force her into paying attention. "Green thoughts," she drew out deliberately. "A green thought?" It was not a hint, but a test.

Julie did not exactly get up, but began to move her body off the chair in a hollow, lithe, collapsible way that seemed both lazy and well executed at the same time. Clearly she believed that her legs themselves would lead her to the bathroom, though Louise could see no sign of where it might be.

Rebecca said, "No. Of course not. You don't know. You don't even have the vaguest idea of what I'm talking about. Why should you? You might have had to *learn* something! You might have had to read a poem! It's your own mother's book—I don't know whether to be furious or just disheartened. 'A green thought in a green shade'—it's from a poem by Andrew Marvell. 'The Garden.' Green! Hope! So that people could keep their hopes and their beliefs and not run away! And not turn their backs on society that needs them! Or go looking for phony prestige in big lawns and commuter trains! And *that's* what your mother meant, Julia! You *can't* turn your back. Because no man is an island! And even though Manhattan *is,* there's no reason why you can't make it pleasant and beautiful and as *green* as you want it. Not that she was saying it's Paradise. Because life never is—though that's all *you're* ever looking for! Because even up here, where it *is* Paradise, there are still drawbacks. . . ."

"Green thoughts and green shades I think I *did* hear about," Maria said. "When I was putting out the garbage, the newspapers. Because Matthew doesn't like to—I *know,* baby, angel, but if you leave them, there come only more roaches. And newspapers you must keep always separate. Anyway, I didn't realize, Julie, that it was your mother. I didn't know the picture. I didn't meet ever your mother. I only once spoke to her on the telephone."

How had Julie's mother looked in the newspaper? Like Elisabeth? So that only if you knew her could you realize who it was? Or if you did recognize her instantly despite the purposeful subterfuge, would you still not have the slightest inkling of who she had once been or what her life was like?

Julie said, "The picture was probably terrific. Now all you have to do is get it together with the voice on the phone. Which is more than she ever did."

"There's nothing I can say to you anymore, Julia. Because I'm sure that Maria would come to an entirely different conclusion! In fact, I'm surprised that you *don't* know her, Maria, because she's always had so many friends and so many interests and you and Dennis were—"

"Because she's always taken such a big interest in my life!" Julie burst out.

"And she's an absolutely marvelous person, Maria, and you would love her! And in fact I even know the exact article and the exact interview you have in mind! It was in the *Post,* right? In the At Home section? Where they have an interview and a picture and a recipe?"

Maria shrugged. "I don't remember, really. I saw it in the garbage only."

"Well, I do! I remember it perfectly! *Perfectly!* Because that's one of those things about me, and people are always remarking on it! And I know that's one of the first things that's supposed to go—your memory. And even Simone de *Beau*voir says so—and by the way, Julia, it's supposed to start at twenty-five, so don't think you're going to last like this forever! Although your *mother's* memory couldn't be that bad!" Rebecca's coloring began rising suspiciously. "Because it was *my* recipe she gave in that interview! Danish duck in wine sauce! That interview in the *Post* where you're supposed to be giving your own very *special* recipe. To show your own private, *characteristic* style of entertaining!"

Julie said, "My mother never cooked anything in her life. Except maybe steak. Or lamb chops. Her whole trip is cleaning. *You* know—throw it away, get rid of it."

"Well, maybe she never *cooked* anything, but she definitely ate it! And I know where, too—in *my* house! And with my memory, I can probably even figure out *when*! Years and years ago, when I used to give those enormous, fantastic fundraising dinners that everybody came to and everybody talked about! Because people still remember those dinners of mine, they made a tremendous impression. And in some cases, how *much* of an impression I didn't realize till I saw my own recipe staring right up at me under someone's else's face in the newspaper! Not that it makes any difference to me if she gets the credit—I'm very flattered! I'm only sorry that all those people who are going to cut out that recipe from the paper never had the chance to eat it when *I* made it. Because you have to really love *food*—for its own sake—to really do it right. Just like anything else in life. And food—it *gives* you life! I don't mean alone—so don't start up with me, Julia. You're not the first one to figure out that material things aren't everything! And I remember when lots of people were *really* hungry, and don't think I don't know that there are plenty of people who still are! Just tell me one thing, darling. How does it taste when your mother makes it?"

In the gloomy dimness, which had been increasing, Louise could not tell when Julie had come back from the bathroom and did not know how much of all this she had actually heard.

She said, "I *told* you. My mother never cooks *anything*. She never *eats* anything. She's five four and she weighs a hundred and twelve pounds. Daddy says she's the closest thing to an anorexic he's ever seen. All she ever does is play tennis."

Because of the darkness, which was now nearly total, Louise had a sudden sensation of blindness. All she could see was an outline of Julie's familiar slouching form, and hearing her voice—a grudging whine—was certain that the expression on her invisible face was sour, sullen, and superior. It was unfair and not to be trusted: she was toying with the idea of blindness as if it *were* an idea, and easily playing out to herself this character of Julie—undeserving but lucky—lucky, lucky Julie, as if she were just that, simply a character. She could not see Rebecca, either, who now said, "*Tennis?* Julia, darling! Does your mother *still* play tennis? I think that's absolutely marvelous. People who want to stay alive and vital and open to the future have to find their own way of doing it. And if tennis is *your* mother's way, I think it's a wonderful thing! It's not *my* way, but I'm not the kind of person who has to wait around tennis courts, making small talk in ridiculous outfits, and then get crushed at cocktail parties! For *me,* being young and staying young is always inside me. But that's just a difference of outlook and attitudes. And someday I know you'll understand . . . Tell me something, darling. It just occurred to me because I know some *wonderful* people who *also* used to have a house on Martha's Vineyard—where do your parents play tennis?"

"I didn't *say* my parents. I said my *mother.* Daddy wouldn't—"

"Oh, that's even *more* marvelous. You see that? She does it by herself! The one thing I have no patience for is people who *stand still.* And if that means having to lie about your age on applications, then, by all means, go ahead and lie! It's what I tell all my friends and I *know* that I'm shocking them. Because they know how deep-rooted a principle honesty is with me. But if you're living in a society as primitive as ours is—primitive and *callous*! So that if you even whisper sixty-five, just the number itself makes you totem and taboo, and everyone's ready to throw you away! Not that anybody believes how old I am anyway! So that when I was in the city the last time and I went to get my special discount bus pass—"

"Bus passes!" Maria said. "Oh my God, Matthew! I forgot again to give you milk money! Again for a whole week you'll have nothing to drink. Bus passes you don't need, it's anyway not so far. You must only be careful about enough money with you. For muggings."

"It's too windy, Mommy," Matthew said. "That's the part I don't like. It's too windy when you have to go around the corner."

"*Your* corner, Maria, darling? Is that what he means? Because if it is, I don't blame him for one minute. And as much as I always loved to walk."

Maria said, "'*Der Wind, der Wind, das himmlische Kind*' . . . I think, Rebecca, on all streets between West End and the Drive, it's all over the same."

"What's that *from,* darling? Wait a minute—don't tell me! I know that I know it—you're quoting Goethe!"

"Mommy, it's too dark in here," Matthew began to whine. "I can't *see* anything. When are we going to Jamie Laufer's?"

"Rebecca will maybe put on a light, baby, angel. It *is* dark. Because really it's already late."

"It would be dark in here anyway," Julie said. "Just like our living room. No matter how many lights my mother turns on or how many exposures she has! Do you know that people can live in caves and still feel completely suffused with sunlight?"

"Matthew, sweetheart! Of *course* I'll put on a light for you. It's just that with all the electricity problems here, and all the times I've had blowouts, the whole thing makes me nervous. And furious! All because of that damn electrician! . . . Let me start with the plugs and we'll hope!"

Rebecca crept around on the floor, apparently tugging at wires. Raising her head, she said, "I've got it! I'm positive! It's not *Faust,* right? It's the 'Erlkönig'!"

The "Erlkönig": a Schubert song Louise could not stand. A man who sees that there's suddenly something wrong with his child becomes desperate to save him. From what? What's wrong? Is he sick? The piano part: a horse, a horseman, galloping, galloping. *Tell* me, *say* something. What is it? You're getting paler and paler. *Tell* me. Galloping, galloping. Father, Father, help me! Save me! Listen to it! It's getting closer and closer, I can't even—What? What are you *talking* about? What shall I listen for? Galloping, galloping. Galloping, galloping. Father! Father! In the distance there is an eerie wind blowing. *Tell* me, *tell* me, your voice is so faint. I can't *hear* you. Your eyes are closed, you're not moving. This is no time to fall asleep! Wind, galloping, silence, sleep—that's all and the whole thing is over. And now, finally, the father understands: his son is dead. He's been carried away, kidnaped by the galloping horseman—the Erlkönig, a figure from legend. The father sings about his grief, berates himself for his own stupidity in not recognizing the notorious villain, and that's how the song ends. The song is a lie; the legend is a lie. The only thing it's about is suicide and the child doesn't want to be saved from its seduction. Gallop, gallop, gallop: how is the father supposed to do something about an inaudible, invisible horseman?

"What?" Maria said.

"What you just *quoted,* darling! *'Der Wind, der Wind, das himmlische Wind.'* You're so *erudite,* Maria! I don't know how I could forget that about you. I *didn't,* really, because I am too in my own way. Not that I know German, but I come from a very musical family, and people are always amazed at the things I can recognize even though I never took a lesson in my life!" Rebecca managed to plug in one dim, heavily shaded antique hurricane lamp; the bulb went out immediately. "Do you see what I mean? That's exactly what I'm struggling against!"

"I think it could be maybe only the extension cord. Or other wires—not exposed, I hope . . . What I said now is from *Hansel and Gretel*."

"*Hansel and Gretel!*" Rebecca said, immediately beginning to hum the theme of *Peter and the Wolf*. "Does that take me back years! I always used to take my daughters and all their little friends. Every single year! Every Christmas! Even if in my opinion it *is* on the sugary side. Still, you have to let children build and develop their own taste. When I think of all those pushy parents! What did they get? Midgets who could parrot!"

The antique hurricane lamp went on again, seemingly of its own volition, and Maria said, "Ah! It *does* work, Rebecca. Only you have I think intermitting current."

In the sudden burst of light, Matthew rubbed his eyes, making them seem smaller and suspicious. "*That's* not from *Hansel and Gretel*, it's *Peter and the Wolf*! We have the record in school. In my *old* school. If you don't believe me, you can call up Jamie Laufer."

"What's this Jamie Laufer business, Maria? Why do you want to see the Laufers?"

"I don't," Maria said, and with her hands in her pockets, looked toward the windows. "Only Matthew does. It's who he remembers from around here in the summer, and it's what I promised. I told him probably you would know who is up here now in the winter and who comes only for special weekends."

"Well, of course I do! Because whoever comes here in the middle of winter? Leon thinks I'm crazy, *he* won't come! Nobody comes! Unless it's a holiday or unless they're running away from each other. And with the Laufers, what good would that do them? In *that* family, each one is crazier than the next! And don't think people don't notice it! And I'd say it's a pity on the children. But that Jamie! With that mouth on him even *I* can't feel sorry! I'll tell you something, Maria, and I hate to even *think* of it coming out of my own mouth—but you listen to that child for five seconds and you can't help coming to the most *atavistic* conclusions! The acorn doesn't fall far from the tree! *Trees!* Because you look at that marriage and you don't know who to feel sorrier for."

Maria nodded noncommittally. "They went to the same school," she said. "*Used* to."

"And you're not going to try to tell me he was any different there! All you have to do is watch him run around with that dog—a *beautiful* Irish setter! Or it *was,* anyway. Because even *studies* have proven it! A dog reflects the personality of the people who own it. And the Laufers made that poor dog as crazy as they are. And that was a *very* expensive dog!"

"What do you think, Matthew, angel? You think the turtle reflects your personality, that's why it's getting lost always? Or the cat? What do you think?"

The light blew out suddenly, as unpredictably as it had gone on before, and Rebecca said, "Even the *bulbs* go out on me here, and I can't tell you how new they are."

Maria, standing in the darkness, clicked the lamp's switch on and off several times. "For intermittent current, you need only something to tap it. You break the circuit. You make the circuit? I don't know which one, it's contact only. *Not* a spoon, definitely, because of conductoring electricity and shockings. It's what happens if you put a fork inside the toaster. I scream it at Matthew always, yes, baby?"

Julie said, "But what do you do when bagels get stuck? I *always* use a fork and nothing ever happened. Daddy even does it and he's *into* all that scientific shit . . . I really loved those breakfasts, he did it every single Sunday. When he bought the *Times* and Nova and cream cheese and everything . . . My fucking mother didn't even make the *coffee*. She used to have her own little private tiny teapot so she could have it with her sickening, plastic Melba toast. Or her *grape*fruit!" Julie shook herself in remembered disgust; Louise heard the various zippers on her fatigue jacket jangling in the darkness like the key chain of a Victorian housekeeper. "That's probably why I *still* can't stand grapefruit. Even when it's been grown pure and organic and *right* for you."

At Birch Hill the one Indian social worker also ate grapefruit. Raised as a vegetarian, she could not accustom herself to eating meat, she explained. Flesh . . . it disgusted her. So, every single day at noon, the bracelets and bangles on her thin brown arm falling and ringing together, she reached into the bottom of her English leather purse to pull out her lunch: a grapefruit. Using no utensils, she peeled the grapefruit whole and pulled apart each section. With tiny, quick gestures she thrust the grapefruit sections into her mouth, and as she crushed them whole against her tongue, Louise always felt newly the meaning of the word *flesh*.

Still moving around in the dark, Rebecca said, "You see how you underestimated your mother, Julia? Tea! Grapefruit! Melba toast! Even *you* have to admit that there's nothing wrong with it and how wonderful and healthy and natural it is. Although God knows how anyone could go on putting that into their mouth year after year and pretend to themselves that they're eating. Or living, for that matter! But—each to his own! I was always very tolerant and open-minded about individual differences and *mishugassen*. It's what you owe to your fellow human beings, not that I like the word *owe*!"

Maria, standing over the lamp, began tapping the glass funnel.

"What are you *fid*dling with, Maria? For God's sake! What are you *doing*? I don't know what's going on and I can't even *see* you!"

"Something with a wooden handle you need, I think. Not really *handle*—you know, a mop, a broom. It wouldn't *fix* it, but only for making it work temporarily."

"Wooden? *Wooden?* Where do I have something wooden?" Rebecca said, clapping her heavy-gloved hand against her forehead.

"It's her head," Matthew whispered to Julie and began laughing.

"All right, Matthew! All right! . . . I heard that because I'm still not deaf! And if I believed in hitting children—*any*body's children—and God knows I never did. Because otherwise right now, with your mother sitting right here and your father lying in a hospital, you'd be the first one to get it! And I mean *get* it! Because I'm not fooling around, and you're just very lucky that I have a sense of humor about these things. And about myself! Which I always had! Which is why I—"

"Matthew!" Maria said. "You must apologize. Right now. Say you're sorry. You *must*."

"Maria, darling! Stop it! *Please!* You're being so *harsh*. After all, he's only a child—a baby, practically. And anyway, since when can't I laugh at myself? Where would we be—all of us—if we couldn't laugh at ourselves once in a while? And anyway, am I the kind of person who would take offense at something like that? *Am* I?"

Maria said, "In the car I have usually somewhere an umbrella. With a wooden handle. I *think* wooden, not plastic. If plastic makes a difference I don't anyway know. What do you think?"

"An *umbrella*! Maria, darling! What a marvelous idea and leave it to you to think of something original like that! Because the umbrella that *I* have is so unique that someone could offer me a million dollars for it and I still wouldn't part with it. Because it's beautif—"

"I hate umbrellas," Julie said. "That's *another* one of my mother's things. She's always sending me these new kinds of umbrellas. That fold up. Or are tiny. Or that attach to something. I think it really freaks her to think that I could go out in the rain without an umbrella. I mean, for *her* all they have to do is say on the news that there's a *chance* of rain. Of *showers*. And there she is—marching out with her little matching umbrella set . . . Daddy says that she should have lived in England—you know, London. And that her whole umbrella trip is just part of her obsessive, compulsive, bullshit neurosis. Only *I* think it's because she's so into *things*. Possessions. She'd probably feel naked without it."

"She worries maybe you would get a cold. Get sick," Maria said. "Only people have always more resiliency—resilientness? *I* think."

In London, England, Louise's mother emerged from an underground station. Life, bitterness, and a variety of demeaning climates had taken away from her that striking, high-colored, youthful bloom which had once been the outward sign of her true promise and deeper distinction. Even her hair, once fair, was now almost entirely white. Worry, injustice, and general mistreatment would have been her explanation for this. But there were those who saw in her white hair, as it fell over her ears and wound about her head, stylish still, an old-fashioned, gracious, otherworldly beauty. These were usually students and could have no idea at all of what her life had been, and what she had rightfully expected of it. It was possible, in Louise's opinion, that her white hair and forced, distant smile (secretly contemptuous if you knew what to look for) lent her a false, suffering wisdom, an idea of herself she had come to enjoy. At least she could extract some pleasure from it—bittersweet—her favorite kind. Enough pleasure, in any case, to diminish the edginess of her gestures, the impatience of her expression. Still, with her graceful smallness, she walked up the steps determinedly, purposefully—the otherworldly calm in her eyes entirely misleading. Alighting from the underground at Swiss Cottage, she put her hand out to test for rain and, accustomed now to a climate where rain was constant, she opened up her umbrella. She did not dislike it: its faded rosy shadow both above and before her temporarily gave her back the coloring and outlook of her youth. Hooded, protected in this way, she managed packages, completed errands, and greeted people with unexpected ease and a certain lightness. Her resilience was remarkable; everyone said it. She did not debate in her mind why this quality had not been passed on to her younger daughter. It was a long-standing misfortune and she did not dwell on it.

"Here it is and I knew I'd find it!" Rebecca said, her thoroughly pleased bustle stirring up the deadness of the room. She held the umbrella out to Maria, but did not let go of it. "Wait a minute, darling! Wait *one* minute. The *reason* that it's so special and people would be shocked at me for using it as if it were just an ordinary umbrella for everyday—not that I care!—is that this umbrella, hand-painted and bamboo and everything, comes from China! And I don't mean Hong Kong and I don't mean *Bloomingdale's* China. Although all I read about in the paper was straw baskets, and you'll have to excuse me, Maria, but any dope can make a basket. And that's the one thing that you'd expect those hotshot fancy society chippies to know about. Because what kind of colleges did *they* go to but basket-weaving ones . . ."

Maria said, "Bamboo. That would definitely, I think, be all right."

"And hand-painted, Maria! Every single stroke! It's from the Canton Trade Fair—and never *mind* the kind of Americans who ended up going there! The people who brought it back for me have lived practically everyplace! India! Japan! England! So they're the last people in the world who could just get taken! And get stuck with junk! Because merchants are merchants— and never mind Cultural Revolution and New Orders! Because I don't care *how* many rivers he swims naked in the cold! When it comes to rooking people, salesmen are the same all over."

"If you swim naked in the cold, you could join the Polar Bear Club," Matthew said. "I saw it on TV."

"Do you see why I object to television, Maria? Did you hear him? That's *exactly* what I mean and *exactly* what I always *tell* people—oh my God! The telephone! The telephone is ringing and I bet I know who it is! It's that wonderful Carla Saltzman! And anytime she just *talks* to me it means something very special for her. As a woman and as a doctor. Because it's so different from her *own* parents! 'I can't get over it, Rebecca,' she always tells me. 'You just *defy* the whole syndrome of old age!' Defy! Every single symptom!"

Rebecca hurried off to answer the phone, and Maria, with the Chinese umbrella on her arm, knocked lightly on the bulb of the antique hurricane lamp. It lit up immediately, and facing away from its brightness, Louise watched Maria tap the bamboo umbrella handle. She moved her fingers over its strange texture and knobby grooves, and in a distant voice repeating, "Bamboo," Maria looked as if she were in a different world.

"I don't know whether that was a wrong number or the God-damn party line or what!" Rebecca said as she rushed back into the room with the door swinging behind her. "And after all that running! I don't even know why I bother!"

Matthew, too, looked as if he were in another world. In the darkness he had found a narrow, raised platform like a ramp that Louise thought was probably intended as a showcase for Rebecca's antiques. Only the one shaded light was on and Matthew seemed unaware of it: with his eyes half closed and his arms partly raised, he walked carefully, one foot exactly in front of the other, inching his way across the ledge as if it were a mountain in an unexplored country. It was a child's game played in private. Every so often his eyelids tightened: he was daring himself to open them, but would not.

"Look at him, Maria! Look at the way he walks—he looks just like Dennis."

Maria said nothing. She nodded slowly in the gloom and her face, suddenly longer and narrower, seemed to have an unnatural pallor that Louise had not seen before. Because of the red glass shade of the hurricane lamp, the light rose up through the funnel like the close glow of a candle flame. Matthew was balancing now in a far-off corner of the room. Half in shadow, his skin, too, looked unhealthily translucent. It was *not* the eerie, borrowed bloodlessness of Dennis's illness, Louise told herself, but merely the peculiar, distorting light of the lamp.

"I'm not saying that he shouldn't." Rebecca laughed, reddening and grabbed at Maria's arm. "I only meant with the way he looks and the way he walks, maybe *he'll* be a dancer, too. Or with all his picture-drawing, *some* kind of artist."

"I hope not. It's a terrible life," Maria said. She had put down the umbrella, regained her characteristic expression, and, still standing, was rapidly pushing things back into her purse. "Come on, Matthew. No more climbing and no Jamie Laufer. It's already late now and time definitely for us to go. My watch says it even."

"Oh, Maria, darling! You don't know what you're saying! How *could* you? Who could blame you? It's only because of your bitterness at life! At fate! At the *cruelty* of Dennis's illness. It's your *grief* that's speaking—not you! Of *course* you want him to use his creativity! Of *course* you want him to be an artist. What mother wouldn't? What greater thing could you want for your son?"

Maria shrugged. She said, "It's my opinion only. I can't decide what will happen to him, but definitely that's my opinion. It's a terrible life."

"Because it's *extreme,* darling. The highs, the lows, the excitement, the agitation, the constant, intense turmoil—of fertility! And delight! That's what it is! By definition. You can't object to the unconscious. It doesn't *know* in-betweens! And who would want it to? That's *boring.* And that's one thing, Maria—" Rebecca shook her hand, forgetting that it was still mittened, like a prizefighter's. "That's one thing that even all the reviewers always agreed about! He was certainly never boring."

Maria was folding Matthew's long green woolen scarf and did not look up. "Maybe on stage not. But in life, always. Chronical. Like his disease now—also chronical."

"You mustn't give *up,* Maria. They're doing *marvelous* things with Hodgkin's disease! Radiation! Remissions! All *kinds* of wonderful things."

Predictably, Maria said, "Well, they're not doing wonderful things for Dennis. It has to do with—I don't know what— stages. What they can do for him now, I don't know. What they can do for *me* at least is better parking places. It's in my opinion disgusting—parking places only for doctors!"

"I *know,* darling! It's an old story. A profession that *guards* its privileges—and all of them undeserved! From the largest to the smallest. And in my opinion"—Rebecca suddenly looked at Julie—"Opinion nothing! Why am I suddenly being so ladylike? It's not opinion! It's the truth. The worst ones were psychiatrists' wives—the very worst! They thought *they* were God and they were *married* to God, and that's how they looked at the world and that's how they brought up their families. And everyone knows how *that* paid off!"

How had it paid off? Louise knew: sullen in her expression, but easy in her gliding strides, Julie dropped in and out of schools at will, at her own pleasure. If she did not like a course, it would not be different for her from not liking a particular flavor of milkshake. No one would think it strange; no one would consider her "not ready." In no one's eyes would there be the accusation that she was unable to cope. If she happened to be taking a bus somewhere, she would just lope onto it on the spur of the moment. She would never have laid out the exact fare the night before, and though she would have to fish for change in her knapsack, she would not lose her balance as the bus lurched. Once seated, she might well miss her stop, but not because other people's lives beckoned her.

"Oh, God *damn* it, Matthew!" Maria said. "*Again* God damn it! *Again* that's something I forgot—your dental slip for school. Because the girl there gets very mad, you can't blame her, if you say it's for rush but not emergency. She has always too many phones to answer, it's a very crowded clinic."

"Maria! Since when do you take him to a *clinic*? *Why?* Why don't you take him to Leon? It's true he doesn't like to work on children, but that's because of the parents. And for you! You *know* he'd make an exception! Gladly!"

Maria said, "It's too far for him to go by himself. And coming home then in the dark, it's what I don't like."

Matthew, his eyes now fully open, came down off the ramp. He said, "Yucch, Mommy! I *hate* the dentist. I hate the drill and I hate the needles. I hate *everything*. And they have these stupid gold stars—for babies."

"You see that, Maria? He'd *love* Leon . . . Matthew, darling,

I know you would. He'd *never* treat you like a baby. And besides that, he would tell you what he's doing and then it wouldn't hurt."

"It always hurts," Maria said. "It hurts for everyone. He must only get used to it. He has already very bad teeth."

"Is Leon a painless dentist?" Matthew asked. Zipped into his jacket, he was standing near the ledge again and squinting up at Rebecca suspiciously.

"Any dentist can be painless," Julie said. "You just have to put your head in the right place. Nitrous oxide is good, though. It gets you started."

Rebecca, whose face was still red, disjointedly pulled herself away from Maria and, turning to Julie with her gloved hand upraised, said, "Julia. I have a *bone* to pick with you, you know."

"It's a duck bone," Matthew said, and once again lapsed into giggles. The suspicious squint was still in his eyes and it occurred to Louise that he so often looked this way because he neglected to wear his glasses.

She heard the motorcycles zooming around the hilly roads again, and this time, in the early twilight chill, they managed to sound ominous and mournful at the same time. They were other people's energies moving and rushing away, and Maria, standing up with her heavy bag on one arm and Matthew's Magic Markers slipping out of their case in the other, raised her voice to match the motorcycles. "I think now we really must go. Because in case later on there are icy roads or too much traffic, I am clearing steer of it."

"Maria, darling! You can't leave yet! I haven't *shown* you anything! My marvelous antique jewelry!"

Maria pulled Matthew's gloves out of her raincoat pocket; they smelled of wet wool. "It's better I think if we come back another time," she said. "It's already dark and I'm nervous for the roads. Also, because they used all day my apartment for the Block Party, I'm afraid for what it could now look like."

"Well, darling, of *course* you'll come back! But here—it'll just take a second! I have them in beautiful little velvet cases and I'll show you my jewelry. It's Victorian and early American—and early everything! Because everything I have is very beautiful and everything I have is very old—and all kinds of vital, wonderful people *all* love it. And *that's* what I wanted to talk to you about, Julia!" Rebecca suddenly turned from her velvet cases to find Julie, who was already on her way out, slouched against the door. "Your *father,* Julia, wrote a paper in some kind of psychiatric journal about people who like to live with antiques. And he said that the reason they do it is that they're incapable of dealing with adult conflicts and adult sexuality! And that they're attempting a Peter Pan–like retreat! Schizoid and unresolved! Those were his exact words! Peter Pan–like! Schizoid and unresolved! Since when does *he* know anything about antiques? Or people who buy them? I'd just like to know what makes him such an expert!"

"I don't read my father's papers," Julie said, and, banging her knapsack behind her, slammed the front door.

"Peter Pan–like retreat!" Rebecca repeated. "Although I'll tell you something, Maria. When you've been through as many failed political movements as I have, you understand something about retreat. About the *temptation* to retreat. Only it's not what *he* thinks—it's a retreat into beauty, a retreat into aesthetics."

"That's what people said about Dennis always—that he was ascetic. They meant it for a compliment, but it's true, really. It's what he was good for. He should have been a priest. He would have been better off, maybe. *I* think."

"Well, *really,* Maria! Dennis would have been brilliant at anything! And naturally there's no question about it. But religion! I don't see how you could wish *that* on anyone! I refuse to have *anything* to do with it! And I made up my mind a long time ago—I'm definitely going to be cremated."

"Dennis wants also to be cremated," Maria said. "To give his old bitch mother, very Catholic, even more heart attacks. I don't know. . . ."

"Memorial meetings are one thing. Because, after all, who do you know who wouldn't want to be remembered? But funerals! They're not going to catch *me* involved in a barbaric and atavistic ritual! I didn't do it in life and I'm not going to do it in death! Because I've thought of everything and I have everything planned! And if people want to call it morbid, that's their business and their problem. Because I'm not afraid to face the future—and I don't need any cushions for it. Or any crutches, either!"

"Daddy had crutches," Matthew said. "And cushions, too."

"*Maria!*" Rebecca screamed. "You don't mean to tell me that you've allowed that child, this adorable *baby,* to see his own father in such a degenerated state! What's the matter with you? Of course, I *understand*—you don't want to deprive him of the relationship, you don't want to cut off the give-and-take. But *this*! You can't let him see his father so passive and incapacitated. What will it do to his identity? And how will it make him feel about getting older and growing up?"

Maria said, "No, no—it's from a long time ago. Dennis twisted once his ankle. A filament only, I don't know. It was *not* broken. Retched? Wrenched? That's for plumbing—anyway, he made then such a fuss over it with crutches and a cane and sitting always only with special pillows that Matthew still remembers."

"But that's very *pain*ful, Maria. And especially for a dancer! That's a *terrible* thing. It makes him a man without an occupation."

"Yes." Maria nodded. "It's true. He stayed home all the time."

The Chinese umbrella began rolling off the kitchen table, and Maria said, "Come on, Matthew. Let's go. No more standing here. Now it's *really* late, now we must really go."

"But Louise isn't ready yet, Mommy," Matthew said in his peculiar, aloof, sneaking voice.

Louise was not ready: in one of the drawstring velvet bags there was a pair of dark gold dangling earrings with a roundish gold-brown stone the exact color of her own hair. They would be worn, these earrings, by a girl who walked quickly, whose hair blew freely in the wind. Running to a bus stop, there would be nothing unusual about her—nothing to make people wonder about the clumsiness of her movements, the awkwardness of her life. Her earrings would fly out freely for a second and then pass along sunlit through the windows of the bus.

"Oh, I *see* what you're looking at!" Rebecca said. "As *soon* as I heard your name was Weil, I knew you'd have marvelous taste! And I'm glad that I was right! But as beautiful as they are, I can't find anyone who knows what—"

"The door is already open, Matthew. If we stand here anymore, it will make it for Rebecca only *more* freezing, and that's not fair. So, move now. Let's go."

The opened door let in a stream of air so dark, raw, and piercing that Louise felt as if nothing outside existed: no path, no steps, no far-off lights or cars. Not even motorcycles—only a suggestion of massed and massing trees which did not knock, but merely bent and might just as well have been imaginary.

"You're really going, Maria," Rebecca said very slowly.

Where were the motorcycles? Where was the highway? Where?

"Well, I'm *very* glad this is the day you chose to come, not that I wouldn't be delighted to see you anytime. Even if I *am* constantly busy! Because you have no idea what it's *like* for me around here most of the time! The letters, the people, the *phone* calls! No matter where they are! *I'm* still the one they think of and I'm still the one they want—"

Matthew said, "I'm going to the car, Mommy."

"Look at him, Maria! He's so sure-footed—just like his father! And don't worry, I understand *completely*. I *know* what you're going through and—"

"Good-by, Rebecca," Maria said firmly. She had already started down the unfinished steps herself, and now merely half turned to wave.

"Oh, *don't*, darling. *Please* don't! I *know* you're emotional and you believe in expressing yourself, but if you *start* that, it'll only make me cry. Just give my love to Dennis and to everyone and tell them that I think of them constantly and they're always on my mind, no matter what! And tell the Dresner girl to give my love to her mother and father and I'm sure they'll remember me. Even if after all these years, between the two of them, they never came up with an original idea. Or in his case, an accurate one. Although, who can say now what might someday be considered—"

It was the last thing Louise heard Rebecca say. Running down the hill with Maria in the windy cold, she felt as if they were fleeing.

"*Damn* it if I can't now find my car keys. From this fucking dark!" Maria said, and with nervous speed flung the contents of her purse onto the roof of the car. "Open the door up for some lights, Matthew! Quickly!"

In the dark, with Julie asleep in the backseat, the car began to move out slowly on the gravel driveway—past the sign that said ANTIQUES—R. RELKIN, past some trees and recessed, shadowy houses, past Marzano's—desolate, white-shingled, and ramshackle.

"Mommy, Jamie Laufer! We passed it already. We passed where you turn for his house."

"Maybe next time, baby, angel," Maria said very softly. "Another time when we come." There were no other cars around them, and it seemed to Louise that Maria's voice was taking on the dreaminess of the small road. Melting snow dripped down from the bare, bending branches of the trees on both sides, making the road seem even narrower and the small, uneven houses closer. In a lit-up upstairs window there were children writing on the glass with their fingers. Downstairs, behind sashed curtains, someone was playing the piano. Soon they would all sit down for dinner: it was the feeling of evening everywhere, and driving quickly in the darkness, the feeling was complete.

"God *damn* it!" Maria said, fumbling for a tissue. She sneezed loudly, waking up Julie, who sat up with a start.

"Shit! What a horrible woman," Julie said, fishing some ChapStick out of her knapsack. "What a total monster-lady! I can't believe it. I can't believe she exists."

Because she had to turn the car onto the main road now, Maria began peering anxiously through windows and mirrors, one hand on the steering wheel and the other still holding the tissue to her nose.

"Where?" she asked, her voice coming through nasal and muffled. "Which one?"

Julie swung her thumb backward. "Her," she said sourly. "Rebecca."

"*Rebecca?* Rebecca is *not* a horrible woman, Julie. Not *horrible.* I don't know how you think things, really. I don't know how you think people's lives. You're not a child—like Matthew, who complains she *touches* you. Or her hands are too fat. I don't know. There *are* really people who are horrible—and don't tell me now your mother. Because *that,* in my opinion, is horrible."

Louise could not put the day together: families are shit, Maria had said, I'm completely serious.

Julie, too, seemed amazed. She stretched back uneasily and said, "You know what I mean, Maria. Her attitudes. Her head."

"What attitudes? You wouldn't even speak to her. You were very rude."

Matthew said, "She *talks* all the time."

"Exactly!" Maria said, and banged down on the steering wheel. "*All* the time. Anything . . . She has, maybe, some reasons."

"She does? What?" Julie asked. Louise heard a surprising note of gossip creep into her voice as she leaned forward with grudging, unfamiliar animation.

"Oh . . . I don't know . . ." Maria shrugged, and suddenly seemed reluctant to answer. "Some things—many things didn't come out the way she thought. With her children. Other things, too, but mainly that, I think."

"What?" Julie repeated.

"Oh, the one married a man she doesn't approve, and the other she doesn't approve because she had always many different men and many different jobs. And is always changing everything lock, barrel, and stock . . . They live very far away, both of them." Maria's voice faded with the distance. "She doesn't ever see them."

"Why does she think she has to *approve* of them? How can she think she has the right to run their lives?"

"She doesn't, Julie. She can't. But she was very disappointed for them. For herself, for them. She had, I don't know, better hopes."

"Because they didn't marry whoever *she* wanted them to?"

"Because—the second one, really, I don't know. The first one went to the Peace Corps," Maria said. "To Malaya? Malaysia? Rebecca was very proud of her, she was very brilliant always. Only she met there a man who was an Islam. A Moslem? And Rebecca told her: In his country they have still women in veils, and you were not raised to be inferior. But—I don't know—she stays there still. She married him. With children and many servants. They send her often plane tickets, but she doesn't use them. It's true—she doesn't want, really, to see her mother."

"Because she *is* horrible. That just proves it."

"Nothing *proves* people, Julie. You can't even that way explain them. I think it's wrong even for me to say that Rebecca is *this* way or *that* way for a reason that I know. That I can *tell*. I know only definitely that it's very hard for her to think about her daughters and not see them. It's her fault, maybe. But maybe it's not. . . ." Maria reached her arm back and put it around Matthew's shoulder. "Families . . . children . . . They all grow up and leave you. You won't leave me yet, Matthew, baby, angel, will you?"

VI

ON BOTH SIDES OF THE STREET, PIECES OF BURST BALLOONS AND STRANDS of blown-apart macramé marked out the length of the block so that it looked to Louise like a trail left by clever captives or uncertain explorers.

"They probably broke some things, I don't hope," Maria said, as they ran through the wind into the building. "I don't anyway *care*—I don't use them. But Joan, especially, will bother me with apologies and replacings. To come with her. Just what I hate!"

In the lobby Louise felt the stuffy, pleasant smell of steam heat mix with the building's customary stench of garbage. A curly-headed, blondish man in a long, striped djellabah came out of a ground-floor apartment and began picking up the stacks of flyers that announced the Block Party in English, Spanish, and Japanese. Padding around the lobby, barefoot and smiling, he had the uneven look of a man without his glasses.

"Hi, Matthew," he said, without turning. "What would you say you liked best? I'm taking an informal survey."

"Say the rides," Maria whispered, pinching Matthew for urgency. "They had an—I don't know—merry-go-round. Tell him that was best. *Quickly*. All I need now is arguings—that's Kopell, the Block Captain's husband." And then, turning and rebalancing her packages, Maria said very loudly, "You are going to be our great new television star, Larry. It's a good thing everyone has now cable."

"*We* don't, Mommy," Matthew whispered crankily.

"*We* can't afford it, Matthew, baby. It's too expensive. You know that. Shh!"

"It's wonderful, Maria, isn't it?" Larry Kopell said. He had put down the flyers and was still nodding and smiling distantly. "That's just the spirit I hope I can get across on those programs—the sharing, the movement, the looseness . . ." He waved his arms in awkward happiness and seemed, Louise thought, as if he would be unable to continue, stymied somehow by his own helpless, foggy joy. "The day was great, the people were great, the kids were terrific . . . You were wonderful, I was wonderful. Even the things that didn't really work seemed right. Didn't it remind you of childhood?"

"Childhood!" Maria said, bursting directly into the elevator, which had just come. "Now I'm *really* glad we weren't here! . . . Childhood!" she repeated, shaking her head. "Whose?"

Inside the elevator, the garbage stench was even stronger. Matthew said, "Yucch!" and, screwing up his face, buried his nose in the Magic Markers. A taped-up, unevenly lettered sign read: FOUND—A SEGAL KEY IN LAUNDRY ROOM ON SAT. IS IT YOURS??? SEE SUPT.

Leaning her packages against the wall, Maria turned to Louise and said, "See Supt! See Supt!" She pronounced the abbreviation exactly as it was written; it made the derision in her voice even more emphatic. "That stupid bastard, he is always so *drunk*. He can't find to turn on even the hot water! Supt! Wait—now they will take definitely the money they collected from the Block Party and come with petitions for him to go to encounter groups for supers! It's anyway what *I* think . . . God *damn* it, I must find now quickly my keys. Or they maybe left open the door, probably, I bet you."

Very few lights were on in Maria's apartment, but misshapen candles flickered everywhere. Through their uncertain glow, Louise could not tell whether the people and objects spread out in equal crowded disarray were an indication of some great, nearly secret carousing, or whether, having laid themselves out beside batik hangings and wine bottles, both people and objects were spent.

"Filthy dishes—exactly what I can't stand!" Maria would certainly say momentarily; and looking at the mounds of unraveling, hand-crafted projects, Louise was reminded of Patient Bazaars at Birch Hill.

"Chicken parts, twenty-nine cents a pound! I found the sale in a new supermarket opening!" Maria called out triumphantly, diving into a large grocery bag. Still in the narrow entranceway, behind both Louise and Matthew, she stood in the dim light, waving a package of chicken high above her head like a torch. "And so many opened-up wine bottles!" she said, immediately snapping on a light and sweeping through the room. "That's what I'll do! I'll make for everyone *coq au vin*. Only I think definitely I don't have enough mushrooms. What do you think? Quickly! Who has some?"

"Maria!" they all called out, jolted by the light, but happy to see her. Joan squinted and, stretching sleepily, said, "I think you got a call from the hospital. But I wasn't the one who answered, so I'm not sure." And Arthur, who managed to get up at once, shaded his eyes comically, saying, "Again mushrooms? That's the first thing she requisitioned every time she conquered a country."

Maria put down her bundles and walked around the living room blowing out all the candles. "You don't ever believe me," she said, already carrying off overflowing ashtrays and bowls filled with apple cores and nutshells, "but it's true. You have only to look for specials, on sales, in big supermarkets and it's much cheaper. Even if it's not near you, if you see it—notice it? You just stop. From the bus, it's naturally easier—you just run out. From the car, a big pain in the ass because of double parkings. But this chicken I got—I don't know where—on the East Side someplace. When I was dropping off Julie."

Large pots of leftover food had been set down carelessly throughout the room, and over them floated the smell of burnt-out candles. It was exactly what Louise had expected: after so many hours of just sitting, she now did not know where to move. Even Reba Axelrod stood up slowly. Her face looked pink from the wind or from sleep, and running her finger through a wedge of runny cheese, she tried, too suddenly, to speak briskly.

"You're right, Maria!" she said breathlessly, trying to avoid a pot of Greek beans. "It's what I've been telling them about for months. All we have to do is form a food coop. Food collective. *You* know. Every week—or depending on how we decide to set it up—somebody else, very early in the morning, can go up to the market at Hunts Point. The savings are incredible! And besides, you find out all about these fantastic new vegetables." Reba widened her eyes and luxuriously licked at her cheesy finger as if she were right then and there savoring a vegetable whose taste she had never before known.

"Glasses?" Maria said, back in the living room, her eyes searching, her hands out. "Cups? No? Nothing? You used paper?

Good! Ah! *Wine*glasses, I'll be very careful, don't worry. But what you'll do with all that cheese, I don't know."

Reba said, "Come on, Maria! You're on my side. What do *you* think?"

Maria shrugged her shoulders and said, "Well, it's already all so runny and ripe. You can't use it tomorrow, we better eat it tonight. Brie, in any case, you can't feed to the cat . . . Matthew! No TV! Come right now and help me dry! But be very careful—these are expensive, special wineglasses and anyway not ours."

"Maria!" Reba pleaded. "You could save a lot of money! You *need* to—I mean, we *all* need to. What about it? All we have to do is get them organized."

"That's right, Reba," Arthur said. "That's the *Obersturmführer*. She certainly can get them organized."

In the kitchen Louise watched Maria bang down a cast-iron frying pan and fill it with cooking oil. "Onions!" she cried out wildly, half to herself. "But never mind, I'm sure I have at least *some*."

"You see that?" Reba said, coming in to join her. "Do you have any idea how cheaply we could get them up there?"

"Now I'll maybe cry a little," Maria said, rapidly peeling the onions. "Probably it's good for me. What do you think?" She turned around, and seeing that it was Reba who stood next to her, she sliced down hard on her chopping board and, tossing her head in the direction of the onions, said, "Hunts Point! I anyway get up very early! And run out in a hurry to be with junkies! It's what I do all day. And always being careful to watch my purse! And where I have the car—for stealings! I don't for that need Hunts Point!"

Joan yawned and, picking at the label of a wine bottle, said, "I think it *is* really dangerous up there. They had a whole series about it on television."

Maria threw the onions and chicken parts into the pan and, muttering "God *damn* it!" as the fat spurted out, repeated, "Hunts Point! Exactly what I don't absolutely need—a bus-driving holiday!" She climbed up a stepladder, shoving around cans of food with the same frenzy that had woken Louise so early that same morning. "Bay leaves I know I definitely somewhere have, but *mushrooms* . . . Well! All right! Too bad, we'll have to use cans and hope for no botulisms."

"A bus-driving holiday," Arthur said, shaking his head. "I can see why that's not for you. But what about a Firemen's Ball? The helmets, the boots, the uniforms—just for old times' sake."

On her way to the bathroom, Joan wobbled a bit in her clogs and called out, "Oh, Christ, Arthur! Don't pay attention to him, Maria. He's really disgusting."

"He is," Maria agreed, and from the top rung of the stepladder began laughing so that she had to grasp the sink.

"Why?" Arthur said, smiling. He carried in two of the big clay pots and emptied them into the garbage. "Why am I disgusting? I'm only giving her the encouragement to remember. Isn't that what you pay thirty-five dollars an hour for? With the meter running?" He held on to the arms of the stepladder just below where Maria was standing, and said, "What do *they* know, Maria, *liebchen*? A bunch of skinny Jewish broads! Come on down and tell it all to Uncle Fritz before the U-boat comes back for you."

"Oh, shit!" Maria said, trying to steady herself, though, with her hand on her face, she was laughing and blushing. "You people!"

"Ah *hah*!" Arthur wagged his finger in the air. "'You people!' Notice that? *You* people! Already she's separating out the population."

Reba said, "I'm serious, Maria. You shouldn't dismiss it so easily, you're not being fair. For one thing, you'd be terrific at it—it involves a lot of bargaining. That's the whole point of these wholesale markets. You buy in huge quantities and you bargain for the best price. You'd be absolutely perfect for it! I can just *see* you."

I did always exchanges from when I was very little, Maria had said. When I was *very* skinny.

"Bay leaves I have," she said now, throwing down a package. "Also some thyme. A pinch, only. A pitch? Mushrooms from cans, not great, but OK, we can use it. Wine—too much is already out, we'll drink some. What else? I can make noodles, maybe, or rice, but French bread would definitely be better. Also later for the Brie. What do you think?"

"If you're really against going up there early in the morning, we could use your apartment to store things," Reba said, and as she widened her eyes and licked her lips Louise thought of a child embarking in secret on a grown-ups' project.

Joan, in her clogs, came clattering back from the bathroom. "Shit," she said crankily, pulling and picking at the threads of her shift. "This thing has split ends, I swear it. And it never even hung right. What should I do next time, Maria? Use a different pattern?"

"I don't *use* ever patterns. It's not what I got used to and now, too bad, I have no patience. Come here to the light and let me see it." Still on the stepladder, she held out her hand and waved it like a traffic cop. Or maybe, Louise thought, like a crane-driver: I drove then a giant something, Maria had said. It was very noisy.

Stepping into the full bright light of the kitchen, Joan said, "My God, Maria! It smells fantastic in here! And you did it in about three minutes. What did you do?"

"I didn't yet put in the wine, it will then smell *more* fantastic. Matthew didn't yet set the table . . . Matthew! Come here! *Quickly,* baby, angel! I think I'll maybe send him down for French bread. Italian—it doesn't matter . . . Look, Joan," she said, stabbing the material. "Look right here. It's not I think the pattern, it's you. You did here a hemming stitch, but it's a seam. For a seam, you must do a backstop—a backstitch. Entirely different! . . . Matthew! Take from my purse one dollar and not more. I think around the corner the little Spanish store is maybe open still, I hope. I can show you later a backstitch, Joan. It's very easy, no problem . . . Matthew! Get your coat and go! Quickly! You have still to set the table."

Joan observed lazily, "I think it started to rain again. For a change." She stretched and leaned her head all the way back so that her long, dark hair, in a ponytail for the freedom of the day, reached nearly to the seat of her dungarees. There was a certain restless languor about her still; she looked, for the moment, the way she must have years before—a teenager mooning around her mother's kitchen. Was this what Julie did as soon as she got home?

"A raincoat, Matthew!" Maria called out, but the door had already slammed.

"I'll set the table," Louise said, but thought, really, that she was the one who should have gone out. She had still not taken off her coat and felt as if she alone were standing there, caught in a black-and-white frame while everyone else was moving around in color. Reba, for instance, was plumping up and down on her heels as if she were looking for something; perhaps her feet had merely fallen asleep. Still doing this, looking like someone on a pogo stick, she said, "Melissa won this *enormous* fish tank. I don't mean a goldfish bowl—which die as soon as they hit the house anyway. It's a *tank*. Huge! I told her we have no room for it, but she *won* it. How can you argue that with a six-year-old?"

Maria said, "It's what Matthew has. You keep it on the windowsill. It fits."

"That's what Bert told her. But the thing *is,* Maria, in her room the windowsill is right on top of the radiator. We'd have poached tropical fish."

"Take it to the country," Joan said. She had taken her hair out altogether and was now braiding it listlessly.

"They'll *die* in the country. And then she won't go to the toilet. That's what happened every time we had to flush down the goldfish."

Maria poured wine into the pan, popped a mushroom into her mouth, and as the winy chicken smell rose up through the room, said, "Salt pork, *that's* what I should really have. Or bacon grease." She shrugged her shoulders, clanked an oversized lid on the pan, and said, "Reba, it's exactly what Matthew has. I already told you. You put down on the windowsill some asbestos, aluminum. It works. It's only all that fish business is completely crazy—much too expensive. So—if they die, too bad. No more."

Joan said, "Maria, really you should have *been* here today. Maybe Matthew would have won some fish. And anyway, *everybody* missed you."

"I know," Maria said grimly. "I met downstairs Larry Kopell."

"Don't tropical fish—the mothers eat the babies?" Reba asked. "I'm not sure I want Melissa to see that."

"You can make then a terrarium, it's the other thing you can do with a fish tank," Maria said. "Some other things, too." She was counting out plates and utensils, pulling things out from shelves and drawers. "We'll set this table in here. A little crowded, but all right! . . . Reba, is your husband coming?"

Joan said, "You're wrong, Reba. How else do you begin explaining about death? It's better if they see it first with things like fish."

Reba began going up and down on her heels again and said, "Maria! What a terrific idea! I *never* would have thought of something like that! You should write a book about it. *You* know—

all your sort of household hints and your projects! And then we could give out a copy to everyone who joins our food co-op!"

Joan, looking serious, said, "I know it sounds brutal, but actually it means more with animals. It takes on more reality—the way farm children learn about it."

"Funny," Arthur said, and smiled up at Louise so that she began having trouble with the place settings. "That's not what *I* heard that farm children learn about naturally."

"What do you think, Maria?" Reba asked excitedly. "Isn't it a good idea?"

"What does *she* think!" Arthur nodded his head in mock gloomy derision. "What do you expect her to think about a goldfish? She was once running up gas bills on Grandpa. And don't forget—those were the days before Easy-Off."

"Arthur!" Joan shrieked.

"Oh, it's all right, Joan," Maria said, looking up in annoyance. "He does it only to provoke. And anyway, he's part right. I can't think about it the same way you do. I had, when I was ten, in my street, to pull out the dead bodies. From the houses, buildings that were, I don't know—collapsed. First, really, to take them out and make sure. Because after bombings and so on there were still live people. *Not* so many. Some. Reba, if your husband is coming, Louise can put out now another place."

A very thin, blond, wan-looking child was walking hurriedly down the cobbled street of a small, tree-lined provincial town. Cobblestones, cuckoo clocks, and medieval architecture were strewn around her in terrible disarray, but she went on picking her way through the rubble, which she called "ruble," foreshadowing the money she would one day be trying to earn. "God *damn* it, exactly what I can't stand!" said this child as a falling brick just grazed her. She was wearing old dancing slippers which she knew to be unsuitable; but she did not believe—it was not in her mentality—to change clothes every time she went out of the house. The excessive thinness did not suit her either, and her hair was tied back by an underwear strap or a piece of sock which she had knitted herself and had intended to exchange on the black market—though not for chocolate, whose sweetness she could still not accustom herself to. She scowled up at the sky, exclaiming, "Again, God *damn* it! I think I'll maybe move to Australia," but this time she ducked out of the way in time. And tripped on what was clearly a person. Bending down, she began heaving away bricks and stones in frantic annoyance, and blowing away the dust and silt from the person's face, she grabbed and slapped the arms, saying, "Come on, hurry up! *Quickly!* Or I'll be late! *Again!*" It was impossible to tell what she could imagine she would be late for.

Joan said, "Maria, there's something I didn't tell you and I really feel terrible . . . You know that—"

"The telephone call from the hospital? Don't worry about it, they'll call again. It's maybe about insurance money or something. I don't know."

Arthur, pouring out wine, gave the first glass to Maria, who began drinking immediately. He said, "Insurance? On Sunday? Drink up, *liebchen*! You can use it!"

Maria put down the wineglass, but she was laughing. Defensively she said, "Well, for anything else, how would they call up just one time? They would call—and then call and call again. I know. I've had already many emergencies."

Joan, looking stricken, put her hand over her mouth. "Oh, Maria, now I *really* feel terrible," she said. "I fucked up everything . . . I even broke your coffeepot. But don't worry—I'll replace it. We'll go to wherever you got it before."

"Where I got it before—a long time ago—was in a bank. From starting a new account. I was then so stupid I thought it made it free . . . Can you believe, Arthur, that I was once so stupid?" Maria smiled distantly into her wineglass.

Joan said, "Oh my God, Maria! You mustn't blame yourself for something like that. People do it all the time. Arthur's cheapo idiot aunt in Long Beach practically *lives* that way. And besides, you were new in the country."

"Maybe *we* should do something along those lines," Reba said, craning her happy, squirrel-like face to the side. "See if we can find someone to get us some wholesale woks. Or *crêpe* pans. And then give them out as an inducement. Although why should anyone need an inducement to join a food co-op?"

"That's one thing I don't care," Maria said. "If anyone thinks I'm a cheapstake, too bad!"

Arthur refilled Maria's glass and said, "That's right, have some more. What do you care what people think? *Prosit!* Pretend it's the *Oktoberfest*."

The downstairs bell rang, and Maria said, "Good! Here comes Matthew! Now we can eat, I'm hungry. And I'm anyway getting worried for his being out too long in the dark."

"Naturally!" Arthur said. "Where you come from, the only one who goes out in the dark is Dracula."

Already flushed from the wine, Maria giggled and said, "Dracula! That's not even near! Americans never know anything about geography, I'm completely serious. Where I come from—or anyway, where I stayed in the country with my cousin Klaus—is the same place as Frankenstein. Near. It's true." She stood up, reached over for a large serving spoon, and, rapping it sharply on the frying pan, said, "Plates, everyone! Quickly! It will be much easier this way. Who likes only drumsticks?"

Arthur held out plates for her and said, "Frankenstein! No wonder you never saw anything peculiar about Hitler or Stalin. That explains everything."

"Frankenstein was the man only, Arthur. Not the monster. People make always the same mistake . . . If anyone wants the wings, too bad. I'm saving them for Matthew."

"But that's the whole point of the book, Maria," Joan said. "That it's impossible to make that kind of distinction."

"Frankenstein!" Arthur repeated just as Matthew came in. "What do you think of *that,* Matthew? Your mother comes from the same place as Frankenstein."

Matthew did not come over to the table. He put the long loaf of Italian bread down on the nearest empty space—a scratchy countertop—and in a small, unhappy voice said, "It got wet." Matthew had gotten wet himself, and looked, Louise thought, as if he had brought the raw, rainy darkness inside with him. His glasses were fogged over, his light hair was plastered down; with the collar turned up, he seemed zippered into his green plaid jacket. It made his small face look pinched and pasty, and as water continued dripping down him, he gave off a child's winter smell of wet wool.

Maria said, "Here, baby, angel. Look! Only wings—I saved them for you. Specially. Come."

Matthew took off his glasses and, rubbing his eyes with wet hands, said, "I'm not hungry. I don't want anything."

"*Wings,* Matthew! Everyone else is already eating. Come on now, hurry up! Let's have the bread." And turning around to look at him, Maria said, "My God, Matthew! Why do you only *stand* there? What's the matter with you? Take off the wet clothes!"

Pulling his zipper listlessly, Matthew said, "Can't I take it in to the television? *Please.*"

"What? I can't hear you, angel," Maria said. She had pulled out a clean dish towel and was vigorously rubbing his head.

"Could I have peanut butter and jelly and take it into the television with me?"

"No. And no, Matthew," Maria said, holding up two fingers. "Definitely. Two no's."

Arthur said, "C'mere, Matthew." Beckoning him over, he put his arm around Matthew as if he were about to tell him a secret and said, "Listen. I think there's something you better tell your mother—it's two eyes, *one* nose."

Joan pulled off a piece of Italian bread and, pointing with it, said, "You think he does that with his own children?"

Happily straddling Arthur's chair, Matthew continued to laugh. Arthur said, "Well, Matthew, what'd you do with your mother today? Cross a couple of borders? Did you have a good time?"

Matthew made a face and said, "Yucchy," as if he were thinking of Rebecca's fat hands.

"Matthew, you *know* that's what I hate always. When you say that. It's first very babyish—from TV maybe. And second, it's anyway not a real word. If you want to answer Arthur, if you want to say something, then say it. But say a word."

"A word," Matthew said and, bursting out again, could not contain his own hilarity.

"You should have let him go to the Block Party, Maria," Joan said. "The kids all had such a good time. They were running up and down the street all day—we practically didn't even see them."

"I *always* don't see him all day. During the week. From early in the morning. And then at night, when I have to go to the hospital, again I don't see him . . . Come here, Matthew, angel," Maria said gently in a winy voice, and she tapped the place next to hers. "If you don't eat now, you'll then *later* be hungry. It's true. I have, if you want, apple juice."

Arthur said, "Go ahead, Matthew. Make your mother happy."

Rubbing his eyes again, Matthew squeezed past the sink and leaned against his mother, who said in the same surprising voice,

"See how wet you are still, baby, angel. Your clothes . . ." She nuzzled her head against his, and in a whisper, almost as if she were crooning to a baby, said, "I tell you what, Matthew. Here—eat now, just a little, whatever you want and then quickly, right away, change into dry pajamas. And then you can watch TV—a long time. OK? Yes? It's a deal?"

Matthew did not answer; he seemed content to stand there, leaning against his mother, his body pressed against hers, removed from its own responsibility. Of course he was only a child.

In the terrible clear, cold light of her studio in Stockholm—a light like ice—Elisabeth did not sit perfectly still at her desk, did not intend to. She turned in her high swivel chair, designed expressly for this purpose. Though perfectly dressed, she turned not once, but again and again, rising higher and higher till she was thrown from her chair. Directly across from her, her husband showed no surprise; he was known everywhere for the impassivity of his expression, which matched so perfectly the starkness of his designs. He began to turn on his chair also—these chairs that he had designed—and, thrown from it similarly, made the downstairs neighbor remark to a guest: "Don't be frightened, it's only foreplay." They rose and turned together on the floor just as they had done separately on the chairs. In front of them the enormous window was uncurtained, but, removed from the responsibility of her body, Elisabeth did not care.

"That's probably what my kids are doing now," Reba said, yawning. "Watching TV. That's all they ever do now since they found out we might be going to South America. Someone told them there's no TV there."

In a green, sunny clearing in Central America, just outside their own house, Sr. Weil's four young daughters lay swinging together in a hammock. The hammock swung very slowly, sometimes barely moving at all; it was the time of highest afternoon heat and there was nothing to do. Birds called but did not fly off. Inside the house a servant ran water, or singing to herself, clattered a dish. None of these sounds ran out to their natural ends, but hung on in the air where they'd fallen, suspended by the heat. The four little girls, so similar in appearance, swung on in the hammock; they rocked and rested. By turns, they braided and unbraided each other's long black hair, and holding up small brown arms against the light, they traded bracelets. Smiling and whispering, they fell asleep, curled up limb against limb, lying together like kittens in the sun. How freed they were from the responsibility of their own bodies was something they did not yet know. It was possible they would never need to.

Matthew said, "I'm finished, Mommy."

"OK, baby," Maria said slowly, and with her whole body gone slack, she leaned forward to let him through. "Pajamas, Matthew," she called back. "Remember! . . . Who wants dessert? Coffee? Cheese—that cheese, naturally, I almost forgot. And probably fruit somewhere."

"There's some fruit left over from the Block Party," Joan said. "Apples and oranges. The bananas got squashed."

Agreeably, Maria said, "We are *all*, I think, squashed. Shloshed? Tomorrow, probably, I'll be squeazy." Smiling, she brought over the cheese and a bowl of fruit, and did not bother to clear off the table. "Look!" she cried out suddenly, pointing to an oval ceramic bowl on top of the refrigerator. "That crook? That crock? It's what I used always to marinate sauerbraten in! I don't know now where it came from."

"I borrowed it, I forgot to tell you," Joan said. "And there's something else I almost forgot." From the pocket of her dungarees she pulled out a large black wool sock, saying, "This sock. Someone lost it in the laundry room. I better hang it up in the elevator."

Louise watched Maria pick up the sock and carefully straighten it out on the table; slowly, dreamily, she ran her fingers up and down each line of ribbing. "It's not mine," she said.

Joan cut off a piece of very runny Brie and, partly missing her plate, said, "I think it's a man's sock. It's enormous."

"Mm." Maria nodded. With her fingers still tracing over it up and down, ridge to ridge, she was picking out small pieces of lint. "Not mine."

Awkwardly, Joan said, "Well, I thought—I mean, it *could* be Dennis's."

"Could have *been*." Maria shrugged. "But he didn't have ever such big feet."

Reba scraped her chair back, rubbed her eyes, and said, "God, it's so late, I should really go . . . But I can't move. And besides, as soon as tax season starts, Bert becomes a total maniac."

Maria folded the sock very carefully, returned it to Joan, and picking up an orange, stared at it and said, "April twentieth."

"It's April *fifteenth*, Maria," Reba said.

"No, no. April twentieth, it's what I had always to say in school every day." And smiling distantly at the orange, Maria recited rapidly under her breath in German, saying finally, "For Hitler's birthday. They gave us every year on April twentieth an orange."

"Ah *hah*! The Führer's birthday!" Arthur said. "Was he a Libra? Or a Pisces?"

"I don't know," Maria said, and peeling the orange with a knife, making spiraling circles of the rind, she had begun to smile the way she always did when Arthur teased her.

He put his arm around her now and said, "Come on, Maria. Tell the truth. Those were your happiest days, weren't they? Eating oranges for the Führer, picking mushrooms with Heinrich and Ludwig, strolling up around the mountainside to visit

Frankenstein, just you and Cousin Klaus . . . Those were your best days. And you had no way of knowing what was going to happen."

"I didn't *ever* know, Arthur. Not then, not now." Maria had spat out an orange pit and with her raised face very pale, Louise saw that she was speaking with odd, sudden urgency. "How can you know? Did I think ever when I was a little girl living in that stupid, ugly little town—city—that I would soon, one day, never be there again? To live in the country, a farm girl, with everything different? And then, in the farm with my cousin, to one day be working in a factory? And after to be in a dancing club? And *still* after, to be in America with Dennis? You think every time: This is my life. But it's not. You don't know. You know only always that it can change, be different."

Dennis would die. Maria was a very simple-minded woman; she had only simple-minded thoughts, and took comfort from the commonplace. Louise could not control her own dizziness; she felt the lights change and the table tipping, dipping. The idea of a table tipping is not an idea, but an example of concrete thinking—a serious symptom. You think every time: This is my life. But it's not. In her dizziness, Louise got up to go to the bathroom. You know only that it can change, be different. The sock was not Maria's: it belonged to a man. Dr. Vinograd, for instance, had gone from one life to another, not necessarily all on skis. Maria was crude in her perceptions of life; she understood one thing only—survival. As a young bride during the Depression and the Spanish Civil War, Rebecca had given numberless wonderful parties, had loved being a hostess. She had thought: This is my life. But it wasn't. Once, many years before, Pablo Casals, on a mountain-climbing expedition, had injured his hand. He had thought then with half-deceiving relief: I will never play the cello again. But he did. It was possible that such beliefs had left Maria without a conscience, like Frankenstein. Like Elisabeth, whose life had so changed that it was frozen now in chilly perfection. Just as facing backward on a moving bus, everything slipped away in frozen, exaggerated stillness: a world where no one moved and nothing was translatable. Dizziness was in itself a translation—and a very ordinary one: the table tipped. The woman on the bus with the two sweet-faced, dark-haired little girls had not known: it was why she looked at her lively, chattering daughters with such wonder. Once she had spoken a different language, had learned English with a British accent, never guessing then that the past and this particular present which she knew could not tell her future. You know only that it can change, be different. The sock, which was not Maria's, could have been once.

Dennis would die. Passing through the foyer, Louise looked up at the photographs and saw that these positions and stances of agony which he had worked to refine as an expression of his art were now an exact reflection of the agonized condition of his body. Which could no longer change, be different. You won't leave me yet, Matthew, will you, baby, angel? Maria, peeling an orange, knew perfectly well what had happened to her, but had an odd way of looking at history: she did not think it determined the future, sealing it up. The table tipped. It was a view that was not necessarily true, but simply just as possible.

In the bathroom, the sounds of other people's plumbing rumbled and clanged through the pipes. Soon Matthew, on his way in to brush his teeth, would stop off to stand near his mother. In his pajamas and without his glasses, he would look almost like a baby, his vulnerability extreme, his tentativeness exaggerated and poignant: set, like a photograph, for nostalgia. Chairs would scrape; Arthur, Joan, and Reba would get up slowly and, gathering their things together, begin to move toward the door—as always, reluctant to leave. A bulb in the hallway would be burnt out, Maria would leave her door open for them till she ran off to answer the phone, which might or might not be the hospital.

Louise looked in the mirror and considered the familiar evidence of her own face, which had said always: This is my life. And it was, but just like a photograph, set and bounded in one time, it could not tell her anything more than what had already happened.

SICKNESS

In books, radiators hum and sing; in my house, the radiator howls and yelps as if a baby were locked up in it, an angry baby who, though he cries and cries, still does not bring his mother running. Not that she isn't longing to. But there is an older neighbor around or an aunt maybe, and her philosophy is: He's crying? So he'll cry! And the baby in the radiator—how can he know all this? So he sends up a last, raging yowl and I am woken up.

Here, in the brief, early whitish light, the march of neighbors has already begun. For even though it is barely morning of my first day home from school, the news of a sick child has shuttled through the building like steam through the pipes, and my mother's voice rises from the kitchen in bitterness.

"What's a doctor? He sits and sits studying long enough so that finally in one place his bathrobe wears out."

It is not a question now of tissues and aspirins, of swollen glands or a throat that won't swallow. This time it is serious: Lichtblau, the limping *Golem* with MD on his license plate, has made a house call. Dragging one heavy foot behind the other, he has announced measles and a high fever, and in a stingy mumble as dull as the one that sends black years to the Irish kids on his new Buick in the street, he has even mentioned the possibility of hospital. But this doesn't worry me because what's a hospital? One, nurses: quick-stepping, white-clad girls whose heads are all blond and faces *shiksa*-silly. And two, doctors: bald, heavy men, sad-eyed and Jewish, who walk slowly on dragging legs, their bodies wrapped up in old maroon bathrobes, shamefully all worn away in one spot.

What would I do in a place like that? Where would I keep my glass of sweet, lukewarm tea that sits, whenever I am sick, like lightened liquid honey on a folding chair by my bed? Where would I put all my books? Where would I get my neighbor stories? As I lie back against the pillow, my room flies up before me like an airy, pastel balloon. From the window, slats of sunlight sift in, off-spinning ballerina twins to the clumsy elephant slats of the fire escape: the sun is playing a game of potsy on the linoleum. Hopping each time to a different cone of color, the sun has zoned my floor so that it's a country counter of homemade, fruit-flavored ice creams, or else great clean pails of paint from which I can choose new, sweet, custardy colors and order the painter to paint my room.

Outside, other children's feet thump off to school. Some are shouting: they just got to the corner, shoelaces dragging, and now, for spite, the light is changing. And some are crying: people with bad work habits, maybe they forgot their consent slips or their gym suits, and because it's too late now to go back, the crying buttons them into their storm coats even tighter and their whole bodies knead with what's coming. But I am inside, I am home, and sickness is all pleasure.

"Some tremendous achievement," my mother says, and from the kitchen her voice in anger and sourness closes in on itself till it's black, black as the telephone, a mother jungle—steamy from her tears and sour from her breath. If she listened to me, she'd be completely different, even wear nail polish, but if that's what I'm looking for, she says, what I better do is go out and get myself another mother. As it is, though, the one I have plucks pinfeathers out of a chicken, and because her fingers get clumsy and impatient instead of elegant and neat, the knife point nips them so they bleed a thin, crooked trail that maps out spongy yellow Chickenland: a bridge across the legs, a mountain pass to the wings, and all the way back through to the interior where the tiny stomach and liver lie hiding together, breathing like brothers.

"Some tremendous achievement," she tells Birdie. "To sit and sit and study and study and nowhere in the whole process is there a head that comes into it or a brain that's involved. In medical school the big expense is in bathrobes."

Birdie is puffy-brown and stuffed, the awful splendor of a Florida suntan. Her voice, too, is bleached—thin and hard from the sun and sandy from cigarettes. With aqua earrings, an orange dress, and two orange-painted big toes that pop out from aqua open-toe shoes, Birdie is herself a sunstroke.

"Let's face it, Manya," she tells my mother. "You'll never get satisfaction. A Jewish doctor is a Jewish prince."

A Jewish prince! Joseph Nasi, Joseph the prince . . .

THE CHAMBER WAS THICK WITH INCENSE AND PLUSH WITH SILKEN PILLOWS. In the distance a droning voice was chanting the name of Allah, summoning the faithful to prayer. But within the richly adorned room not even a palm frond dared stir, for in the center, seated upon the largest and most sumptuous silken pillow of them all, was the Sultan himself, brocade pantaloons loose about his legs and a gleaming scimitar at his waist. Behind him stood his fierce, mustachioed guards, before him veiled and scented dancing girls. All awaited his pleasure and command. Beneath the imperial turban, however, the Sultan's heavy brow was clouded and his darkened visage bespoke distress. Besides all this, he was very ugly, had a fat, puffy face as if mosquitoes couldn't keep away from him. With a soft rustle of silks, a graceful, veiled maiden appeared before him, bearing a silver tray of sweetmeats. But barely raising one languid hand, the Sultan sent her away. On hot days, sweetmeats probably made him a little nauseous. A richly garbed courtier bowed low before him.

"Sire," he said, "an emissary just arrived from the mighty King of Spain urgently begs that Your Majesty receive him." But bidding him rise, the Sultan merely looked away, saying, "I shall receive no one." A thin, hurrying Vizier flung himself at the Sultan's feet crying, "If it please Your Majesty, a messenger stands at the palace gates with a plea of grave import from Your Majesty's heroic general now engaged with the Infidel in battle far afield." The beetle-browed Sultan sighed.

Suddenly a great clatter was heard from without and finally even the fat, sitting Sultan started getting a little curious.

"What occasions this disturbance?" he demanded of his court.

"It is nothing, Your Majesty," replied a saber-bristling guardsman. "Nothing His Highness need concern himself over. It is merely a Jew."

"A *Jew*?" cried the Sultan, hastily rising from his cushions as color flooded his features. His eyes were popping, too, and probably by this time there was even a vein twitching somewhere. "A Jew? *What* Jew?"

"Merely a Jewish doctor who calls himself Joseph."

"Joseph!" the Sultan cried out with great emotion. "All praises to Allah Who has sent him to me this day. Bring Joseph to my presence immediately."

Hustled in between two armor-laden guardsmen was a slight, bearded man of modest dress and bearing and proud, intelligent eyes.

"Sire," he said, stepping forward, carefully lowering his eyes, but not bowing his head or bending his knee, for there was only One to Whom Joseph bowed. And not every other minute either because he certainly wasn't Catholic.

"O Joseph," the Sultan called out in great agitation. "What news do you bring me? What of my son, what of my ships, and what of the terrible apparition of my nightly slumbers?"

"For your son, O great Sire, I have prepared a special salve and now the lad's eye is as bright as ever it was."

"Selim," the Sultan breathed. That was his son's name in Turkish.

"Of your ships, Your Majesty. Though one was lost in a storm at sea, the cargo of all the fleet has been rescued in a foreign port by a friend and member of my faith, one Mannaseh ben Levi. Further, he has sent a message to me with the news of a worm, Your Majesty, who through his own cunning can spin silk. He offers to send to your court as many of such creatures as Your Majesty desires in the shipment with the lost cargo."

"Allah be praised!"

"Of the apparition. It was a warning to Your Majesty of the storm at sea which distressed your ships. Now that the cargo is safe, the dreaded apparition will trouble you no longer."

"O Joseph, physician to my body, my soul, and my coffers. How shall I reward you? What is it that you wish?"

"For myself, Sire, there is nothing I desire. But for my people, I ask that they may always live in peace within your walls, free to pursue their daily lives and to worship, harming no one, according to our age-old laws and beliefs."

"Granted, Joseph. Most swiftly and easily granted. But what of yourself? What do you ask for your own person?"

"Only that which is granted for my people."

"Then, Joseph, if you will not ask, I must bestow unrequested. And I, His Imperial Majesty the Sultan, name you, Joseph, a Prince of my Domain. No longer are you merely Joseph the Jewish doctor. Henceforward you are to be known as Joseph the Prince! Let cymbals sound and gongs strike!" Right in my ear: it is Birdie's Atlantic City charm bracelet sounding and gonging on the Formica table.

"UH-TUH-TUH AND LOOK WHO'S HERE!" SHE SAYS, SMILING AT ME, HER lipsticked lips wide and bright as a sideways orange Popsicle.

Uh-tuh-tuh and look who's here. Yellow kindergarten clowns hop all over my pajamas and red spots climb through my flesh. That's who's here.

"*Ketzeleh*," says Birdie. "Are you hungry? Do you want some bread and peanut butter?" But I'm not sure what I want; my head is spinning off in a dead man's float all by itself and is strange to the rest of me—luggy limbs and scratchy skin.

"Oh, Manya," Birdie calls to my mother. "Watch how your daughter spreads the peanut butter. I love the way she does it—so perfect and so exact you'd think the knife is a paintbrush. Look how she sits there with that peanut butter like an artist."

"Some artist," my mother says. "She has no hands, she's just like me. She couldn't even tie up a goose, my father used to say about me, and that's what it is—no hands."

In the back of the siddur, in the Song of Songs, it says: What shall we do for our little sister, for she has no breasts? But there is nothing in it about no hands.

"Look how she makes it smooth and how she goes over and over it. By the time she's through, it's a shame to eat it."

But my mother doesn't even bother to turn around because in her opinion peanut butter and nail polish are the exact same thing: both of them made up inside the head of Howdy Doody.

Birdie has nothing against peanut butter, though. Why should she? She chews gum, plays mah-jongg, goes to bungalow colonies, and eats Chinese food. Altogether she would be a cow but for one thing—cows get the best boys and end up with the best husbands. And this is Birdie's story: she didn't. So far did she miss in this one way that even though she has been divorced for years, she still cries to my mother in the kitchen that when she wakes up in the morning she feels that there is no taste in her, and sometimes when she stands with her shopping cart in the aisle at Daitch's, everything starts to get cold, sour, and far away. Her one son, Salem, is eighteen and goes to pharmacy school in Philadelphia: by a coincidence, an accident, the city where his father lives. Really he should be named Shalom, but from being ashamed that it was too Jewish, Birdie named him Salem and what she didn't know was that he would get called Sal—a name for an ordinary Italian hood. Still, he is very good-looking, Salem: tall, black wavy hair, and a long, rocky face like Abraham Lincoln's. Every couple of months he comes home to visit his mother, and takes back all her saved-up empty soda bottles for the deposit, pulling them along University Avenue, her shopping cart behind his long, skinny Abraham Lincoln legs all the way to Daitch's. When he's not there, I don't think she bothers about soda bottles, and anyway, when her allergies come she goes to Florida, when it's too hot in the city she goes to Monticello, in between sometimes she goes to Lakewood or Atlantic City, and for what's left she comes back to the Bronx and starts right in playing mah-jongg as if she were just a cow with other cows, her life the same as theirs.

"Sometimes that's what I wish for you most, Miriam," my mother tells me in the late afternoon when she sits drinking tea and her narrow, nervous face gets dreamy from the steam, and her worn-out, angry voice gets swallowed away with the heat and sweetness in the cup. "I wish you could grow up to be a cow."

BUT IT'S TOO LATE FOR THAT BY NOW AND I KNOW IT; DONNA SCHOEN-baum, in my class in public school, is one already—and if not yet exactly a cow, then definitely a calf. Her flat, moony face tilts in the light when she raises her hand for the pass, the slow, sleepy look stays on her even in city-wide reading tests. In her father's dry-goods store, woolen underpants creep through the shelves and flannel pajamas hibernate in the window. Once, coming back from an errand for Miss Devlin, just to waste more time, I took all the barrettes and bobby pins out of my hair and stood with it just like that in the fifth-floor girls' bathroom. All of a sudden, behind me in the mirror was Donna Schoenbaum, her dirty blond hair in two fat rubber-band curls on her shoulders, her face like two wide, white, empty clouds that stand still, her eyes tiny and tight and, without her glasses, even dumber.

"Ooh, Miriam, you look just like a witch," she said with her high, naggy, baby-cow voice. "I never saw you before with your hair down and that's what you look like. All your long, black, messy hair with your long, thin face and your *nose*. You look like a witch, I swear it."

In camp once I learned a Yiddish song about a cow, a calf really, and this the chorus of it: *donna-donna-donna-donna,* instead of *la-la-la*. So, into her face in the mirror I said, "Donna, Donna, Donna, Donna." A calf, all tied up, is being led off to slaughter in a wagon. Right up above it, following along in the sky, is a bird, a swallow, who flies back and forth, up and down, anywhere he wants while the cow with her dumb eyes just lies staring. The wind, seeing all this, starts laughing, keeps it up day and night, till finally the farmer driving the wagon takes pity, looks around at that stupid-eyed, tied-up calf, and says: Who told you to be a cow? *Donna-donna-donna-donna*. Donna's father's store is right next door to the kosher butcher where the huge, split bodies of killed kosher cows, hanging on deliverymen's shoulders, wobble between the entrances of the two stores. Sometimes the bodies stain the sidewalk.

"You even have yellow skin like a witch," Donna said. Because I am named Miriam, my skin should be different: dark and lit up as a crayon color, polished and sunny—olive skin like Gracie D'Onofrio's, who has a private house with white statues and vegetables in the front and her father's exterminating business in the basement. Gracie is the prettiest girl in my class and, except for Marty Weintraub, the person Miss Devlin hates most. Gracie talks all the time: in line after the bell, in the lunchroom after the whistle, in the auditorium even in front of the principal, and in the room when she isn't whispering, she's sending notes. "If you don't know how to stop that tongue, I'll call your father and have him exterminate it," is what Miss Devlin's always threatening her. But worst of all, in Miss Devlin's opinion, is that Gracie no longer goes to Released Time, playing hooky from her Catholic lessons. Once in line in the Girls' Yard, in one of her after-the-bell talkings, Gracie said, "They're all mean, and I have to get stuck with Sister Mary Joseph, who's the meanest. All you have to do is talk once, and she takes you downstairs and beats you."

"It's a terrible thing that your religious education can't manage to do any more for you," Miss Devlin screams at Marty Weintraub, a person who calls out and throws spitballs. "You're a rude young man, Mr. Martin Weintraub, and the Sisters would surely know what to do with a rude young man like you."

If I were in school now, the morning nearly over, where I would be, probably, is walking slowly up the back stairs on an errand for Miss Devlin. On these stairs there is a window at every half-landing, and on the higher floors the windows, through the gratings, skip the fat yellow brick of the Annex next door and fly straight to the Reservoir—the round blue beginnings of a strange little country far away from the Bronx. In the fall this little country is a colonial village settled by the Dutch: a bright, curvy shore full of tiny-roofed private houses in shapes and colors as jumbled and leaping as the changing trees, and higher than all of them, one white-topped church, sunny and placid. But in the winter, when the snow sticks to the little houses beyond the Reservoir, sealing them in long after it's become slushy in all the neighborhood streets, the little country, pale, poor, and half buried, seems even farther away—Russia. A Cossack horseman rides these backstairs windows: Anton, the custodian's helper, belted to the ledge with a pail, sits astride the sill, his stallion, and washes the windows. Pressed against the glass, his forehead is wide and empty like a Russian steppe and his cheeks are as red as my mother's were when she was a girl in Poland. From squinting in the wind, Anton's eyes get a tight, slanty, Tartar-tribesman look, and when he's working hard, his mouth curves down around a matchstick between his lips—a thin, sneering curve, practically Chmelnitski. . . .

Heavy, endless snows were falling, and throughout the bitter winter the land became a lonely, frozen waste. At night wolves howled in the dark forests and icy winds cried out through the trees. Through these trees, too, flew terrible stories: of unwary souls who ventured forth in crude wagons and were frozen to death in the deep while landowners in fur-rugged sleighs galloped by, their sleighbells jingling. In the snowbound countryside the peasants (poor farmers) could carry no wares to fairground or marketplace. And in the villages within the Jewish Pale of Settlement, families sat in their bleak, chilled houses, huddling closer together around the steaming samovar. Artisans and tradesmen, rabbis and scholars lived in these villages, and not often could they voyage abroad. For as bitter as were the Russian winters, more bitter still were the cruel and unjust restrictions placed upon them by the harsh rule of the Russian Tsar. As long as they had lived with poverty and hunger, so long had these pious, simple folk lived with fear. "O Lord," they pleaded, praying to the Almighty One with fervor and devotion, "Thou Who hast vanquished our ancient oppressors, how long must we suffer under this terrible yoke?" Thus they prayed in synagogue and study house.

In such a study house, in just such a shtetl (for so these villages were called), a tailor, Mottel, and his five sons sat poring over the Holy Writ as the afternoon deepened into evening. Suddenly, amidst the dull hum of men's voices chanting the Scriptures and disputing over the commentaries, a great clatter was heard at the door, soon followed by an icy blast of chill air. It was the red-bearded beadle, a lantern swaying on his arm, as he cried in a terror-filled voice, "Brothers! Brothers! Bestir yourselves! Hide! Run! Save yourselves and your sons!"

"What is it, Beadle?" asked the tailor. "A pogrom?"

"Not that," the beadle replied, his voice still shaking. "Oh, hurry, brothers, hurry! It's the Snatchers, the Tsar's kidnapers, and with them ride an army of Cossack soldiers."

"The Snatchers!" the cry went up in alarm as all hurried to their homes, for these Snatchers were the cruelest, most heartless measure the Tsar had ever devised. Eager to rid his lands of Jewish subjects, the Tsar, pretending benevolence, had offered first-class citizenship to all those Jews who would convert to Christianity. But the Jewish people remained steadfast, and the Tsar, even further angered by these "ignorant, stubborn wretches," sent out bands of kidnapers to those areas of his empire where he permitted Jews to live. The evil purpose of these kidnapers was to snatch little Jewish lads, not more than seven or eight years of age, tear them from their mothers and their homes, and send them to peasant Christian families in distant reaches of the Tsar's vast realm, where in hapless servitude they would daily be forced to go against the teachings of their faith. For twenty-five long years such captivity was theirs to endure, the latter part to be spent as unwilling conscripts in the Tsar's brutal army. By that time, gloated the ruthless Tsar, all ties with their heritage and origin would be forgotten.

As the tailor and his sons hurried through the darkened streets, fierce Cossack soldiers already crowded the pathways. Troops of burly, red-cheeked young men sat astride sturdy stallions, and the mouths of these sleek beasts foamed and steamed in the frost. A wail went up throughout the village, and from one end to the other could be heard the voice of the cobbler's widow, Teibel, crying, "Please, sirs, please! I implore you! Take pity on me! What am I but a poor, lone widow? And what is he but my one, only son and barely an infant?" But the widow's pleas were of no avail and the screaming, woebegone youth was dragged off amidst his mother's weeping.

Quickly the tailor bade all his family hide so that when the louts arrived, they would think they had happened on an empty house. But the baby, cradled in its mother's arms under the bed, began to whimper in fright when he heard the heavy, crunching footsteps stalk through the door. Frantically stuffing a cloth a bit farther into the infant's mouth, the tailor's wife suddenly gasped in horror. For her sons, hiding in the yard, began to let out terrible, piteous cries: they had fallen into the hands of the snatchers. Hurriedly crawling out of her hiding place, the anguished mother clutched her youngest son to her breast and saw that the infant in her arms had gone limp and lifeless, suffocated by the tiny cloth. Late that night, peasants of the neighborhood, emboldened by drink and encouraged by the Cossack forays, swept through the miserable village, pillaging and plundering as they went.

Just as the drunken peasants are finishing off, a noise starts to come from the kitchen like a hundred toilets flushing. Ppshh, wuschsh, swishchh, it comes and goes: my mother is speaking Polish with Eva the Refugee. In Poland, my mother said, it rained constantly from Rosh Hashanah straight to Simchas Torah and rained again from Purim all the way to Pesach, and that's why when people speak Polish it sounds like a rainstorm. Not that Eva the Refugee thinks so. She comes up to see my mother when she gets the feeling that she has to speak Polish. As far as I'm concerned, if she opened up an umbrella and used a little imagination it would be just as good. But there's no one else around she can speak Polish to, not even her husband, Fritz, who's so German-looking—with his glasses that have no frames and his strange smile—that he lived underground in Germany for the whole war without anyone finding him out. What happened to Eva, though, wasn't so lucky; every time she wears a short-sleeved dress, the whole building has to see the blue number on her arm and think of the terrible life she had. When she first moved in, it was this blue number that made all the other women in the building, the cows especially, keep away from her completely, but when they found out how talented she was in gossiping, all her worries were over.

In her tiny ground-floor apartment where she lives with her husband and her fat little son, Eva sits at her window that looks out on the front court and watches everything, from early in the morning when I leave for school till very late at night when all the mah-jongg games are over. And these are the things she knows: what person's daughter who goes to art school and is engaged for the second time had a big fight with her boyfriend in the lobby at one in the morning, and refused to give back the ring till he tried to pull it off her finger; what very skinny woman with no children went running down to someplace in the South and came back with a baby girl that she says isn't adopted but when you take a good look into the carriage what you see is the face of a Southern shiksa; what boy's mother got so furious when he didn't make the SP that she went to school and tried to force the principal into telling her her son's IQ, and when he wouldn't, how this person's mother carried on so much that the principal was ready to call the police; what person's children have to go running all over the building looking for televisions to watch even though there is one in their own living room, but all it gets is snow and ghosts because this person's husband is so cheap that he won't give Rappaport a two-dollar-a-month increase for a roof antenna. There are smaller things she watches, too. To my mother she says, "I didn't know your daughter was starting a new fashion with high socks—one up and one falling down all over her ankle." And to Stuie Greenzweig's mother, "In case you never thought about it, it's possible for a boy to walk out of the house every day at three thirty with Hebrew books in his hand and where his feet take him doesn't have to be Hebrew School." So there are people who would be happier if Eva would move, just to a different apartment.

Even Dora Rappaport, the landlord's wife, begs Eva to go into a bigger apartment: every time she sits in her beautiful house in Long Beach and thinks of Eva with the number on her arm in that tiny apartment, it makes her nauseous. But Eva isn't interested. To Rappaport and anyone else who asks, she says that she and her husband are saving up for a house on the Island. But the truth is that if Eva ever had to give up her ground-floor front-courtyard window, she would have no place to put her talents.

Anyway, what Eva really wants has nothing to do with apartments or houses, it doesn't even have anything to do with watching people from windows. What Eva really wants is a baby daughter, and what it has to do with is the blue number on her arm. Once, a long time ago in Europe before the Nazis came, Eva was married to someone else, not Fritz, and had two little daughters. When the Nazis came around and started taking people away, they told everyone that they just needed people to do work, and that they would put all the children in special nurseries so that the mothers, who were working, wouldn't have to be bothered. But when they got to Eva's older sister Anzhia, who was beautiful, with long red hair, and played the flute like a bird, she refused to be separated from her children, and what happened to Anzhia was that she and her three children were shot with a gun right then and there. When Eva saw this, what she should have done is hide—quick, one, two, three—with her two little daughters under the bed, and then be very careful about how she stuffed cloths. But what she did do was let her children be taken separately, and because she never saw them again, what she would like to have now is a daughter.

What she *does* have now is a son, Stevie, who's almost five years old, with a fat pink face, blond hair, and a tooth in the front that got broken by Jeffrey Bugatch one time when Stevie pushed Jeffrey's baby sister Sherri off her bike and then, for good luck, stepped on her finger. Because of his habits with younger children and because he looks so much like his father, people call out

"The Nazi's here" when they see him coming, and all the mothers in the neighborhood can't wait till Stevie goes to kindergarten, where if he gets the morning session with Miss Callahan, Nazi activities will definitely be over. But that's not why Eva can't wait till he gets to school. She tells everyone around that she doesn't care how many children get into SPs, Bronx Science, or walk off with fantastic scholarships; she is convinced that as soon as the teachers in public school get a taste of her Stevie, every other smart child they ever taught will immediately drop right out of their heads. In the meantime, she dresses him in perfect clothes, and anytime he goes near the sandbox or forgets to put a napkin under his ice-cream pop, she screams out, "Stevie! Stevechen! Daddy doesn't let!" If Eva were a little more perfect with her own clothes, maybe she wouldn't have a smell of so much refugee perspiring that I don't even like to stand near her. But I wouldn't get out of bed to stand near her now anyway. Right this minute, for all I know, she could be telling my mother that the reason I got sick is that there were days last week when I didn't button my top button, or that I almost never wear my gloves except when I leave in the morning. I have no way of knowing, though, because the sounds from the kitchen are still Polish. Swischhh, plishch, chwushh they go, slower and slower, so sleepy a rain that I only know it's over when I hear the bell ring.

DR. LICHTBLAU'S NAME MEANS LIGHT BLUE, BUT THE WAY HE RINGS THE BELL is gray, heavy, and nervous. In his whole life put together, he said only one funny thing, and even *that* was only because I asked him a question. I wouldn't have asked it either, but I was sitting in his office waiting for him to fill out my medical form for camp, and all he did was stand by the window in his white coat and peek out through the venetians to see who he could catch sitting on top of his car. Outside children were skating and screaming, upstairs someone was practicing the accordion, but inside Dr. Lichtblau's ground-floor office there was such a strange, snowy quiet that I looked at the medical form and said, "What's St. Vitus Dance?" "St. Vitus Dance, hah!" Dr. Lichtblau said to me. "With the camps your mother sends you to, the only dance you'll ever have to worry about is the Horah." And then, because I gave him a dirty look, "Not that I have anything against Zionism. I wouldn't want you to think so. As a matter of fact, and this is the truth, somehow, somewhere, distantly by marriage I'm related to David Ben-Gurion." It's not David Ben-Gurion's fault if in a big family some distant cousin somewhere goes out and marries a moron.

In my room, seeing the books on my bed, Dr. Lichtblau says, "What are you reading there—Nancy Drew?"

"No."

"What then? Sue Barton? No? What?"

What I am reading is this: It was a warm, sunny day in Düsseldorf, Germany, in the year 1809, but the gray, stuffy classroom held no hint of the lovely spring morning without. Throughout the long rows small, diligent heads were bent over the copybooks on the desks, and over the sound of busy, scratching pens only a clock ticked. Occasionally, one of the bolder, more daring lads would stealthily look about him, hoping that his raised head had not aroused the stern eye of the severe Prussian schoolmaster, for stiff, exacting discipline was the unquestioned standard of this sunless room. In the back, however, in the row closest to the windows, sat a pale, thin youth whose dark, brooding eyes turned not to his copybook but to the green, budding world beyond the window. He stared longingly, his gaze seeming to fix on a point so distant that only he could see it, and suddenly as a wave of light burst across his gentle face, he grabbed his pen and began to write furiously. But before he knew it, a dark figure was looming over him, snatching the very paper from his hand.

"Ah, and what have we here?" said the schoolmaster, lifting his pince-nez as he glared mercilessly at the dismayed youth. And as the titters of the class rose, the schoolmaster, his voice harsh and mocking, read aloud: "'*Du bist wie eine blume*—You are like a flower. So pretty, pure and sweet.' You are like a flower indeed! How dare you scribble such twaddle in my classroom? Heinrich Heine, explain yourself!"

He doesn't, though, so finally I tell Dr. Lichtblau, "What I'm reading is a story with a poem inside it."

"As far as my daughter is concerned," the doctor tells my mother, "Nancy Drew is the one and only. Not that she's such a big reader, Andrea, but when it comes to Nancy Drew, she even has trouble eating if she didn't finish it."

"Andrea," my mother says very slowly, her mouth making it sound as round and ridiculous as a clown who flops around on TV shows. "She must be in junior high by now, your daughter. How does she like it in Mount Vernon?"

"As a matter of fact, right now she's in Miami with her mother, but what their schools are like down there nobody told me."

"Such an adorable child," my mother says. "All ninety-fives in Florida-going and her mother the same in mink-wearing."

When the Lichtblaus lived in the building, before they moved to Mount Vernon, Andrea's mother used to come back from Alexander's and Loehmann's with so many packages that she had to take a taxi. These taxi-takings were counted up by Eva, but could be seen by anyone who was outside. Sometimes Andrea was in on them, too, but most of the time she wasn't, because in the whole neighborhood Andrea was a girl who was famous for always being busy. Once she was busy trying to be very smart so badly that she went to the library every single day after school, looking so hard for smartness that she forgot to see if she was getting good books. Then she decided to be a brilliant pianist, and practiced "Spinning Song" day and night, till people in her father's waiting room got dizzy and complained. Then she tried to be a brilliant Girl Scout, but not many people in the building had sympathy for her cookies because they knew that where the Girl Scouts met was the Catholic church. Finally, just before she moved, she tried to be very religious, waiting around for Jewish holidays to come and crying because her mother wouldn't send her to Hebrew School.

After she moved, I saw her only once and that was in Alexander's on the Girls' Wear floor, where my mother was bending over a counter of marked-down polo shirts and picking out the ones in my size, saying, "I know it says seconds, Miriam, but they're only polo shirts and besides I can't find any imperfections." "I can," I said. "They're all ugly and how much more imperfect than that can you get?" Just as she was starting to tell me what a bitterness I made of her life, Andrea's mother, her arms so full of packages that she needed a taxi on the spot, came running over and without even bothering to say hello, immediately said, "I don't know how I'm ever going to get out of here. With all the building that they're doing and the banging and hocking, you can't get anywhere near an escalator."

"*What?*" my mother said. "You mean they're expanding again? God Almighty, I can remember when Alexander's was only a lousy little Sephardi dress shop."

"I'll never make it to the elevator with all I'm carrying," Andrea's mother said. "And even if I could find the stairs, how can I manage when I'm so loaded down?" All the time she was saying this, Mrs. Lichtblau kept going up and down on her tiptoes, looking around her in the same nervous way her husband does when he's worrying about who's standing on his car. And all of a sudden, right in the middle of Alexander's, Andrea's mother started crying. Andrea, whose hands were also all full of packages, was standing on the opposite side of the polo-shirt counter, and as soon as her mother started crying, she moved about two baby steps away from her so that she was facing me almost exactly. Except that she was taller and had different glasses, I couldn't see that there was any new and special Mount Vernon feeling about her.

"Hiya, Miriam," she said. "Are you still so smart or did you get a little dumb yet?" Especially since her mother was crying I didn't think it would be nice to tell her that anyone who could think up a question like that had to be on the dumb side herself, so I only said, "You got new glasses."

"They're not new," Andrea said. "It's just that I don't live in the disgusting Bronx anymore, so you don't know what things I have."

"What things do you have?"

"A bra, for one. And as a matter of fact I needed to get a bigger one so badly that we had to come straight to Alexander's. I don't think you'll need anything like that for a couple of years at least." This immediately made me start worrying about the Song of Songs: What shall we do for our little sister, for she has no breasts? If she were really only a *little* sister, naturally she wouldn't, but what if they were just being polite and she wasn't so little anymore?

"What else do you have?" I said.

"Gorgeous underpants. And I just got a whole bunch of new ones that are even more gorgeous." Although you're not supposed to open up your packages in the middle of the store because if they see you they might think you haven't paid yet, Andrea tore open one of her top bags and pulled out a whole pile of underpants that were all exactly the same: white nylon with two bright red hearts stitched on in the middle. Holding them up nearly over her face, Andrea said, "If you think they'll run, you're all wrong. It only happens with the cheap kind." Because it seemed to me that these nylon underpants with two little hearts dancing over the crotch were the most ridiculous things I had even seen in the whole of Alexander's, I began to stare at Andrea and the underpants as she held them to her face, and suddenly I got the idea that if Andrea had underpants with two hearts embroidered on them, maybe if someone ever got a good look at her heart, they would find two little pairs of white underpants stitched on it. Though it's not exactly a medical question, it's something I still wonder about whenever I see Dr. Lichtblau and think of Andrea. But Dr. Lichtblau is not very talkative. Finally, as he's getting ready to leave, he turns to my mother and says, "She looks a lot better to me today than she did yesterday. I'm not saying that she still doesn't have the measles, but between yesterday and today there's a difference between a very severe condition and an ordinary case running its course."

"Between yesterday and today," my mother says before he's even slammed the door, "he either looked up a medical book or else called a doctor. Or who knows? With a man like him it could simply mean that he won't make any more house calls." Still, she closes the venetian blinds as he told her to and warns me about no more reading.

"When I think of how my older sisters were blind for days and days when they had scarlet fever," my mother says. "And who ever thought they would be able to see again?"

"What I have is the measles," I tell her. "Nobody gets scarlet fever anymore besides."

But she isn't listening to me; the look on her face is all Poland. "They just stayed there in the bed, all three of them together, till they couldn't walk and they couldn't move and if you looked at their faces you could see they were burning up, and if you looked at their tongues, what you saw was strawberries. I couldn't stay with them in the room anymore even though it was my room, too, so I used to stand outside and watch them lying in the bedclothes. The room was so dark they thought it was always night, and they would cry out such strange things, things that didn't make any sense to me, till I started to think that everything in the room was black—the windows, the air, the bed, the blankets, and even my sisters. When they couldn't even see any more, something had to be done, so my mother decided to give them castor oil, but because of the terrible taste, they twisted and turned in the bedclothes and wouldn't take it. As sick and weak as they were, my sisters, they simply fought her off. And all day long the same thing went on till my mother became frantic. Finally, very late that night, my father came home and without saying anything, he pulled out from his pocket an orange. How he managed to get it, he never told us, all I can tell you is that it was the biggest orange I have ever seen in my life—a Jaffa orange from Palestine. Of course Palestine was nothing then—no country, no people, hardly even a place, but even at that time they had Jaffa oranges, and they were so big that just to hold it for a minute, I had to use my two hands. I can still tell you how it felt: very round with a thick, bumpy skin and a strange smell—deep and sweet and very distant, the first fruit God created on earth. My father went right in with it to my sisters and gave it to them with the castor oil, and I stood at the door and watched them eat it, and because I was foolish I stood there and wished that I could get sick, too."

"Oranges get caught inside your teeth and make your fingers sticky," I tell my mother, but she doesn't answer me because I'm a prima donna and there's nothing that pleases me. She keeps standing by the window, though what she can see there I don't know; with the venetian blinds drawn, I hardly know if it's night or day. All I'm sure of is that it's after school: from downstairs you can hear Mindy Simons practicing the piano, playing "Für Elise," and Richie Lazaroff with his cheap and noisy trumpet playing "Malagueña."

Because it's so dark in my room and I can't read, I decide to tell myself my favorite story in the book, the story of Chayim Nachman Bialik, another one who sat around in school all day just staring out the window, and then after that turned out to be a poet. Not that he was like Heinrich Heine, who couldn't wait and had to rush into writing a poem the second he saw a flower. Chayim Nachman Bialik had it much worse: his dreaming in school got so bad that he practically couldn't learn how to read and because of that the rabbi used to beat him. His trouble was that every time he saw a Hebrew letter, it would look to him like a person—a man chopping wood or a woman washing clothes, and in his head he would make up stories about whatever person the letter made him think of instead of just reading the letter aloud the way it was. And not only in that way did he have it worse; his family lived in a tiny town in Russia and was very poor, and the only thing he really liked was running around in the fields outside the town. His father worked in a tavern and hated his job so much that he used to sit there reading the Talmud while he was pouring out drinks. Meanwhile, Chayim Nachman Bialik sat upstairs in his room, and when he heard the noises from the tavern—the screaming, the yelling, and the horsing around—he got terrified.

Things did not get better—his father died and he and his mother had to move to another town. When this happened, he felt so miserable that all he did was think about the field he used to run around in and wish himself back into it. Naturally, this didn't do him any good, he wasn't Mary Poppins. Besides, by this time they were even poorer. His mother tried to make some money by doing little things around in the village, but she had no luck. She used to get up so early and work so hard that every time he looked at her, her hands and face seemed so thin, weak, and tired that he was afraid she would get worn away. Because he was suffering so much, he started to spend a lot of time thinking about it, and it began to seem to him that all his mother's suffering and his own were like all the years of suffering of the Jewish people, and the more he thought about it, the whole thing from beginning to end made him sick. He wished that the Jews would snap out of it and get back to the good things they had going for them in the time of the Bible.

One day while he was sitting around dreaming as usual, he fell asleep and had a real dream. In this dream, he was in a land so strange and desolate that it could have been another planet or even the middle of the moon. All there was around him was a desert—terrible, hot, empty sands, orange-brown and wasted. Occasionally there was a squat, ugly palm tree and sometimes a rock. Vultures were screaming somewhere or maybe jackals. Above, the sun was so hard, yellow, and unending that it wore away the sky and left you with nothing to look at. After a while he realized that there were people walking through this desert—a bunch of hideous, broken-down old men. They all had beards, long cloaks, and staffs, and kept walking and walking in a slow, sickly way as if they were blind or didn't know where they were going. He tried to call to them, but they paid no attention, and when any of them came closer they were so old and disgusting, with sour phlegm on their beards, that it made him sick. The old men walked away, but the sun kept burning and draining him like a fever or a terrible sickness, and he lay stretched out in the sand helpless with thirst and with sweat. Suddenly, from the slow pull of my legs and the sweat running through my body, I realize that I've been sleeping, too, and cannot tell whether this was all the story's dream or my own. I get up and look around my bedroom, but there are no hints. Through the wall next door, Stuie and Arlene Greenzweig are watching *Howdy Doody,* and outside, past the venetians, the last of the sun is getting itself together over all the roof antennas in the Bronx. A thick orange globe, it floats in the sky like a bumpy Jaffa orange, a streaky golden desert, the land of Israel itself.

SOUR OR SUNTANNED,
IT MAKES NO DIFFERENCE

What could make sense? The Israeli playwright had such long legs it was hard to believe he was Jewish.

"Little girl," he said, coming up to Miriam with his very short pants and his heavy brown sandals that looked like they were made out of a whole rocky gang's Garrison belts, "little girl, which languages you are speaking?"

But Miriam had not been speaking to anyone: she was walking around the canteen with a milk container going gummy in her hand, and waiting by herself for all the days of camp to be over. There, in the rain, the entire room was sour from milk and muffled from rubber boots and raincoats. The sourness clung to her tongue and whined in her sinuses; locked away from rain and from mud was the whole camp. Soon, some other day, it would get sunny and Snack would be outside on long wooden picnic benches. If you made a mistake and sat down on these benches, splinters crept into your thighs, and if you sat down on the grass instead, insects roamed your whole body. For milk containers and Oreos, this was summer.

"Listen to me, please, little girl. Why you are walking away? I am asking only a simple question. Which languages you are speaking?"

"Right this minute?" Miriam said. "I wasn't speaking anything, can't you even tell?" How he could be smart enough to fix tractors or fool Arabs, let alone write plays, Miriam did not see, not that she said it.

"No, no," said the Israeli playwright. "Bring me please your counselor."

"She's right over there with the garbage," Miriam said, but because she was not at all sure of how words came out of his mouth or went into his head, walked over with him to Fran, who was going around with the basket.

"Amnon!" Fran screamed with her thin sparrow's voice, and immediately dropped the basket and the empty milk containers like people on TV shows who walk backward into sewers. Miriam had never seen her look so lively: Fran's flat paper face was like the front of a brand-new apartment house, and even though she was nineteen years old, did not wear lipstick. Instead, she got up very early in the morning, before any of the girls in the bunk, just to make sure that she would have enough time to stand in front of the mirror and put on all her black eye makeup. It was how Miriam woke up every morning: Fran standing at the mirror, patting and painting her eyes as if they were an Arts-and-Crafts project. Right after that, Gil Burstein, a Senior boy, went to the loudspeaker to play his bugle, and from that time on there was no way at all to stop anything that came after. Every single morning Miriam woke up in the cold light of a strange bed.

From behind all the black lines, Fran's eyes looked as if she was already set to start flirting, but even so her arm would not let go of Miriam's shoulder. It was just another thing that Miriam did not like. Simply going from one activity to another, the whole bunk walked with their arms linked around each other's waist; at flag-lowering, you joined hands and swayed in a semicircle; in swimming you had to jump for someone else's dripping hand the second the whistle blew; and at any time at all there were counselors standing with their arms around kids for no particular reason. They were all people you hardly knew and would probably never see again; there was no reason to spend a whole summer hugging them.

"Miriam," Fran said, smiling at her as if she were a new baby in somebody's carriage, "do you speak Yiddish?"

"What do you mean?" Miriam said. "Every second? I can, if I have to."

"It's all I ask you," Amnon said and, for the first time, smiled too; from way above his long legs, his face crinkled and seemed smaller, as if he wrote most of his plays right under a bulb that was going bad.

Fran said, "I don't see it. She's very quiet—her voice is much too soft."

"It's not making a difference. In America you have microphones falling from the ceiling even in a children's camp you're using only for summer."

"On that huge stage? Are you kidding? She'd fade into the woodwork. Nobody would even see her. I told you—she's very quiet."

"She is *not* quiet," Amnon said. "Not quiet, only unhappy. It's how I am choosing her. I see her face: unhappy and unhappy."

It was the last thing Miriam wanted anyone to think of. "Everything's perfect," she said, and with all the tightness inside her, quickly gave Fran a smile that tired out the corners of her mouth.

"Probably she wouldn't forget lines. But if she doesn't remember to scream when she gets up there, you're finished."

"I don't believe in screaming," Miriam said, but not so that anyone could hear her. Beneath the ceiling, there were Ping-Pong balls popping through the air like mistaken snowflakes, and behind her, some girls from her bunk were playing jacks. In the close, headachy damp, Miriam looked at Fran and hated her; in the whole canteen, that was all that there was.

It was getting to Amnon, too; the whole sour room seemed trapped in his face.

"Frances Wishinsky," he said as he watched Fran walk away with the basket. "In England are *boys* named Francis. In England, Wishinsky would already be Williams. England is a worse country, it's true. I have suffered there for eleven months."

Miriam said, "I read that it rains a lot in England," and wondered if the rainy day and gray, stuffy room were what was reminding him.

"Weathers are not so much important to me," Amnon said. "Other things I don't accustom myself so well. For me, terrible weathers I find not so bad as terrible people. For example, I think you're not liking so much your counselor Fran."

But Amnon was a stranger. "She docks us from movies a lot," Miriam said, "but with what they've got here, it doesn't even matter. The last time we went, all they had was Martians. An entire movie about a bunch of miniature green guys running around in spaceships."

"You're not liking science fictions? Which kind of films you like to see?"

"All different ones. I just don't see why they can't find enough movies to make up with real people's colors and sizes in them."

"Ah," said long, stretched-out Amnon. "Look here, Miriam, you have been ever in a theater?"

"A children's theater," said Miriam. "They took us once from school." The children's theater, in the auditorium of a big high school in Manhattan, was in a terrible neighborhood: in a building right across the way, a left-alone little girl was standing up completely naked, her whole dark body pressed right against the window in the cold. "She's only a little baby," Miriam had said, but there were people who giggled all the way through the play and couldn't wait to get outside again just to see if she would still be there.

"Children's theater," Amnon said, nodding. "This play we do is also children's theater. Only because it's in Yiddish, the children here will not understand. But what can I do? I am not choosing it, it's not my play, it's not my language."

It was not Miriam's language either, so she said nothing and watched Amnon stare around the room, more and more dissatisfied.

"It is not my medium. I am playwright, not director. What can I do? Many people are coming to see this play who are not interesting themselves in theater and they are not interesting themselves in the children. They are only obsessing themselves with Yiddish. For *this* they will come."

"For what?" said Miriam. "What are they all coming for?" There was a program every Friday night—nobody special came and nobody ever made a fuss about it.

"It will be performance for Parents Day," Amnon said. "In two weeks is coming Parents Day. You know about it, yes?"

But more than yes: Miriam was sure that any parents, seeing what camp was like, would be only too glad to take their children out of it. How much more than yes? It was the one day she was certain of and waited for.

EVEN BEFORE SHE GOT THERE, MIRIAM HAD A FEELING THAT CAMP MIGHT not turn out to be her favorite place.

"It's terrific," was what her cousin Dina told her. But it was the same thing that Dina said about going on Ferris wheel and roller-coaster rides in an amusement park. Coming home from school, her arms full of all her heavy high-school books, she would tell Miriam, "Wait till you start doing things like that! Everybody screams and it's terrific."

"I get dizzy on the merry-go-round," Miriam said, and was very suspicious. Only a few years before, Dina used to lie around on her bed, setting her stringy strawberry-blond hair and reading love comics. With her extra babysitting money, she would buy different-size lipstick brushes, close the door in the bathroom, and completely mess up all her perfectly good but strange-colored brand-new lipsticks. Naturally, Dina's mother did not approve, but all she said was, "All the girls are like that. They all do it, and Miriam will be like that, too." But because she was not like Dina, who and what she would be like was in Miriam's mind very often; it was the reason she looked so closely at people's faces on the street.

"If you'd only smile once in a while," Miriam's aunt said, "you'd look like a different person." But her aunt was a liar, a person who spent her life thinking there was not much children could understand. Just to prove it once, when Miriam was in kindergarten, she gave her aunt a special lie test on purpose: on the day that Israel got started as a country, everyone had the radio on all day and many people put out little flags in their windows.

"Why do they have Jewish flags out?" Miriam asked, very pleased with herself because she had thought up the trick and knew the answer.

"What Jewish flags?" Her aunt's arms were all full of bundles and her fat, soggy face looked very annoyed. "Where? In the window? They're left over from Shabbas."

So Miriam saw she was right, but even when she got older said nothing, because she knew that for the times her mother was sick, she would still have to stick around her aunt's house, listen to some lies, and watch Dina fool around with her friends or do her homework. Whenever her aunt bought fruit, she would say, "It's sweet as sugar," even if it was unripened grapefruit; and when she made lamb chops, she said, "Don't leave over the fat, it's delicious," even though it wasn't.

Sometimes, when Dina and her mother had fights, or when her uncle was yelling on the phone about Socialism, it would seem to Miriam very funny, so to stop them from noticing her giggles, and also to drown out the screaming, she would go into the living room and play the piano. She played from her head songs she had learned in Assembly or Hebrew School, or, even better, melodies that came into her mind like ideas: not real, official songs that people knew, but ones she made up on the spot and could change and fix up if she wanted. It was separate from things that she knew about and completely different from people; often when she played the piano, it seemed to Miriam like reading Chinese in a dream.

"I don't see what's so great about playing without piano books," Dina said. "You can't even read music. Just wait till you start taking lessons from Mrs. Landau and have to start practicing from *books,* then we'll see what a big shot you are."

"I'm not ever going to take from Mrs. Landau," Miriam said. "My mother says she's a very limited person who shouldn't be teaching anybody anything."

"Your mother tells you too much," said her aunt, but in what way this was true she had no idea. "Stalin" was what Miriam's mother called her uncle, and what she said about him was that he simply had nothing in his head and had no way of telling what was true from what wasn't. For this reason, all of his talk about Socialism was just noise-making, and all he was, she said, was a big talker who would believe anyone who was a bigger faker.

The other thing Miriam's mother most often told about was her own life when she was a child, but when she got to that, she talked only half to Miriam and half to someone who wasn't there at all.

"Who could have believed that any place could be as big as Warsaw?" is what she would say. "Streets and more streets, I couldn't understand it. I was the first girl from my town ever to be sent there to school, and I was so smart that when I got there I was the youngest in my class. But all my smartness did me no good—I looked at all the stores and the people, the streetcars and the houses, and all I did was cry constantly." This, Miriam never had any trouble believing; it was a habit her mother never got out of. Whenever the boiler broke down for a day, her mother cried all the time that she washed in cold water, and if the butcher ever sent the wrong kind of chicken, or one with too many pinfeathers on it, she cried for hours after and then started all over again when they were ready to sit down and eat it.

Still, with all the things that she did tell, when it came to camp Miriam's mother said very little.

"You'll meet children from all over. When Dina went, there was a girl from Winnipeg, Canada."

"Was her father a Mountie?"

"How could he be a Mountie?" her mother said. "Ask Dina, I think he was a dentist."

"Then I don't see the point."

"It isn't a question of point, Miriam. In camp you'll have grass and trees and get away. Here all you'd have is the hot city."

But it was the hot, empty city that Miriam loved. The flat, gritty sidewalks, freed of people, widened in the glassy, brilliant glare and in the distance fell away like jungle snow. Hard, strange bits of stone came bubbling up through the pavements: glazed, heated traces of another city that once drummed and droned beneath. In front of all the buildings, just where landlords had planted them, low, wiry shrubs pushed themselves out like rubber plants, and the buildings, rougher and rocklike in the ocher heat, seemed turned into brick that was brick before houses, brick that cooked up from the earth itself. From the sky, the city's summer smell sank into Miriam's skin, and walking along with the slow air, she felt her thin, naggy body skim away to the bricks and the pavement that streamed, in belonging, to the sun. What she would do with a bunch of trees, Miriam did not know.

ONLY DODGEBALL, IT TURNED OUT, COULD HAVE BEEN INVENTED BY HUMAN beings: if somebody kept throwing balls at you, it was only natural to try to get away from them, and if you would just be allowed to go far enough, there wouldn't be a problem in the first place. This was what Miriam decided on for all games, so in basketball and volleyball she let other people push and scream for the ball as if there were a sale, and in badminton she watched them jump and yell, "Look at the birdie," like photographers with black cloths in an old-time movie.

Folk dancing was no improvement. "Right over left, left, step, right behind, left, step," Naamah the Yemenite folk dancer sang out instead of words in her dark Yemenite voice, while all her heavy silver jewelry sounded behind her, a rhythm as clear and alone as somebody cracking gum in an empty subway. In a way, Naamah was the most Israeli-looking person Miriam had ever seen; with her tiny, tight, dark features and black, curly hair, she flew around the room like a strange but very beautiful insect, the kind of insect a crazy scientist would let loose in a room and sit up watching till he no longer knew whether it was beautiful or ugly, human or a bug. Sometimes Naamah would pull Miriam out of the circle and sing the special right-over-left song straight into her ear as if *Miriam* were the one who couldn't speak English.

"The grapevine step," she screamed over the music. "It's necessary for all Oriental dance. Not just Israeli. Also the Greeks have it, and it's found modified with the Druse." But it seemed to Miriam like doing arithmetic with your feet, and finally Naamah let her go back into the circle, saying, "Westerners cannot do our dances. They do not have the body."

"I don't know what *she* acts so fancy about," Miriam said in a half-whisper to no one. "Everybody knows that when the Yemenites first came to Israel, they never even saw a toilet before, and when the Israelis gave them brand-new bathrooms, what they did was go all over the floor."

"Shush, Miriam," said Phyllis Axelrod, a tanned, chunky girl in Miriam's bunk. "Don't answer back. If you feel bad, just cry into your pillow. I do it every night and it works."

"What does your pillow have to do with it? That sounds like putting teeth under your pillow so that fairies will give you money."

"You get dimes that way, Miriam. Don't you even want the dimes?"

"If I want a dime, I ask my mother for it. I don't hide teeth and expect fairies, that's not something I believe in."

"My mother wouldn't just hand out dimes like that," Phyllis said, and Miriam immediately felt sorry. She liked Phyllis, though she often seemed not too brilliant; sometimes they were buddies in swimming, and once they snuck out of the water together because Phyllis heard a radio playing inside the little cabaña that was only for counselors. It was the reason that Phyllis cried into her pillow at night: she missed listening to the radio and knowing what was on the Hit Parade, and this gave Miriam the idea that when Phyllis got to be a teenager she might spend all her time hanging around cars in the street, holding up a radio and looking for boys. Sometimes Phyllis also cried because she missed her oldest brother, Ronny, who had just come back from Korea and immediately got married.

"You're not glad about being a sister-in-law?" Miriam asked her.

"It's not that great," Phyllis said. "I just wish I had my regular brother back again, no army and no wedding." Still, she had a beautiful red-and-gold silk scarf that Ronny had brought back for her from Asia; once she wore it as a shawl when everyone, already in white tops and shorts, had gone out on the road to pick wildflowers for the Friday-evening table. On that road, outside camp but just behind the bunks, most of the flowers were tiger lilies, and when Phyllis bent over to pick one, she looked, with her straight black hair and broad brown face, like an Asian girl herself.

It was the closest Miriam got to "children from all over": except for a girl from Teaneck, New Jersey, everyone in her bunk was from New York, mostly from Brooklyn or Queens, both places Miriam had not been to. Still, from what they said, the only difference she could see was that they called Manhattan "going into the city," while people from the Bronx called it "going downtown." Besides Miriam, that meant only Bryna Sue Seligman, who, because she came from Riverdale, would not admit it. Everything that belonged to Bryna, her recorder included, had specially printed stickers, made up by her father, who was in the printing business, that said in giant yellow letters BRYNA SUE SELIGMAN, and her favorite book in the world was the Classic

Comic of *Green Mansions.* On the very first day they were in camp she asked Miriam, "Don't you wish you were Rima? Isn't *Green Mansions* the most beautiful thing you ever heard of?"

"It's OK," Miriam said; she could not see constantly going barefoot in a hot jungle and having to depend on birds when you had any trouble. But Bryna liked the whole idea so much that just in order to be like Rima, she kept her long red hair loose and hanging down her back, walked around without shoes when she wasn't supposed to, and blew into her recorder, which she couldn't really play, when she lay in bed after Lights Out. Whenever there was any free time, Bryna the bird-girl spent almost all of it either brushing her hair or dusting herself with bath powder, all in her private mirror with the yellow label, moving it constantly from side to side so that there was no part of her she would miss.

"I don't know what I'm doing here," she would say as she stared at herself and brushed all her red hair. "I'm going to be a bareback rider and my mother promised me a camp with horses."

"Jewish camps don't come with horses," Miriam said. "You should have figured that out for yourself. Besides, I thought you said you were going to be a poetess."

"Oh, I am one already," Bryna said. "Anytime I feel like it, my father prints up all my poems."

"In yellow?" said Miriam.

"In any color I want. Once I wrote a poem about a rainbow and my father made every line in a different color."

This sounded like a bubble-gum wrapper and no poem, but watching Bryna trace around her suntan marks in the mirror, Miriam decided not to say it.

"I could be going horseback riding in Riverdale right now. Where I live, it's practically the country."

"Where you live is the Bronx," Miriam said. "On your letters you put Bronx, New York, and you even write in a zone number."

"It just so happens that lots of people put Riverdale-on-Hudson, and any time I wanted to, I could."

"You *could*," Miriam said, "but it would probably end up in a museum in Albany."

Because their beds were next to each other, Miriam and Bryna shared a cubby; with all Bryna's yellow labels shining through the shelves like flashbulb suns and the smell of her bath powder always hanging in the air, there was no place that Miriam felt was really hers. Her bathrobe and bathing suits hung like blind midgets in the way; they even got the Bryna bath-powder smell. It made them seem as if they were someone else's clothes and, like everything else in camp, had nothing to do with Miriam and her life.

"I could be in a special dramatics camp on a fat scholarship," Bryna said. "The only reason I told them no was that they didn't have any horseback riding, but at least *there* they would have had me starring in a million plays."

"I'm in a play here," said Miriam. It was turning out to be what she had instead of a cubby, and completely faking calmness, she waited for Bryna to faint.

WHO COULD HAVE BELIEVED THAT ANYPLACE COULD BE AS BIG AS WAR-saw? Probably not anyone in the play: who they were, all of them, were Jews, Nazis, and Polish partisans in the Warsaw ghetto—but where all the streets, more streets, and streetcars could be, the stage gave no idea and Amnon didn't ever say. On the stage was a tiny, crowded Warsaw filled with people who had phlegmy, sad Polish names—Dudek and Vladek, Dunya and Renya—just like in Miriam's mother's stories, and though they were always fighting and singing, there was no way for them to turn out not to be dead. Even the Yiddish song that Miriam had to sing at the end was about a girl who gets taught by her boyfriend how to shoot a gun, and who, one night in the freezing cold, goes out in her beret and shoots up a truckload of Nazis. When the girl is finished, she falls asleep, and the snow coming down makes a garland in her hair. Probably it also freezes her to death, though all it said at the end of the song was: "Exhausted from this small victory, For our new, free generation."

How could a girl who ran out all alone shooting soldiers let herself end up snowed under? And what was the point of people's running through sewers with guns if all they turned into was corpses? It was very hard to explain to Bryna, whose big question was, "Are you starring?"

"Nobody is," Miriam said. "It's not that kind of a play. Half of the time I fake being dead so that nobody finds out and they leave me."

"You mean you don't even *say* anything?"

"I do," Miriam said, "but what I say doesn't do any good. I'm a little girl in braids and I sneak out of the ghetto with my big brother."

Bryna said, "That's your big part? What do you tell him?"

"Nothing. While he's out getting guns, I hide and I hear some Nazi soldiers being so drunk that they start screaming out their plans. And that's when I immediately run back to the ghetto and warn everyone."

"Oh," Bryna said. "So the whole thing is that you copy Paul Revere."

"The only kind of Paul Revere it could be is a Jewish kind. Everyone dies and there are no horses."

Bryna said, "Some play! When we did *The Princess and the Pea,* I was the star, and then when we did *Pocahontas, Red-Skin Lady of Jamestown,* I was the heroine. In *this* moron play, I bet that there isn't even one person with a halfway decent part."

"My part's good," Miriam said. "I'm practically the only one who doesn't turn out to be killed."

"That's because you're a girl."

"No, it's not," Miriam said. "I don't even *know* why, that's just the way the play is."

"Listen, Miriam, I've been in a million plays. Little girls never get killed in any of them."

"Well, in this one they do. In this one the only people who don't wind up dead are me and Gil Burstein."

"*You're* in a play with Gil Burstein? You? Just let me come to rehearsals with you and I'll let you use my expensive bath powder anytime you want."

"You can't get out of playing badminton just like that," Miriam told her. "That's only for people in the play."

But play or not, camp was still camp. At night, cold air flew in through the dark from Canada and mixed on the screens with mosquitoes; 6–12 and whispers filled up the air in the bunk and stayed there like ugly wallpaper. How could anyone sleep? Miriam played with the dark like a blind person in a foreign country: in the chilly, quiet strangeness, her bed was as black as a packed-up trunk, and her body, separate in all its sunburned parts, was suddenly as unfamiliar as someone else's toothpaste.

In the daytime, too, camp was still camp: a place dreamed up to be full of things that Miriam could not get out of. Whenever Amnon saw her face, he said, "What's the matter, Miriam?" It was how he kept starting out rehearsals.

"Look here, Mir*iam*," he would say, pronouncing her name the Hebrew way, with the accent on the last syllable. "Look here, Mir*iam,* say me what's wrong."

"Nothing," she said. "Everything's great."

"Why you are saying me 'Nothing' when I see you are crying—have been crying?"

"I wasn't, I'm not, and anyway it's not something I do."

"All girls are sometimes crying."

"Well, not me," Miriam said. "I don't believe in it." For a reason: it sometimes seemed to Miriam that if a person from a foreign country—or even a miniature green man from Mars— ever landed, by accident, in her building and by mistake walked up the six flights of stairs, all he would hear was screaming and crying: mothers screaming and children crying, fathers screaming and mothers crying, televisions screaming and vacuum cleaners crying; he could very easily get the idea that in this place there was no language, and that with all the noises there were no lives.

But crying was the last thing that Miriam thought of once she got to rehearsals. Still in camp, but not really in camp at all, it felt like a very long fire drill in school when you stayed on the street long enough to be not just a child on a line, but almost an ordinary person—someone who could walk in the street where they wanted, into stores, around corners, and maybe, if they felt like it, even disappear into buses.

As soon as Miriam put on her costume and combed her hair into braids, there was nothing on her body that felt like camp, and away from the day outside, nothing to even remind her. On the stage, Jews, Nazis, and Polish partisans were wandering through the streets of shrunken Warsaw, and in a corner, where in the real Warsaw there might have been a gas streetlight, a trolley-car stop, or even her mother's Gymnasium, Miriam and Gil Burstein played dead.

"What's the best can-opener?" Gil whispered.

"I don't know," Miriam said.

"Ex-Lax," said Gil, and laughed into his Ripley's *Believe It or Not.*

"Rest!" Amnon called out. In the middle of the stage, a Polish partisan had just kicked a Jew by mistake and suddenly the girl was crying. Nazi soldiers and Jewish resistance fighters started stampeding across the stage and charging, and Amnon, looking at no one, said, "Always they are playing Indians and Lone Rangers. It's for me completely not possible."

"Rest!" he yelled again; what he meant was "Break." Once, in one of his terrible-English times, Amnon said, "Ninety-Twoth Street Y," and Miriam, thinking suddenly of a giant tooth-building with elevators full of a thousand dentists, could not stop herself from laughing. Other times she thought of asking Amnon why she and Gil were the only ones who managed to end up not dead, but usually during breaks Amnon sat with his long legs stretched out across a whole row of chairs and just talked. He hardly even noticed who was concentrating on Cokes and who was paying attention.

"In Israel now it's not the right climate for art. You understand me?"

"It's much too hot there for people to sit around drawing pictures," Miriam said, and wished that the Arts-and-Crafts counselor could understand this, too.

"No," Amnon said. "For me it means in my own country even people are not interesting themselves in my work. Here it's not my language, it's not my country, there is no place for an Israeli writer, there is nothing to do."

Gil Burstein said, "He could always take and autograph butcher-store windows or foods for Passover. I'm getting sick of this. Who wants a Coke?"

"Me," Miriam said, but knew the truth was that she didn't mind at all. From lying stretched out on the wooden stage for so long, her mind felt empty and the whole rest of her seemed dizzy in a sweet, half-sleepy way. Soon, in this dark auditorium, only the stage would be full of light and the plain wooden floor would hold up for an hour all the mistakes of a place that once had existed. A girl with braids and a too-long dress would run out into the mixed-up streets, and sitting in the audience with many other people, Miriam's mother would know what this place once was like way before and could tell how it actually looked. The girl with braids would sing the last song, and all Miriam's days of camp would finally be over.

PARENTS DAY DID NOT START OUT WITH GIL WAKING PEOPLE UP WITH HIS bugle; instead, from the loudspeaker in the office came records of Israeli songs—background music for the whole day, as if it were a movie. The melodies ran out quick and flying, and framed by the music, the whole camp—children, counselors, little white bunks, even trees and grass—seemed to be flying away, too, as if after all these weeks they were finally going someplace. Not exactly in the movie herself, Miriam went to the clothesline in the back, checking to make sure no bathing suit of hers was still left on it.

"Miriam, you better come in the front," Phyllis said. "There's a whole bunch of people here and they're looking for you."

Right outside the bunk, some girls in a circle were doing the dances that belonged with the melodies, and squinting there in the sun, practically trapped inside the dance, were Miriam's aunt and uncle, and with them a couple she had never seen before. The man, very short and with gray, curly hair, was dressed just like her uncle: Bermuda shorts, brown cut-out sandals with high socks, and a kind of summer hat that always looked to Miriam like a Jewish baseball cap. His wife, who was taller, had thick, dark braids all across her head, and though her skirt was very long in the sun, there was such a round, calm look in her clothes and on her face that Miriam was sure she had never had to be anybody's mother.

Miriam's aunt said, "There's my niece. Here she is. Miriam, this is Mrs. Imberman and that's Mr. Imberman, they came up with the car."

Miriam's aunt looked exactly the same: every part of her heavy face drooped like the bargain bundles she always carried, and stuck to her cheeks like decals were high pink splotches the color of eyelids—extra supplies of tears she kept up to make sure she was always ready.

"What are *you* doing here?" said Miriam. "You're not my mother. Who asked you to come?"

"Mr. and Mrs. Imberman came here to see a play," her aunt said, "and we're staying right next to them in the same little hotel, and it's not far, and they came with the car, so here we are."

"I didn't say what are *they* doing here. I said what are *you* doing here? And where's my mother?"

"Your mother couldn't come. She was going to write a letter and tell you, but I told her not to because I *know* you, Miriam, that if you knew about it you'd make a fuss, and now I see how right I was."

Turning around, Miriam stared at all the trees and grass that she had there: if they were so wonderful, the least they could do was pay attention to the music and do an Israeli dance.

"For you, your mother is your mother, but for me, she's still my little sister and there are plenty of things still that I have to tell her."

The trees, with all their millions of leaves, did not do even half a grapevine, and Miriam's uncle said, "Imberman, feel how hot it is already here and it's still early. Can you imagine what it's like a day like today in the city?"

"Hot," Mr. Imberman said. They stood there, the two of them, with their Jewish baseball caps, and Miriam thought how her uncle looked when it got too hot in his apartment: he would walk back and forth in his shorts and undershirt, fan himself with a newspaper, and say in Yiddish, "It's hot today in the city. Oh my God, it's hot!" If her uncle and midget Mr. Imberman got together, they could both walk back and forth in a little undershirt parade, fan themselves with two newspapers and, in between saying how hot it was, could have little fights about which countries were faking it with Socialism.

Miriam said, "If my mother were here, she would take me home."

"Why should she take you home? It's good for you to be outside and it's good for you to get used to it."

"Why should I get used to it if I don't like it?"

"Look how nice it is here, Miriam," her uncle said in Yiddish. "Look what you have here—a beautiful blue lake, a sky with sun and clouds that's also blue, big strong trees you can see from a mountain—with birds in them, wide, empty green fields with only grass and flowers. Look how nice."

"The lake is polluted," Miriam said. And it seemed to her that he was describing someplace else entirely—maybe a place in Poland he remembered from when he was young, maybe even a picture on a calendar, but definitely not camp on Parents Day. All the empty green fields were filling up with cars, the grass and flowers were getting covered over with blankets and beach chairs, and pretty soon the birds from the mountain would be able to come down and eat all the leftover food that people brought with them. Except that there was no sand, the whole camp could have been Orchard Beach.

"Let me tell you something," her uncle said. "First I'll tell you a little story about your cousin Dina, and then I'll give you some advice."

"I don't want any advice from you," Miriam said. "You can't even figure out which countries are faking it with Socialism, and if you're supposed to care about it so much, why don't you just write a letter to a person in the country and ask them? All they have to tell you is if they're selfish or if they share around the things they've got."

"Straight from her mother," said Miriam's aunt. "With absolutely no sense that she's talking in front of a child."

"And don't think I can't understand it either. My mother calls *him* Stalin."

Mrs. Imberman said, "Sweetheart, are you in the play?" She bent her head in the sun, and for a second her earrings, turquoise and silver, suddenly turned iridescent.

"Yes," Miriam said and looked up at her: somewhere a man with a sombrero and a mustache had gotten off his donkey and sat down in the heat to fold pieces of silver so that Mrs. Imberman could turn her head in the sun and ask questions of strange children.

"Ah-ha," Mrs. Imberman said, "an *aktricekeh*. That's why she's so temperamental."

"I am *not* an actress," Miriam said. "I never was one before and I don't plan on being one again, and what I'm definitely not going to be is an explorer, so I don't see why I have to get used to so much being outside."

"Listen, Miriam," her uncle said. "Let me tell you what happened with Dina in case she was embarrassed to tell you herself. It happened that Dina didn't feel like giving in her chocolates to the counselor, so she put them under her bed and only took out the box to eat them when it was dark in the bunk at night and she was sitting up in the bed and setting her hair. She figured out that if anyone heard any noises she could tell them it was from the bobby pins and curlers."

"Such a woman's story," Mr. Imberman said in very Polish Yiddish. "I didn't know, Citrin, that you knew such women's stories."

Miriam's aunt said, "You know my Dina. She could set her hair anyplace."

"Anyway, what happened, Miriam, is that once somebody put on a light and saw her, and that's how she made some enemies, and that's why she didn't always love it here."

"I don't set my hair," Miriam said. "It's the one thing I'm lucky about—it's naturally curly, and now I have to get it put in braids for the play, so goodbye."

"So quick?" her aunt said. "Goodbye, Miriam, look how nice and suntanned she is. Nobody would even know she has a sour face."

JUST BEHIND THE CURTAIN, MIRIAM WAITED BUNCHED UP WITH EVERYONE in their costumes on the hot, quiet stage. Sunk into the scenery, not even Gil Burstein was laughing, and all the Jews, Nazis, and Polish partisans were finally without Cokes in their hands. Amnon, still walking around in his same very short pants, gave Miriam a giant Israeli smile that she had not seen before and could not feel a part of. He said, "Now I don't worry for the play and I don't worry for the audience."

But why anyone would worry for the audience, Miriam could not see. All through the play she kept looking out at them—a little girl in braids and a too-long dress who would end up not dead—and could not tell the face of anyone. Who they were she did not know and did not want to think about: people, probably, who cried and screamed in their houses, fanned themselves with newspapers, and took along hard-boiled eggs if they went in a car for a half hour.

The stage did not stop being hot, and lying stretched out on it with Gil Burstein, it seemed to Miriam that they were playing dead right underneath a gas streetlight from a stuffy summer night in the real Warsaw. Way above their heads hung a fat yellow bulb that was surrounded by a thousand insects. In all different shapes and sizes, they kept flying from the empty blue darkness backstage toward this one single glare, till the bulb, ugly and unshaded in the first place, seemed to be growing a beard as sweaty and uneven as a grandfather's. Back and forth, over and around, the different insects crowded and buzzed, all with each other, so that, watching them, Miriam started to wonder whether these were Socialist bugs who believed in sharing with each other what they had, or else bugs who were secretly wishing to keep the whole bulb for themselves and, by politely flying close together, just faking it.

In the woods, just outside the finished-off Warsaw ghetto, the night was bitter cold. Miriam stood up to sing the song of the girl with the velvet face who went out in the blizzard to shoot up the enemy, and knew that no matter how big the stage was, when she sang and played the piano there was nothing about her that was quiet at all. "'Exhausted from this small victory, For our new, free generation,'" Miriam finally sang, and the curtain fell over her head like the garland of snow on the girl who could end up snowed under.

Left all by herself behind the curtain, Miriam heard crying coming from people in the audience: they were the parents of no one in the play, but were crying now because, like somebody's stupid, stupid parakeet, they had learned how to do one thing and one thing only. If anyone yelled out "Budgie!" right now, the entire audience would immediately get up and start flying. Amnon would fly out, too, and Bryna, always a bird-girl, ran up now to Miriam on the stage and right then and there began chirping.

"Guess what?" she said. "Now there are *two* people in my family with red hair. My mother got her hair dyed and I didn't even know it was her till she came over and kissed me."

"Oh," Miriam said, and because she could see that Bryna had big things on her mind—counting redheads—listened from somewhere for the sound of Amnon's voice letting out his one Israeli-parakeet line: Say-me-what's-wrong-Mir*iam*, Mir*iam*-say-me-the-matter. Standing there on the stage, a little girl in braids and a too-long dress who would end up not dead, Miriam promised herself that never again in her life would anyone look at her face and see in it what Amnon did, but just like the girl who could fake being dead, she would keep all her aliveness a secret.

DRAGON LADY

SAIGON (AP)—Police indicated today a woman arrested in connection with the shooting of a Nationalist Chinese intelligence officer may be the Dragon Lady who has been gunning down people from the back of a motorcycle.

The National police director, Brig. Gen. Nguyen Ngoc Loan, said Miss Phung Ngoc Anh, a 24-year-old Vietnamese of Chinese descent, was arrested carrying a .45-caliber pistol which ballistics tests show was used to kill five persons, including two Americans. Loan said the woman admitted three of the shootings.

The Dragon Lady has been variously described as having long hair and short hair and wearing a red scarf and a blue scarf. Loan said a search of Miss Anh's apartment turned up a red and a blue scarf and two wigs.

"Draw your own conclusions," Loan said.

The Dragon Lady shot most of her victims from the

backseat of a motorcycle driven by a male accomplice. She operated in Cholon, Saigon's Chinese quarter.

Loan said the woman had admitted she was a Viet Cong who learned to shoot a .45 at a secret base in Cu Chi. "She shoots with both hands," Loan said.

"MISS PHUNG NGOC ANH, A 24-YEAR-OLD VIETNAMESE OF CHINESE DESCENT"

THERE ARE PLACES WHERE IT DOES NOT RAIN EVERY DAY AT A CERTAIN TIME, but the girl tripping over the mosquito netting in the heat does not know them. Not that she really hears the rain—it rains every day and she's used to it. She pays no attention to the whirring fan from the gambling club across the street, and can even disregard the clatter of dishes and pans from the cookshop through the alley. What she cannot stand is the goat: every time he moves, the bell around his neck rings, and as he hops back and forth on his tether in the back, there is enough sound of bells to make it seem like a pagoda. Many people could gain calm from this idea, but she doesn't—all it does is make her trip, and ring up through her mind certain things she has to live with.

I built my hut among the throng of men
But there is no din of carriages or horses.
You ask me how this can be.
When the heart is remote, earth stands aloof.

It's her grandfather's favorite poem, this one, by T'ao Yuan-Ming, and on long walks he often recites it for her, in a way, as a lesson. But as it is, her heart is not remote enough. Not yet. When will it be? And who is she?

First of all, her name is not Phung Ngoc Anh. Not yet. From such a Chinese family, how could it be? She is named Sut On (Snow Quiet), and from the Ling family, so Ling Sut On, and for most of the years before she was twenty-four, lived in Cholon, in the rooms above her uncle's godown. He is her First Uncle, her mother's oldest brother, and though all he's supposed to have downstairs in the warehouse is rice, what else he might have his stained fingers into is a secret between them and his abacus, which, no matter what else is going on in the world, never seems to stop moving. Really there's not as much there as Wu and his round-bottomed wife always like to pretend, but still, even Sut On's grandfather, First Uncle's own father—who cannot complain of being thrown out or not supported (it's not as if Wu were actually unfilial)—even Sut On's grandfather says to no one in particular when Wu is around and looks as if, for a minute, he might have stopped moving beads in his head, "'If a state is following the Way, it is a disgrace to be in poverty and low estate within it. If not, it is a disgrace to be rich and honored.'" And sometimes, when Wu's gambling cronies come upstairs, Sut On's grandfather smiles, looks straight ahead of him, and, pretending that he's talking to himself, says, "'Ill-gotten wealth and honors are to me as wandering clouds.'" With that kind of smile on his face, he looks as if he might *be* a wandering cloud, and half the enjoyment for him is throwing them all off and leaving that impression. Wu gets the point, though. He puts down his teacup, makes a quick bow, and heads down the stairs, his friends clacking after him like mah-jongg tiles. His attitude is well known: One—you're not in Canton anymore, Old Man. Two—I don't care *who* you were there. Three—what good did all your study and Confucius-quoting do you when famine came? And four—if it weren't for me, every single one of you in this house would be out on the street and starving. Not that Wu would actually ever dare say this to his father himself: he leaves it for his perfect, quiet wife to shriek it out to Sut On's mother. In Wu's presence, you could think that First Aunt, Ping, had no tongue at all—stolen by the fox-fairies maybe. She is silent and sweet-faced as she bends down in her cheongsam to give him things, and always cooing with her children, but as soon as Wu is out of the room, and especially when he takes his old secondhand Renault and goes out buying rice in the Delta, Ping begins shrieking and, for all her concern with perfection, suddenly doesn't even care how much she offends her husband's father. "It's my house," is one of her favorite beginnings. "Everything here is mine, and when we move, even if we let you stay here, you would be left with nothing." And another one: "When we move, even if we let you visit us, you wouldn't know what to do."

"And the goat?" says Sut On's mother, very familiar with this conversation. "Will he know what to do when you take him?"

It's not much of an argument, though, because everything in the house does belong to Wu, goat included, but he is a miser and would never move. Besides, who would watch the godown? Not his sickly brother Lim, who also lives upstairs with his whiny wife and children and cannot even watch what he says or to whom he says it, so busy is he darting around in his leather cap and dreaming up schemes for anyplace else—Hanoi, Macao, Bangkok. Nor would Wu trust Sut On's father—a man who could not even properly take his wife to his own home. This is what makes it so hard on Sut On's mother, who is in any case practically a barren woman: two sons stillborn, and another one so puny he did not last a month. Of course, there is Sut On, but she is only a girl, and naturally there are people (one of them Sut On's father) who blame it on Vietnam: what kind of country has *women* for heroes, keeps up statues of women who drove off invaders mounted on elephants? But Sut On's mother never gives up, goes to fortune-tellers constantly, and every morning before she sets out rice cakes and tea (while French ladies are having coffee and long hot rolls), she lights her joss stick and prays to Kwan Yin. With no sons, Sut On's father could take another wife if he wanted, but this is impossible to imagine. Once, in the time of the Japanese, he ran a public letter-writing stall, but for as long as she can remember, her dim, red-eared father has always worked for her uncle and usually smoked enough opium pipes to not even know who she is. If anyone spilled tea on him, he wouldn't feel it. So no one pays attention to him, least of all her mother, who never suspected how lowly she had married, and there is no respect for him in this house. Every so often, though, his face changes, and suddenly, as if he were one of the Forty-seven Beasts, he is forced out of his thinness and quiet, and above all the usual racket, even over explosions or bombs, he begins to scream and stamp his feet, cursing in peasant Cantonese that Sut On cannot even understand. Which one of the Forty-seven Beasts is what she tries to figure out when this happens. For instance: there once was a man who spent all his days and nights in wickedness and unbelief. His family pleaded with him, his friends argued and cajoled, his neighbors warned him, but it was all useless, for in his arrogance he would not change his ways. Suddenly, in the middle of his life, he was overtaken by a strange and mysterious illness: for ten years he would neither speak, receive visitors, nor move from his bed. His son, who was dutiful, hovered by his father's doorstep, and finally one day heard the old man call for a bundle of hay. As quickly as the hay was brought, so quickly was the door now shut again, for, to the poor obedient son's horror, he saw that his father had been turned into an ox.

Or another one: in a village a farmer, known for his idleness and covetousness, one night stole into the yard of his friend and neighbor and, in the false glow of darkness, came away with his neighbor's most prized duck. Swaggering in the moonlight, he cooked the duck that very night, ate it, and later, in the midst of his sleep, felt his skin begin to itch. In the morning his body was covered with a thick growth of duck's feathers, so painful that he cried out. "Quack," came the farmer's voice in his agony: he had been turned into a duck.

If Sut On were a French girl, she would not have to listen to such scenes of stamping and cursing; they would not happen, and if through some accident they ever did, she could go off and turn on the water faucets, tremendous silver spigots known to shine through French villas, and in the rush of French water, drown out all the noise.

How does Sut On know so much about what happens in French houses? In a roundabout way, the answer is her grandfather, and in an even more roundabout way, it's certain big-time Cholon merchants, much richer than Wu, so much richer, in fact, that when they appear at the house unexpected, it sends Wu running up and down screaming orders and bumping tea things. By mistake, he even bowed at a no-good friend of sickly Lim's whom he had forbidden to ever come back. This is the perfect situation for Ping, who is always waiting for the time her smiling smug ways will get a deserving reception. But it's not Wu these whispering, dark-suited merchants have come to see. Instead, it's Sut On's grandfather—whose reputation they have not forgotten, whose words and even name, because he was once their teacher, can still recall them to fear.

"'Man's life span depends on his uprightness,'" says Sut On's grandfather immediately. Naturally, they are up to something. Why waste time? "'He who goes on living without it escapes disaster only by good fortune.'"

"My grandfather was a *lettré*," Sut On would say later on in her school years, simply to make an impression, because otherwise she was ashamed of her household. But in much later years and in a very different place, this old misused sentence came back to her head with a certain surprise.

The merchants leave without even saying good-by to Wu. This is the reason for their visit: they have managed to secure an extra place for a Chinese child in the French school, and they wish to honor their old teacher by offering it to him for one of his grandchildren. Sut On's grandfather is very pleased—not so much by the offer, but because they remembered to quote for him from Feng Guifen: "There are many brilliant people in China. There must be some who can learn from the barbarians and surpass them."

Wu is furious, he stalks around and cannot even go back to his abacus. What does he care about French schools? The richest men in Cholon have been in his house, drunk his tea, have come and gone as if he were nonexistent. If they truly want to honor his father, then help make the old man's life more prosperous and comfortable by entering into business arrangements with the son. But Ping sees it differently: "Think of Chen. When he goes to the French school, he'll be able to help *his* father"; and because Wu is still fuming, children on the floor are crying, and Chen, a loping, sneaky boy, is nowhere around, Ping shrieks out in an unwifely voice, "Chen! Find Chen! It's his grandfather who wants him."

"Do they think I have no ability?" says Wu. "Do they think my contacts in the Delta would be of no use to *them*?"

"If you don't find Chen immediately," Ping screams at all the other children, "you are disobeying your grandfather!"

Lim's listless friend, who has taken off his shirt, yawns very loudly, the goat rings his bell in the back, and Sut On's grandfather, who does not at this moment look like a wandering cloud at all, says, "It's time for my walk with Sut On."

There is nothing at all unusual about Sut On's grandfather

taking her out for a walk. It's been a habit of his for years, and rarely is the walk itself very different. For years he has held her hand and walked slowly through the different streets in Cholon, only speeding up a bit or ducking into an alley when he sees the face of someone he does not respect and would rather avoid. Occasionally they go along the docks, and this is the only part Sut On does not like: the coolies, wearing no shirts and sweating, load things on their backs and mutter to themselves peasant Cantonese curses, just as her father does in the times when he is angry. Her grandfather does not allow her to look away, but because he knows she does not like it, he buys her a slice of pineapple or a fruit drink to suck on. Usually, though, they walk slowly through the streets and the stalls and he tells her about his life in his village in Canton, which even her parents have never seen, tells her stories from ancient China, and sometimes when he thinks of it, recites pieces of poems. What she likes best is the story of Chuang Tzu, who was a philosopher, a real person, but was never sure of it. One night he dreamed he was a butterfly, and when he woke up he couldn't decide whether he was Chuang Tzu who had dreamed he was a butterfly, or whether instead he was really a butterfly who kept on dreaming he was Chuang Tzu. "Is it I, Chuang Tzu?" her grandfather says, changing his voice when he comes to this part of the story, and thinking about it now, Sut On is about to ask her grandfather to tell it to her again, but he is holding her hand more tightly and walking along so quickly that they are no longer even in Cholon, but in Saigon itself, where Vietnamese live, and there are no more signs in Chinese.

"Look very carefully, Sut On," her grandfather says, and being in a strange place, how can she do otherwise? She knows hardly any Vietnamese, having lived in Cholon all her life and always gone to a Chinese school. Once, in one of his strange, unpredictable fits of anger, her father knocked down a Vietnamese policeman, leaving him sprawled out right on the street. Probably he had said something against the Chinese or looked at her father in a way that made him think so, but since it had happened in Cholon, even though there were many people watching, naturally it had all come to nothing, except for her mother, for whom it was just an extra reminder of how she lived in shame.

Sut On looks around her and knows what she will never be: a lithe Annamese girl, pretty in an *ao dai*. Her bones are too broad, her legs are too heavy, and even if she ever put on an *ao dai* and got accustomed to the material, just above it her face would be a dead giveaway—she will always look Chinese. That's not what her grandfather has in mind, though.

"They have nothing," he says, and will not even look at all the Vietnamese who crowd through the street. "No empire, no culture, no language, no energy. They couldn't even keep their alphabet, which in any case was really ours. What do they have that isn't borrowed?" and walking along in his long Mandarin coat and his beard, Sut On's grandfather does not dodge around trishaws or pedicabs, but passes right by them as if they were shadows and not there at all.

And soon they aren't: they have walked so far, Sut On and her grandfather, that by this time there are no more trishaws or bicycles, only Frenchmen in cars. Their eyes blink too much against the sunlight, their feet seem stuck as they push them, in big shoes, along the street.

"I've never told you this story before, Sut On," her grandfather says. But she's in no mood for a story. No other street is so wide and so shiny, no other street has no markets or stalls. Instead, people walk in and out of glass-covered stores wearing the same kind of clothing that stares out from the glass. With their very pink faces, they climb to the top of high-windowed buildings, and when they get tired of being so high, they come down to the street, tip back in strange chairs, and, unfolding their newspapers, they sip cups of coffee and don't suck their gums. Not one of them knows enough to hold a cup with two hands, and despite this, they live in big white houses hidden by gardens, where maybe occasionally they take off their wide shoes. Even their little children have pink faces and red and yellow hair and, when they take rides on airplanes, do not come home to goats.

What story can have come to her grandfather's mind? Heng O, the Moon Lady? The Sisters in the Sun? How the Eight Old Ones Crossed the Sea? What on this street could make him think of any of them?

"A hunter went into the woods and in them found a young deer, a fawn so lovely that he could not kill her. Instead, he brought her back with him to his home, and let her play there within his yard. At first he worried that his dogs would attack the shy creature, so different from themselves. But it was not so. For months on end the fawn played and frolicked with the dogs in his yard, and grew up with them so well that the hunter saw no reason to return her to the forest. One day, however, when the gate to his yard was open, the deer ventured forth and, seeing some dogs in the distance, she scampered up to play with them. But these were strange dogs who had never seen a deer before. They tore her up from limb to limb and that is the end of her story. For so long a time had she lived with dogs, she no longer knew she was not one of them."

"I've never even seen a fawn," Sut On says, though she's never made this objection to stories about fox-fairies. But they're no longer on the Rue Catinat now, so she skips on the streets that are increasingly familiar, and her grandfather buys her a slice of pineapple.

"A deer is a fleet animal," he says very carefully: it is Sut On who will go to the French school.

"DRAW YOUR OWN CONCLUSIONS"

IN FRENCH BOOKS THE PAPER IS VERY GLOSSY. TOUCHING IT, IN HER EURO-
pean schoolgirl's smock, Sut On is no longer a girl who comes
home each day to a room above a godown in Cholon, or even a
strangely pink-faced girl whose mother in thin, high-heeled shoes
plays tennis at the *Cercle Sportif* and thinks nothing of walking
in and out of shops on the Rue Catinat. Instead, she is someone
named Françoise or perhaps Solange, whose face she cannot
quite imagine, but whose feet take her along broad, tree-lined bou-
levards, broader than any in Saigon, and down into underground
trains where people around her sit down politely with armfuls of
long, thin breads. Sometimes this Françoise or Solange takes her
small dog, Coco, for a walk into gardens called the Tuileries. She
is totally unfamiliar with goats, though sometimes in August she
and her family—mustached, firm-voiced father, smiling mother,
and perhaps a small brother named Jean-Claude—take trips in a
car which they own, past farms to the countryside. Here, there
are animals, maybe even a goat, but Françoise or Solange occu-
pies herself with the fruit orchards. She sings a song to herself in
a perfect French accent about a shepherdess, all the while she is
picking cherries and dropping them one, two, three into a basket.
She is very careful to avoid picking any mushrooms, and when
it is time for a meal, eats veal in a sauce of wine and butter, and
potatoes that have been cut up thin and fried. Never in her life
has she tasted bean curd, and if she saw a lichee nut, she wouldn't
know what to do with it.

"She'll grow up to be a taxi-girl," Ping shrieks whenever she
sees Sut On in her smock, carrying home her schoolbooks and
writing out her lessons. It's the one thing Ping ever learned from
Chinese literature: educated girls may bring great pleasure to
men, even emperors, but never, never are they marriageable. Sut

On's mother pays no attention to this, goes on pouring out her many cups of tea as usual, and worries only that her daughter, almost grown now, has become much too concerned with ordinary noises and everyday smells. Because of this, Ping has begun to call her Madame Oo-la-la, and still rails to Wu about his father, "How can he have shown such preference? He must have been as blind and deaf then as he is now."

He's not truly deaf yet, Sut On's grandfather, but he is blind enough so that it's very difficult for him to read. Instead of taking walks together, Sut On reads to him from old issues of a Chinese newspaper whose office has been bombed. Luckily he cannot tell that these are articles which he's heard before, and is pleased enough with Sut On's blurry presence and the rising and falling of her voice as she reads. After his death, when his picture—taken so far back in his youth that Sut On does not even recognize him—is hanging on the ancestral altar, her mother says, "He was a very fair man, your grandfather. He had no illusions about his children." What, in Sut On's opinion, was there to have illusions about?

There are things about her, though, which he has never known. First, her greatest mistake at the French school: a picture in drawing class. The drawing was in honor of Christmas, a feast day celebrating peacefulness and serene joy. Sut On drew a great-winged bird flying slowly from high mountains to a quiet pond. All around her, other children drew a fat, bearded man, *Père Noël*, or a pink, yellow-haired baby surrounded by donkeys. The French girls laughed aloud, the Vietnamese girls looked at each other and giggled, the drawing teacher tore up her paper. Sut On looked up at the drawing teacher: blond and doughy, his face looked like a countryside in a European child's picture book—the sheep on hills in French nursery rhymes. So, once again Sut

On drew a picture for the joyful holiday—a pink, yellow-haired baby, and put him right next to a goat.

"Do you *live* in Cholon?" the French girls would ask her sometimes. "My parents like to go there to eat Chinese food. Do you walk all the way?"

Sut On walks all the way, she has never tired of it. No longer a small child on the arm of her grandfather, there are streets in Saigon she has gotten to know as well as Cholon. These days, though, there are almost no French girls left in her classes, and the Vietnamese girls who once giggled at her drawing hop into their brothers' sports cars, wearing sunglasses and giggling still. This time they're off to Vũng Tàu, to the seashore. Perhaps soon they'll go to Paris or even America. In the meantime they buy new scarves, look through *Paris Match,* and watch the American secretaries whose hairdos, incredibly, rise up like so many new buildings: floors and floors of immovable, perfect curls.

Sut On will not go to Paris, nor to the university at Hue as she had wished. In the room above her uncle's godown, cousins' children lie wailing on the floor, Lim sucks his gums with his cap on, the goat rings his bell in the yard. If she takes this teacup from her mother's hands, it will not rest between her fingers, but fling itself in all directions: like a dragon or one of the Forty-seven Beasts, there is nothing that it will not smash.

"A SECRET BASE IN CU CHI"

NARRATOR: "THE VILLAGE OF QUOC TRI, ONCE A PLACE OF CHEER AND hardy, joyous activity, found itself suddenly plunged, through no fault of its own, into one of lassitude and woe. No longer did the sultry winds whistle through the green and gold stalks a happy, continuous melody as busy as the chirping of crickets. It was not floods which were drowning the crops and sturdy spirits of the villagers, but great sheets of fire and flame, falling from the skies, which ruthlessly consumed, sparing nothing: neither fields, nor homes, nor sons. The villagers who remained could not contain their puzzlement. What had they done to so anger their ancestors? The women wept and wailed over the loss of those most dear, and the men, sunk in anger and sorrow, did not know what there was to be done, nor what, indeed, was the cause of this terrible misfortune. As they sat, still tormented by grief and astonishment, soldiers appeared amidst the ruins. From their speech and appearance, the villagers could ascertain that these soldiers were Southerners like themselves, and rushed out to greet them with hope innocent in their hearts. Alas! Neither hope nor innocence lasted beyond that instant. The soldiers, as rude and ruthless as the flames themselves, gave no heed to the cries of their countrymen. Cruelty flickered on their features and they swooped through the desolated village, ravishing its young daughters, torturing its revered Elders and temporary Chief. But still they had not contented themselves, for they began to vie with each other in wringing the necks of the few miserable, squawking chickens scratching mournfully about in the scorched yards. These they carried off to heavy rumbling trucks nearby, trucks whose massive sides were labeled U.S.A. And finally the villagers understood! These soldiers were the puppet troops of a usurper government, and the sheets of flame, the cause of their misfortune, did not fall from the skies, but were thrown upon them by giant planes flown from the country of Hollywood."

What has happened to Françoise or Solange? And where, for that matter, is Sut On? Called Anh now, she is wearing black trousers still strange to her, and standing to the side, watching, as a small theatrical troupe performs a pageant for the villagers. It is an NLF holiday, so members from her base, which is close to the village, have come with the troupe to celebrate. It's not the first time she's been in a village like this one: years before, when Wu drove out to buy rice, Sut On and Chen occasionally went along. Chen would lope along with his father, but Sut On almost never got out of the car. Sitting in it, stuck to her seat by the heat and the sun, she would look out the windows, closed against mosquitoes, and staring at the red-tiled roofs behind small palm trees, at the little orchards of mangoes and jackfruits, and, above all, at a certain slow quietness so different from Cholon, she would wish that she were one of the small girls she could see running barefoot past the monkeys, sucking on a piece of cane or perhaps a coconut. She looks no more like them now than she did then: it's girls like these she's met at Cu Chi, girls to whose bodies black trousers are not strange, girls who have run barefoot for miles and miles through wild panther country and think nothing of it. Bits of rice and *nuoc-mam* are what they're used to, and jungle sounds at night do not make them jump. Their Vietnamese is so quick she can barely understand it. Naturally she is still not trusted.

The troupe is finishing up, waiting for the musicians. They sing with a guitar:

> *An American plane is like a tiger*
> *Ferocious from afar*
> *But helpless against determination!*

Sut On is still watching a small-boned girl from the troupe, a dancer, who played out with slow, huddled movements the grief of a widow. The sadness, which just minutes before crept and bent through all of her, is gone now, transformed. She stands up straight and, in a plain cotton blouse her mother might have worn in the Viet Minh, is singing with all of them, "Helpless against determination!"

"Other women bring forth children, you bring forth rifles," said the official who arrested Ho's sister in the days of the Viet Minh. Her father was a *lettré*. "My grandfather was a *lettré*," says Sut On that night, when they are back at Cu Chi, far beneath foliage. In the darkness especially, the feeling of holiday persists: there are coconuts and an orange or two from the village, and some of the younger boys are strumming on guitars. But Sut On is impatient with it. In a headiness, an elation she cannot explain to herself, she pushes a guitar out of someone's hands, and in her high Chinese voice—she hears her accent but doesn't care—begins to sing:

> *Dors mon amour*
> *Fais do-do mon trésor*
> *On crie chez la voisine*
> *Chez nous une câline*
> *Tu se traînes dans la fange*
> *Tu vas dans la soie*
> *Dans la robe d'un ange recalée pour toi.*

The song is from *Mother Courage,* a record Sut On once found hidden behind books in the French school.

> *Dors mon amour*
> *Fais do-do mon trésor*
> *L'un repose en Pologne*
> *Et l'autre je ne sais où.*

"Why are you singing a French song?" says the cadre. He is a wiry man, quick, nimble, and for that reason called Squirrel. No one's name is his own.

Why is she singing a French song? For a second, in her headiness, Sut On thinks she will tell Squirrel about *Mother Courage*, about the Thirty Years' War, but is afraid that just like with machine-gun fire, when her head drums so quickly that the rounds seem too slow, her thoughts are going so quickly her voice would make no sense.

"It's a lullaby," she says, and, looking at him directly, knows perfectly well that was not the way she sang it.

The cadre begins tapping rapidly on a bamboo length he has sharpened. In his staccato Northern voice, he says, "You should not stay in the jungle any longer."

"A RED AND A BLUE SCARF AND TWO WIGS"

THERE IS NO STREET IN CHOLON, NO HOUSE, NO DOOR, NO STAND, NO stall that Sut On could not find in her sleep. It is in fact this feeling of sleep that stays with her now as she walks through the market in a short wig and a Western dress, seeing no one and smiling dimly, politely, at hawkers who, noticing a stranger, shout out elevated prices in broken Vietnamese. She could tear off her wig, pull out her voice, and scream and haggle with them in Chinese, but luckily the sleepiness stops her. In some ways, nothing even seems familiar, so she walks on, with her sunglasses, to a certain teashop where she picks up instructions. In front of it there is a row of old women who are selling radios and cameras in cartons marked PX. One of them suddenly looks up at her and in a hoarse, tired voice calls out in Chinese—it is *not* her mother.

Inside, the message is more or less what she has been expecting: "The mountains around you do not have higher peaks than the one on which you already stand! There is no going back."

In the bare Cholon apartment rented to Miss Phung Ngoc Anh, Sut On lights a joss stick, and in its old, missed smell folds and unfolds the scarves, staring at the red and blue squares in the dark room. Over and over again she turns them inside out and around and smooths down the edges; it's as if they were someone else's, she has never been so neat.

"Should I wear the red or blue?" she says, and feels like giggling, so much does she want to pretend that this is her dilemma.

Asleep on the straw mat which belongs to the apartment, she dreams that her grandfather is walking through the long, narrow halls of her uncle's godown. He is coming to greet her, but does not call out her name or even beckon to her. He just keeps on walking slowly with a slice of pineapple held out in his hands.

"There is no going back." To what would Phung Ngoc Anh go back? There is a girl with a flowing red scarf who speeds through the streets on the back of a motorcycle. If her heart is remote, she'd be the last one to know it. Fleet as a fawn, she shoots with both hands.

BABYSITTING

This is one of the places where the Marshaks lived: a small stone cottage, probably whitewashed walls, outside some virgin sand and water the color of tinted sunglasses, maybe a clump or two of bougainvillea, and, as far as you might want to see, several endless fields of blinding red anemones.

Theodore H. Marshak, America's enigmatic wanderer-poet-playwright, interviewed for the BBC's prestigious Third Programme, was asked if there was anything about the U.S. that he missed. Confounding both interviewer and audience, Marshak replied, "Yes. Eggrolls and spareribs." Abroad at the time was celebrated N.Y. restaurateur Sy Krinsky, and hearing of Marshak's response, the sympathetic Krinsky immediately arranged for special Care packages from his Jade and Lotus Garden to be flown to Marshak at his isolated Mediterranean retreat.

And:

Topics and Treasures alight on . . . exciting young Ted (Knives) Marshak and his radiant-as-her-name wife, Sunny. No believers in private Illyrias they, but as Ted told us, thoughtfully choosing his words with the quiet, dramatic intensity for which he is *treasured,* "This is a good place. It lets you know that life is where *you* are."

Where *I* was at the time was in high school, and one of the things that preoccupied me in those days was the way people looked. Going to school in the morning, walking up the difficult blocks which were all hills, I used to imagine that just up above us was an overworked pilot in a low-flying plane. Anytime he needed a jolt out of his boredom, he just glanced down from the cockpit and took a good look at us: long hair, dangling earrings, Mexican serapes, and chunky leather sandals that kept winding up our legs as if *they* were the hills. Those were the girls.

The boys, already sensitive to charges of "fruitiness," were careful to look as if they might have been going anywhere, and could only be spotted by the instrument cases or sketchbooks they carried between their loose-leafs. Here and there, in advertisement of something particular, some had longer hair and wore capes.

As we came closer to the tops of the hills, the sounds of instruments tuning up surrounded us. Finally, at the very top was the school itself, famous all over the city for its distinctiveness and nonconformity. An occasional flute or bassoon blew itself over the first warning bell, and certain above all of our distinctiveness, we pulled at our serapes and streamed in through the opened doors.

I say "we": in fact I did not have long hair or Greek sandals, and took very little part in the life of the school, which I called to myself decadent, affected, and sometimes bourgeois, though this word *bourgeois* was known to be out of date, a carryover from other times. Still, these were my favorite words, and were in my eyes constantly as I climbed up the hill or walked through the halls. Because I did not share in the look of the school and seemed overquiet in the recklessness which was its spirit, there were people who began to wonder.

"Are your parents divorced?" the guidance counselor asked me. "Is there something you'd like to tell me?"

"No," I said, and was easily truthful.

"Just tell them you're a mental case, it's the one thing they're always waiting for," said a girl I knew whose father was a well-known sculptor, and who was herself to become briefly famous in her senior year when she refused to take cover in a shelter drill outside Altman's.

"I can't," I said. It was one of the many things I considered decadent.

Partly out of concession, and partly because I liked them, I did get long pierced earrings, and sometimes wore peasant blouses. About these heavily embroidered peasant blouses, my mother said, "Every Polish peasant had a blouse like that. Wanda the goose-girl!" And for the earrings she fell back on Yiddish, calling out as I left the house, "The little gypsy with her jangles."

In my jangles, and with my schoolbooks, I sat opposite the guidance counselor.

"Your teachers say that you don't contribute in classes. Would you say that you were always shy?"

"With *some* people," I said, and looked out for life beyond the shades where a whole city was speeding about its morning business.

She leaned back against her filing cabinets and smiled at me as if I were a convalescent. "There's a wonderful church down-town, and they've asked us if we could find them an organist."

"I don't play the organ," I said, and ran out with the bell to report on this latest bit of decadence to my friend Simone.

Simone and I were not exactly friends. We belonged to rival Socialist-Zionist youth groups, and in citywide gatherings of Zionist youth stood glaring at each other in blouses of varying shades of blue, each washed-out difference in color marking our separate commitments.

"What about the Arab workers who were paid *money* wages and never included communally?" Simone would say. She wore her hair pulled back by a thin, knotted rubber band that nobody would dare call Beat or bohemian, and would not have her ears pierced or even wear olive wood barrettes. Also, she had a policy of never taking a seat in a bus or subway, because if there was an empty seat near a Negro and you didn't sit in *that* one, it could be judged as offensive, and if you did, when there were other seats around, it could easily be thought of as patronizing.

On the train, which lurched past pillars and gum machines, I would stand on my tiptoes, trying to get hold of a subway strap.

"What if it happens that money was what they wanted in the first place?"

But Simone was much better at arguing than I; she enjoyed it for its own sake, and not even the end of a long day, a crowded train, or an upcoming midterm could stop her. What might do it, I knew, was to say, "What about the Prague Trials?" but since I did not actually know what they were, I decided not to try it. Besides, she was the only one in her family not born in France, she lived on the twelfth floor of a doorman building on Central Park West, she spelled her last name, Frydman, with a *y*, had an uncle who was a Communist representative in the French Chamber of Deputies, and her father, who was always taking business trips to

Switzerland, could be found listed in the telephone book this way: Frydman Lucien . . . Imprt-Exprt. What he imported or exported I had no idea; altogether, it was a family of mystery. Once she told me that her father would have to stay in Milan for a few days because they had relatives there who were beginning to feel insulted.

"Milan, Italy?" I said. "How come you have relatives in Italy?"

"Oh, *you* know. Typical Yid story. They were hiding in a convent and now they're very rich."

It was not typical of anyone I knew, so that this sense of their glamour and mystery only deepened. In a way, what I found most mysterious and glamorous of all was that Simone lived in Manhattan, on a street whose name alone, I believed, existed solely for the purpose of certain Hollywood movies when it was necessary to show, through the flash of an awning and a lobby, or a doorman with a whistle at a cab, the backdrop of lives carried on in the ridiculous luxury of obvious make-believe.

This possible movie aspect of Simone occurred to me constantly when I talked to her or listened to her arguing, and made me feel that, in some way I did not understand, she was leading a secret life. If it was true about Simone, who was at least partially my friend, what about all the other girls in school whom I hardly even knew? I began to look for clues of secret lives in the way people braided their long hair or knotted their sandals and, gaining nothing from this but more confusion, turned to other sources.

"Why do you always wear black?" says the schoolmaster in *The Seagull* to Masha, a girl whose father is not rich, but manages anyway for her to be living in the middle of a big estate where there are plays at night.

"I am in mourning for my life," Masha says, and continues to complain in this way, without ever really offering any decent explanation.

In my French class, a girl named Lucy Sperling told everyone that she had gone through her closet and thrown out all of her clothes except the ones that were black.

"My mother may kill me," she said, "but I'm only going to wear black from now on."

So Lucy Sperling was in mourning for her life. Why? You could never have known it from looking at her. It was another case of secret lives.

The guidance counselor, who was still intent on finding out mine, though it was obvious I didn't have one, said, "How do you spend your time after school? Do you ever do any babysitting, for example?"

"Sometimes," I said. From time to time, in my own building, I would babysit for people going out for Chinese food and the movies. After hysterical last-minute preparations, they would leave their bathed, whiny children, *Marjorie Morningstar* with a bookmark in it, and a blaring television. Out of boredom and disapproval, I had, for the most part, stopped doing it.

"The Marshaks always want one of our girls as their babysitter. Last year we gave them Erica Jaffe, but she graduated, and after that they went to Greece. Do you know who Ted Marshak is? Shall I give them your phone number?"

Did I know who Ted Marshak was? Was there any way I couldn't? Aside from Kahlil Gibran and Jean Cocteau, he was one of the few writers anyone in school considered worth bothering about. What he was most famous for was a single very long poem called *Knives*. It was about a random knife murderer who takes joy from his work, but is then caught and imprisoned. He escapes from prison by making a knife out of something in his cell, and ends up by being in a traveling circus or carnival where he is known as "The Human Knife." The book, in paperback, was carried around as a badge, and its beginning lines were memorized and quoted by everyone:

Knives!
Flashing highglint into soft
flesh And blood-
Slash
I cruise/
sluice through yr rivernights (my gore
store)
No
end
end
red
en
Ded

"Ted Marshak, the poet?" I said.

"He's much more than a poet—they're extremely interesting people, the Marshaks. Erica Jaffe loved them. They live in Manhattan, though. Will the traveling bother you?"

"Oh, no," I said. "I take the subway all the time," and being very careful to avoid Simone, I ran all the way down the hill. I was preparing for a brand-new decadence and the beginning of a secret life.

THIS IS ONE OF THE PLACES WHERE THE MARSHAKS LIVED: A GRACIOUS penthouse apartment splashed with all the moonlike winks rising off the New York skyline, vast, pale, painting-filled walls, rosy, expectant twilights echoing with the tinkle of laughter—muted laughter—due naturally to brilliant and witty jokes that were just being tossed off, and in the bathroom a glass-enclosed shower.

"I don't think they *will*," said Mrs. Marshak, "but just in case the kids get hungry, there's some celery in the fridge."

Except for the difference in coloring, Mrs. Marshak looked like a stalk of celery herself. Nothing moved in her face or her body as she talked, and even doing that, her mouth seemed to barely open. With her straight blond hair and loose, boyish boniness, she looked like a girl getting married in the Sunday *Times*. But most particularly what she looked like was a woman I had once seen in the elevator in Bonwit Teller's. This woman, just as straight-limbed and angular-featured, was, it occurred to me when I saw her, what was called "horsey." Whether this meant someone who rode horses or someone who looked like a horse, or even a person who because of too much horse-riding in the family had developed into this strange and specific but recognized mutation, I did not know. As it happened, the woman in the store was English. She was holding the hand of a handsome little boy of about four or five whom she had dressed in short pants and a blazer, and as they entered the elevator, she said to him in a clear, brisk English voice, "Caps off in lifts."

"The babysitter's here, Ted," Mrs. Marshak called out, still slouching calmly in exactly the same spot. She had obviously just put on eye makeup and sprayed herself with some perfume, but I was sure that this made very little difference in her appearance. Prettier than the English woman in the elevator, she had the kind of good looks that would in no way be changed by standing in front of a mirror with bottles and brushes, and would probably look the same—expensive and clear-skinned—even if she wore dungarees. "Ted," she said again, and her voice was not nagging, not even impatient. "Sascha, Pietro."

From somewhere in the back, children's voices screamed, and soon, with a naked child on either side of him, out came a short, round-faced man with a head of wild, outstanding black curls. He was practically naked himself: no shirt on at all, and there, as he came walking along, was just putting on his pants. Staring at his fly, which he was zipping, he said, "What happened to Erica Jaffe?"

"I don't know her," I said, "but I think she graduated."

He looked up from his fly and said, "You don't look like her."

"I'm not her sister. Why should I?"

"All the girls from your school look alike," and turning around, he walked away, leaving his expressionless, long-limbed wife and two tiny, shrieking children.

"Their pajamas," I said to Mrs. Marshak. "Don't you want me to help them put on their pajamas?"

"Pajamas?" She was moving a thin, horsey finger just enough to flick at a cockroach. "They might be in the basement. I don't know if Ted brought up the wash."

Wash? Cockroaches? Fly-zipping? By this time I realized there would not be any glass-enclosed shower; as far as I could see, there was hardly even any furniture. I followed the children into their bedroom and, opening the top drawer of an outsize bureau that looked as if it, too, might have done time in the basement, I fished out an undershirt.

"Whose is this?" I said as the two of them rolled giggling on the splintery floor. I looked at Pietro, the older one, and then at Sascha, a round-faced little girl with wild blond curls; when she leaned back in her crib, flushed and overtired, she looked like a confused, unkempt grandmother. "Whose is it?" I said, and as I held up the little shirt, a huge roach came crawling out of it.

"Roachie, roachie, richie roachie," Pietro sang out. "Wanna see my dump truck?"

I saw the dump truck, found some more underwear, and just as I was getting ready to read them a story or sing them a song, my usual babysitting routine, Ted Marshak, dressed snappily now in a suit and tie—there was even a flower stuck in his lapel—came in saying, "Sunny? You found their underwear?"

"No," she said, "the babysitter."

"The *babysitter*?" He looked me straight up and down in a way I was unused to, and kept squinting and frowning at me as if I were a person too stupid to realize that she had been waiting for hours on what would turn out to be the wrong line. "Where the hell is Erica Jaffe? I don't know how they could even have sent you here."

"I don't know how you could have named your daughter Sascha. It's a *boy's* name, and it's Russian, and it's not even a real name. It's just the nickname they use for Alexander."

"So Little Miss Underwear-Finder speaks Russian, too!"

"No," I said, "I just know it from Russian novels."

"*Russian novels!*" He made it sound as if I had said Cracker Jack box tops. "I suppose your idea of plays is Chekhov. Or Ibsen. And poetry—God knows what! Wallace Stevens!"

"I never heard of him," I said.

From the door, Mrs. Marshak called out, "Good night, niblets." She did not go in to kiss her children or even look at them; she did not tell me "We'll be back around twelve, but if anything goes wrong, here's the number where you can reach us"; she did not say "Pietro likes the little light on at night" or "If Sascha gets up, you can give her some orange juice." Just "Good night, niblets"—a name for goldfish or maybe hamsters. Why didn't she come right out with it: let them eat roaches.

I said, "Goodbye, Mrs. Marshak. Have a good time."

"Oh, *please*—call me Sunny. It makes me feel so old."

"A good time!" Ted Marshak said. "Russian novels! I don't believe it."

I couldn't believe it either: here I was, two minutes in the home of America's famous, exciting, enigmatic, wandering poet-playwright, and already I had managed to make such a terrible impression that my secret life—just barely begun—was practically over. I began to walk slowly through the long halls and dim rooms of the apartment: broken light switches, crayoned walls, torn beach chairs, overflowing garbage bags, dirty plates and glasses on the floor, and no books anywhere. I was walking numbly in this way when the phone rang.

"Hi, baby, let's have the knife."

"You have the wrong number," I said.

"Sunny? You hiding that bastard? He tell you how much he owes me from that crap game last week? Come on, now, put him on! Gimme the knife."

"This isn't Sunny, it's the babysitter. The Marshaks aren't home. Can I take a message?"

"Message? Yeah, tell him Al Carpentier called."

Al Carpentier! So "the knife" was Ted (Knives) Marshak, and Al Carpentier would have to be Alvin Carpentier, the playwright, as treasured, enigmatic, and wandering as Ted Marshak himself. I looked around for some paper to write down the message, though I knew there was no chance I would forget it, and right near the phone, in a raffia basket that had one rotting apple in it, I saw some.

Dear Mother, Daddy and Grandma B,

Well, we're all settled now finally, and it's good to be back in New York. Sorry I haven't written for a while, but I've been busy with the house etc. I hope we'll be able to see you sometime soon but it depends on Ted's plans etc. He says thanks for everything. I was truly sad to hear that you had to have Prince put to sleep. What did you tell Aunt Elinor? A white lie, I hope.

Last week we went to a party and guess who was there? The King of Morocco and Ed Sullivan! Also there were some

Here the letter stopped; she had not finished it, probably having gotten sidetracked by an etc. Underneath it were two things: a snapshot and what was apparently the last page of a long letter:

> *. . . though I doubt it would be similar. After all, it's so long ago that Kate was in Greece.*
>
> *Love to you from Daddy, Grandma B and all the Bradburys.*
> *As ever,*
> *Mother*

> *Dear Pietro and Sascha,*
>
> *Here is a picture of Aunt Betty in Uncle Bob's new boat. You can't see Uncle Bob because he is in the cabin. When you come up to visit he will be glad to give you a ride.*
> *Love,*
> *Grandma*

What kind of world did these pajama-less children come out of?

> B my name is Betty and my husband's name is Bob
>   We come from Boston and we sell boats

I tried to imagine what it would be like when some kindergarten teacher in the nearby public school would look down the list in her roll book and find between, say, Leventhal, Wendy, and Negron, Miguel, this: Marshak, Sascha. The teacher was young— maybe it was even her first year: she had matching accessories and a bow in her hair. "Sash-a?" she would say to herself stupidly, wondering. "Sas-ka?" feeling entirely puzzled.

I looked out the living room window, from which, if you strained very hard, you could see Central Park, and there, past the trees and the snow, was a certain Sascha Marshak, riding in a troika, racing through the avenues of a large estate. Her cheeks were burning, the strains of waltz music made it impossible for her to sit still, but if you looked closely, you could see that everything she was wearing was all black: unknown to all those around her, she was in mourning for her life. Then there was another Sascha Marshak—this one a middle-aged man with rimless glasses and a stern, square, steely face; he had just been thrown off a Central Committee and was sitting grimly in a Prague Trial. On purpose, he had taken special care to wear absolutely nothing that was black.

I was still shoveling this unfortunate Comrade Marshak into an icy grave somewhere between Prague and Siberia when I heard a child's uneven footsteps and a sleepy baby's voice crying, "Daddy, Daddy." It was Sascha. Her feet had gotten caught in the strap of what looked like field glasses, and dragging them behind her, stumbling, she opened the door of what I had thought was a closet. "Daddy," she called into the empty, darkened room. "Daddy working?" I put on the light: it was Ted Marshak's study and I couldn't get back to it fast enough.

CHEMISTRY/SET
by Theodore Marshak

CHAPTER I

The chill fall air gnawed like a knife. This knife which was air and was wind, which was weather and was darkness, which was all the elements, was all his life. He trudged through the darkling Milwaukee streets, his schoolbooks weighing down his arms and knew with a strained heaviness in all his body what awaited him. Past Perlmutter's grocery lined with uncrated produce that were the unopened suitcases of his sorrows, past Tony Di Suvero leaning razor-sharp against his barber pole, there it was. TABAK'S. TABAK'S HARDWARE. Wrenches. Screwdrivers. Pliers. Hammers. Tabak's Hardware! What was Tabak if not hard?

"Murray? You home?"

Murray Tabak. Him. *Home?*

Home? It occurred to me that home was just where the Marshaks might be any minute. I rushed into the living room and picked up the book I had brought with me: Dick Diver was in the middle of effecting a miraculous cure on a woman who couldn't even see him. I thought about her rash, but couldn't concentrate.

When the Marshaks did get home, both looking puffy-faced, and neither of them snappy, I immediately said, "You got a phone call from Al Carpentier."

"Stupid bastard. What did he want?"

"He said that you should call him back."

"Ted plays pool with him sometimes," Sunny said, but the expression on her face was so rapt and far away that I began to wonder if she had just met Ed Sullivan or possibly the King of Morocco.

"Call him back! Call him back! Him and that wife of his— bitch walks around with a scissors between her legs. Do you know what they want of me? Do you know what they *want*?"

"He just said that you should call him back," I said, thinking that he was embarrassed about the money.

"Do you have any idea of what people want of me? Do you have any idea of what they expect? Do you know what *this is*?" He pulled the flower, now obviously fake, out of his lapel and pointed it at me.

"Ted," Mrs. Marshak said. "It's late. Pay her, she's only the babysitter."

"*This* squirts water. *This* is what they want. Ted Marshak, *enfant terrible,* prove it! Show us your tricks!"

"Ted, please, I'll find the money. Just walk her to the subway."

"Show us your tricks! Do something shocking! Say something scandalous! That's what we came for."

"If you really do squirt water at anyone, that's ridiculous," I said. "If you don't respect them, what's the point of doing what you think they want?"

"There's nothing she doesn't know, is there? Underwear, Russian novels, anything else? Jesus Christ! Smart-ass Jewish girls!"

"I know I'm not like Erica Jaffe and I know you don't like me, but if it gets you so angry to be with people like that, I don't see why you do it."

Mrs. Marshak began dumping everything in her purse onto the table and, frantically counting out change, she said, "Are you ever free in the afternoon? After school? Because sometimes I like to go bird-watching."

"You don't have to walk me to the subway, Mr. Marshak," I said.

He was standing at the side window, the one that almost looked out onto Central Park, and without turning around, he said, "Octagonal."

"What?"

"Octagonal. The paving stones along Central Park West are octagonal. You didn't know that, did you?"

The next week I did get a call from Mrs. Marshak. Just as

she had said, she was asking me to come after school; she wanted to go bird-watching. "Ted's out on the Coast," she said. "Big Sur, he's not sure when he'll be back."

Since this meant I would be going in the same direction as Simone, I decided I might as well tell her. She was standing outside her locker, finishing up an argument with her locker mate about socialized medicine.

"My father does *not* rob anyone," the locker mate was saying. "He sometimes works in a clinic and he even makes house calls after dinner."

"You can never justify what your father does. He dares to take money for what are simply the givens of human existence."

"Simone," I said, "I'm going to be in your neighborhood this afternoon. I'm babysitting for Ted Marshak, and they live right around the corner from you."

"Oh, I know that building," Simone said. "It's a slum. I babysit for someone there, too. Anita Selden—she's divorced and she's very boring. She keeps all her old love letters in one corner of her drawer and all her divorce stuff in the other, and all she ever has in her diary is what she says to her analyst."

"In her diary? What does she say?"

"She has these fat twin boys, and she keeps worrying that they'll have buck teeth. And now she has a new one. She's afraid that they're stupid and they won't get into any private school."

"Are they stupid?"

"Oh, *you* know. Bourgeois. Trivial. Like her."

In the Marshaks' apartment, a confusing variety of cartoon animals were quacking and meowing their way across the TV set. They fell down cliffs and pounced on each other while Sascha slept on the floor and Pietro played with his dump truck. Only Mrs. Marshak, field glasses around her neck, stared at the screen and laughed, as if she would not be able to tear herself away.

"I just love him," she said, finally walking off toward the door. She put on an old trench coat and still managed to look as if she were about to go foxhunting.

Who? I wondered. Who did she love? I knew I would not be able to figure it out, but as for the rest of it, there was a certain logic: while she was out spying on birds, inside her house I would do some watching of my own. Most of all, I wanted to know what was happening to Murray Tabak, and in what way his Chemistry was Set, but with the children around, I did not dare. I walked over to the raffia basket by the phone; there was the same rotting apple, but beside it was a foreign air form I had not seen before.

Dear Sunny,

You can't imagine how excited I am that you're coming to England! It'll be a great place for Ted to finish his book, he'll have no trouble getting Dex. Rafe is at the studio all the time and I hardly get to see him. I sit in the park with the kids and am practically the only actual mother *here. All they have here are Nannies, or worse,* au pair *girls— gorgeous and foreign who make me feel like an ancient hag. When you come, we'll be able to sit in the park together, we'll help you find a place. How much $$ did Ted get, it's not cheap here, not like Greece. Let me know details and plans.*
Love,
Barbara

P.S. BBC people are awful, *they keep saying I have a southern accent which is ridiculous since I haven't lived there since I was a baby practically.*

So the Marshaks were going to England and this was my last chance. I was just deciding to go into Ted Marshak's study when I heard the front door open. What had happened to all the birds? Was this the only time they could think of to fly south and brush up on their accents?

But it was not Sunny. Instead, holding on to an old duffel bag, and wearing a bright yellow slicker, was Ted Marshak. He stood in the dim entrance, the shininess of his slicker the only light in the whole hallway.

"Where's Sunny?"

"She went bird-watching. How was Big Sur?"

"Big Sur," he said, as if he were simply repeating nonsense syllables. "Big Sur."

"Daddy! Daddy!" the children began yelling, running over and jumping up on him.

"Daddy was in Milwaukee," he said. "Daddy saw Grandma, and Daddy saw Aunt Marilyn, and Daddy brought you presents." He unzipped the duffel bag and took out two matching sailor-style playsuits with the price tags still attached, and several large wrapped packages.

"Guess which is from Grandma and which is from Aunt Marilyn." His voice had become very cocky; he was not talking to his children, but to me.

"And look what Grandma sent for Mommy! Another present!" Out of the duffel bag came a two-pound box of chocolate mint creams and a small bottle of dietetic French dressing. "My mother," he said. "Jesus Christ. My mother."

"I guess I'll go," I said. "As long as you're home, they don't need a babysitter."

"Wait a minute, I'll walk you to the subway. I have to get cigarettes."

"Are you going to leave them alone?"

"For five minutes? To get cigarettes? Are you my mother?"

"No," I said. "I'm Aunt Marilyn."

All the way down in the elevator, neither Ted Marshak nor I spoke. Finally, not looking at me, he said, "We're going to England."

I could not tell him that I already knew, so I settled on saying, "That's very nice."

"*Nice? Nice?* Do you have any idea of what this means? Do you have any idea of what it could be like for me? Do you know what my father is? Do you know what he does for a living?"

Of course I knew: he owned a hardware store in a bad neighborhood in Milwaukee.

"He's a glazier," he said. "You know that old vaudeville joke—when someone's standing in the way, they say: Did you think I could see through you? Is your father a glazier? *That's* what it'll be like for me in England. My father *is* a glazier."

We were already at the subway entrance; I took out my train pass and was trying to juggle it with my books, sneakers, and oboe case.

"Goodbye, Mr. Marshak," I said.

"It's blinding."

"*What?*"

"The glare," he said. "The glare is blinding."

All the way down Central Park West, the sun, getting in its last licks of the day, was eating its way from one tall window to another, and flashing down off the high metal on cars and buses as they drove off—home and away.

ANITA SELDEN, THE DIARY-KEEPING MOTHER OF THE FAT TWIN BOYS REmarried: an eye doctor, so that if her sons have turned out to have astigmatism instead of buck teeth, they're set for life.

Simone Frydman, on a summer visit with her Milanese cousins, met a friend of theirs, an architect from Turin named Claudio Levi. She did not marry him but decided to live in Italy; I still hear from her occasionally when she comes to New York.

And Ted Marshak? For years afterward I looked in bookstores for *Chemistry/Set*. I never saw it or heard of it, but if it was a good bookstore, I would find a copy of *Knives* in the poetry section just the way it always had been.

That whole period in my life is not one I like to think about very often, but recently, going to the Shakespeare Festival in the park, I had to walk along Central Park West. The paving stones were still octagonal, and in the draining late-afternoon heat, what I saw all around me were girls with long hair and dangling earrings slipping out from the side streets and the heavy, canopied buildings. They wore peasant blouses, serapes, Mexican belts, and chunky sandals: that uniform, once the peculiar distinctiveness of our adolescence, had passed into "fashion."

Bicycle-riding was in fashion, too, and looking out into the street, among the swerving riders, it seemed to me that I saw Ted Marshak. His hair, once so extreme and outstanding, would no longer set him apart, and the man on the bike, despite long, dark curls, was bald on the top of his head. I stared for as long as I could, trying to make up my mind, but the glare was blinding. In what place the Marshaks live now, I could not begin to guess.

LOSS OF MEMORY
IS ONLY TEMPORARY

Only a stone could have thought up the waiting room of a psychiatric clinic as a place to meet for lunch. To make sure, at least, that nobody would think she was a patient, Naomi's aunt wore a certain blue-flowered outfit with velvet trim which, from years before, she was used to taking out only for the High Holidays or sometimes funerals. These clothes turned out to be not a good idea: sitting by herself in the empty light of a fall day, they brought back the beginnings of years that looked no better backward than forward. Luckily, there was nobody watching. At the Reception Desk the two Puerto Rican secretaries did not once look up, but went on drinking coffee from big paper cups. With their curly heads close together, they typed and giggled, giggled and typed, so that between the quick bells of their typewriters and the ringings of different phones, all they seemed to do was fill up the shiny, silent hospital space with ridiculous tropical bird calls. Aside from them, there was only one person who passed through the empty waiting room—a tall woman in a tan pantsuit and a beauty-parlor face, she wrapped a scarf around her head as if there were a mirror in front of her and, with this easy look, went right out to get a taxi.

Finally, from the far end of the long hallway came a thin girl who *did* look like someone getting out of a psychiatrist's office. Her walk was slow and distracted, and a loose smock or raincoat that was weighted down in the pocket kept waving out around her legs. One sloppy blondish braid was swinging on her shoulders, and with her head down, glasses kept slipping from her face. It was no surprise that she wore no makeup and, worse, had a long black pin clipped crookedly to the upper pocket of this odd raincoat that did not begin to fit. The thin girl got herself into the middle of the small waiting room itself, and Naomi's aunt saw that the long white coat was no raincoat, and that on the crooked black pin it said N. DUBIN M.D. PSYCHIATRY.

"Naomi!" the aunt said, jumping up from a green plastic chair that could easily have come from the office of a dentist with no eye for the future.

"I know," Naomi said. "My pantyhose are crooked. I'll go into the ladies' room and fix them."

"*When* did I—"

"All right, then, I'll go into the *men's* room and fix them," Naomi said, and pulling out a bunch of keys from the weighted-down pocket, she locked herself into a room that was only marked STAFF.

There were no years in between: who but Naomi could so quickly, immediately, lock herself into a room, any room, and without any notice just disappear? She even looked the same— the same sleepy eyes and sharp features that always made her look like a girl you couldn't quite recognize because she hadn't come close enough. Even the messy hair and glasses were the same.

People always said she must have been golden-blond as a child, but this was not true. The same dirty-blond braids hung down Naomi's back in a picture from when she was five years old. In this picture she was sitting on a llama in the Bronx Zoo and, wearing a dress that had once been perfect on Toby, Naomi, with her braids and her glasses, sat making faces in the sun. Right in front of the llama, sweating and holding on to a bag—probably popcorn that Naomi never finished—was her father. His sleepy eyes and round glasses passed from his face to her face exactly, and what else could have come from him was hard to tell. Despite the calm, sleepy blondness that ran all through his family—stringing out on his side a line of anemic, whispering, dirty-blond children—it was *his* maniac brother-in-law who managed, in his off-duty cab on a Sunday, also in the fall, to jump over a divider on the Belt Parkway. Left in this cab was a new bed for Naomi and three dead people: both of her parents and the maniac brother-in-law himself. Not in the cab were Naomi and Michael, Bluma's two children, one twelve, the other seven, both alive, both impossible, one a stone, the other a boy who in seven years had learned how to do one thing: kick.

"Look," their uncle tried to explain to them at the time, to try to make them feel a little better. "Look, you're not the first ones this happened to. When I was a little boy in Europe, my mother died at the same time that I was born so that I never even knew her, and my father died when I was five." But all the kicker did was kick the refrigerator right through the wall so that complaints came from the neighbors and the landlord, and he had to go and live with an aunt on his father's side who had a private house in Jamaica. And the stone, already on her way out, already disappearing to a friend's house, slammed a door and said, "In Europe that's *supposed* to happen. That's the whole point of not being there."

People also said she looks so *quiet,* she looks so *serious,* but these were not people who ever had to hear her open a mouth or slam a door, and did not stop to think that this was what, for twelve years, her own mother had had to put up with and did not have the energy or inclination to ever try to stop.

"Naomi, are you the only one who feels bad?" the aunt had said on that day, having to run all the way out to the elevator just to catch up with her. "After all, she was my only sister. And what about your cousin Toby? The only aunts she has left now are on her father's side, and both of them are in Argentina."

"If you just keep crying onto the table, you'll just have to keep on sponging it up," and there, on the day of the funeral, she ran off to have supper at her friend Lenore's.

"YOU'RE WEARING YOUR TASHLICH DRESS," SAID N. DUBIN, M.D., WHO HAD fixed up her braid and put on some lipstick and still looked no more than sixteen. "What sins were you planning to get rid of?" She twirled past the bathroom in her white coat, walked toward a new door, and was ready again to be disappearing.

"Naomi, do you really remember that? When we went to the Reservoir and threw in the bread crumbs?" It was the one thing she *would* remember: she used to sit in the high, coarse grass near the Reservoir, getting her holiday clothes grass stained and filthy, staring and staring for no reason at the plain blue water and the white concrete banks. "The Romans built reservoirs, only they called them aqueducts," she said, without question on purpose to make Toby, who was older, feel bad for something she did not know. "Shh, not when you can see that people are praying," was all her mother would tell her, because to Bluma only one thing had ever stood out—that her daughter had a *"reicheh shprach."* A rich language. To whom she spoke this rich language was anyone's guess. Inside, Naomi sat stone-silent like all the Dubins, looking out at people from her round, cloudy glasses, or if she happened to be standing in the sun, squinting up at them with the crookedness of a beggar. *Not* like her father's family, whose pale, blurry quietness sat in her simply for the look—a disguise; finally, when you least expected it and when there was absolutely no reason, her whiny voice would sneak out like a mimic's—*that* was the *"reicheh shprach."* As it turned out, there was one way in which Bluma may have been right: Naomi was very good in languages, a girl to whom Hebrew teachers lent records and French teachers gave awards.

"Do you remember how you and Toby used to run ahead sometimes and come back nagging for ice cream even though you knew you couldn't have it?"

She was paying no attention: despite her sleepy eyes and slow walk, Naomi pulled out a black notebook and looked at her watch.

"The elevator isn't quicker," she said, and, taking out her keys again, unlocked a different door that turned out to be a stairway. Once, a few years before, when Mark Turkel, a neighbor's son, had finally gotten a part in an off-Broadway play, the aunt had gone backstage with his mother. Strange doors had opened and closed, pieces of staircases jumped out of the woodwork, and rushing people in costumes bumped into each other without apologies. It was this same feeling she had now, walking behind Naomi through shiny corridors that did not end. Arrows and signs flashed through the hallways, oxygen tanks got raced over tiles, and doctors and nurses, outfitted like children for Assembly, passed beside bodies on stretchers; sometimes they nodded.

"Naomi, how do you know where you're going? You—who could get lost on your way to the corner to get a loaf of bread. It drove your mother crazy. Remember?" Nearly running—heavy in her mistake dress—the aunt was trying to catch up with Naomi, who would not stop looking as if she had something else on her mind, something that had to be done in a hurry.

"This is the Coffee Shop," was all she finally said, and, pushing open a door that said EXIT, nodded in her colorless, distant way at a Chinese boy in a white suit and a stethoscope.

"I *heard* that they have a lot of foreign doctors working in hospitals."

"He's not foreign, he's from San Francisco." Naomi grabbed on to a table that was still loaded down with somebody else's leftover lunch and said, "Decide what you want to eat or we'll be here forever. Don't get the tuna fish."

"I'm not really that hungry," the aunt said, still not even sure of the round plastic chair she was trying not to slide out of. "That wasn't my idea of this altogether. Anyway, since when do *you* eat lunch? The only thing you ever liked was French toast, and even that you threw away half of. Remember?"

"BLT on toast and black coffee," said Naomi to a waitress in a yellow dress who was there suddenly, and before the aunt could even say "I think I'll have an egg," a redheaded girl, even younger than Naomi, was standing at the table, saying, "Dr. Dubin, there was a message for you. Dr. Fortgang wants you to prepare Mrs. Grossbard for ECT."

Naomi looked up at the girl as if she had just put down a newspaper. "Fortgang?" she said, a smile slipping into her voice and even up to her wan, washed-out face. "Was it a phone message, Miss Perry? Or did Fortgang rumple his two-hundred-fifty-dollar suit and actually pass through the building?"

The girl, Miss Perry, not only had red hair, but also freckles all over her face, and looked as if she belonged in jeans and a plaid shirt, sitting on a fence with a fishing pole or a lunch box, waving at an orange school bus. Instead, with a nurse's uniform and a slightly buck-toothed, summery smile, she said, "He was here, but it's even funnier. He actually made a note on the chart."

"That *is* funny," Naomi said. "He must be getting ready to send out bills," and there in their uniforms the two of them began laughing as if they were walking down the street together and had just seen something ridiculous in the window of a store.

"Naomi," the aunt said. "What's ECT?"

"Electroshock therapy," she said, and again immediately looked at her watch. "Toby's baby present is upstairs. I'll have to go up again and get it later."

"I didn't come here to collect presents. I was just thinking of Mrs. Lippman and what happened with her son."

"What?"

"She was a very fat old woman with fat red cheeks. She lived on the ground floor. You wouldn't remember her."

"You weren't thinking of her cheeks. What happened?"

"To her? She's been dead for years. She was a very old woman."

"What happened to her *son*? What's the tragedy you want to tell me?"

"Her son?" the aunt said, remembering suddenly his similar fat cheeks and doughy, rumbling body, terrible for a boy. "Her son? He was perfect till he was seventeen. Not only perfect, but brilliant, very mechanical. All of a sudden, when he was seventeen, he started something new. No school was good enough for him, nothing was right, teachers were staring at him, people were monkeying with his walkie-talkie. Even his mother could see that something was wrong, so she took him to a doctor who put him in a hospital, and instead of getting better, he got worse."

"How did he get worse?"

"He started getting very violent, so that every time she went up there to visit him and took the special bus, she saw red marks on his face and bruises all over his arms and she never knew whether he did it to himself or else whether he got it from when they had to hold him down."

Naomi picked up her head, but it was only to wave at a boy in another kind of white suit at a different table, and swallowing some water, she gulped out, "Before phenothiazines. You know—tranquilizers."

"Before *lots* of things you would hear about, you were never good in science anyway. Also, don't forget—these were people who didn't go to fancy Park Avenue doctors. What was his mother? A simple old Jewish woman. She didn't know anything, but she always read the Yiddish papers very carefully, and one day she found an article about a new kind of brain operation that was a brilliant cure for craziness. Naturally, it gave her hope for her son, so the next time she went to the hospital she quick ran to the doctors, and they said if she would sign the papers, it was fine with them. Why would she hesitate over a signature? Naturally, she signed the papers, the brilliant brain operation was done, and Mrs. Lippman was left with a vegetable."

"Lobotomies aren't done anymore," Naomi said, "and you'd have a hard time finding anyone to defend them."

"What about Mrs. Grossbard?" the aunt said, watching Naomi pick up her bacon sandwich, which was stuck together with blue and yellow plastic toothpicks as if it were a wedding. "What about Mrs. Grossbard who you're going to give shocks to? Mrs. Grossbard whose life is so funny that you and Suzy Q. Redhead couldn't stop yourselves from having laughing fits about?"

Naomi could have been a girl glancing up now and then for her subway stop. "Mrs. Grossbard has a fancy Park Avenue doctor," she said. "He's the one who makes the decisions, I'm only the resident. And anyway, you don't have to worry. She won't be a vegetable."

"But she'll *forget* things. I know what happened to Schreibman's sister-in-law. She woke up in the morning and didn't know what day it was, she went to the bakery and couldn't remember a single salesgirl."

"Loss of memory is only temporary," the stone said. "There are conditions in which ECT is indicated. Involutional depression, for instance."

The Romans built reservoirs, only they called them aqueducts—how was this different? "How do *you* know if that's what she had? You don't even know who I'm talking about."

"Severe depression associated with menopause. You know what that is—change of life."

The egg the aunt was putting her fork into was cold. "Whoever expected that you would become a doctor? Your *mother* would never have predicted it. *She* knew you were never good in science. You were good in languages like people on your father's side. Remember that uncle of yours who had a cleaning store downtown? The one who called himself French Cleaner? Some Frenchman!" the aunt said, recalling his squeezed-in, monkey's face: on the way to America, his boat had docked for a few days in Cherbourg. "He could speak any language anyone came in with. You must remember that, Naomi. You used to hang around there so much." It was probably how she had managed to get through medical school—anyone who could stand the smell of a cleaning store for hours on end would have no trouble wading through four years of ether and bloodstains. "You were very close with his older son, Azriel. Remember? Not that you keep up with anyone."

Naomi said, "I got a letter from Azriel last week. He's in Japan."

"What's he doing in Japan?"

"He's studying Japanese. Azriel's very good in languages."

"He's not still in school! I thought he was married and had a child."

"He's teaching at Stanford, he's on leave for a semester, his son is four years old."

"Four? He'll be ready for school soon."

"He goes to a Japanese school. *He's* very good in languages, too."

"I don't see what's funny about it, Naomi. It's the one thing you were ever really good in. Remember that French teacher you had, Mrs. Gelfand, who couldn't stop raving about you when you translated those French poems? And that Israeli engineer who was staying across the hall who said he could have sworn you were a sabra the few times you bothered to open your mouth?"

She managed to open her mouth now, but all she said was, "Hi, Steve," to a tall, suntanned boy whose giant circus-clown's tie bobbed out from underneath his white jacket together with his Adam's apple.

"Nao," said S. SONNENBORN M.D. PSYCHIATRY. "You were beautiful this morning. No shit. First presentation I haven't slept through in months." The tall clown's eyes seemed to follow the glow of his tie the way Naomi's did a windowed distance.

"Thanks," Naomi said. She was trying to fix an earring and in one minute her long white sleeve would be soaking up coffee. "Naomi, you give more to the floor than you put in your mouth," her uncle used to say to her. But it was easy for him to have patience, he was not the one who cleaned the floor.

A buzz from S. Sonnenborn's pocket forced him to pull out a walkie-talkie. "I'm on call," he said. "Talk to you upstairs." His smile trickled out to the bottoms of his sideburns, his tie pulled him out to the door, and the aunt said, "Naomi, why did that boy call you Nao? It's not a name, it sounds like a deodorant."

"For short," she said. "For a nickname."

"But no one in your life ever called you *Nao.* Your parents never called you that, your uncle and I never called you that.

It isn't even your real name—Naomi—it's only your English name. Your real name, the name that your mother gave you, is Nechama."

"I know what my name is. Let's go upstairs, I'll get you Toby's baby present."

"Look how you call it 'baby present'! You don't even know the names of Toby's children. They wouldn't know you if they saw you on the street and you're practically an aunt to them. And what about your brother? You don't even keep up with him and he always felt so close to you."

"We were hardly even brought up together. Anyway, I saw him when I was in California, and if he needs money for bail, he knows my phone number."

"Money for bail?" the aunt said. "Who do you think you are that you can talk that way? What will you have from all this but years of debts?"

"Just like all other medical students. I'll pay it back."

"But you're *not* like all the other medical students. How could you turn out this way? How could Michael? What could he possibly have in common with all those boys rebelling against their parents' swimming pools? He practically had no parents, let alone swimming pools."

"Why don't you ask him? He's the one with theories. I was only good in languages."

"But why did he have to get tear-gassed? What happened to him?"

"You know what happens when people get tear-gassed. You read the papers the same as everyone else."

"But, Naomi, he's your *brother*. Do you think he resented us?"

"I'm not Michael. How do I know?"

"You're a psychiatrist. That's why I'm asking you."

"That's right. I'm a psychiatrist and Michael is a dropout, and those are both categories that everyone can understand."

"I'm not concerned with *everyone*. For you, spilling your coffee and monkeying around with other people's memories are all the same thing, because to you it doesn't matter *what* you forget."

But already Naomi had gotten up and, in her distant, disappearing way, was floating past the cash register.

"That's a cute hat," she said to a foreign-looking girl who had just tumbled through the door in a blue raincoat. The girl pulled the hat off her head as if she hadn't known she was wearing it, and in a fuzzy, foreign voice said, "It was knitted for me by my sister. In many colors. I can give you one if you want."

"Since when are you interested in hats?" the aunt said, but the girl—delicate, fair-skinned, and dazed—continued to look as if she had just been pulled out of an avalanche.

"Na-o-mi," she said. "You won't believe what I have been through. Do you know what his wife said? 'That lovely Danish girl in your department—why don't we invite her for dinner?'"

"He told you that?" Naomi said. "What a bastard."

The girl seemed about to cry. She took off her raincoat and said, "I don't even have many cigarettes."

"Listen, Inga," Naomi said, "let's have dinner tonight. Just come over to my apartment."

"I can't do it. I'm on first call. It's better, I think, it's better for me to be working."

In the corridor, the aunt said, "She's so pretty. Why is *she* a doctor?"

Naomi looked at her watch and, fussing again with her little black notebook, shuffled straight into an elevator where a man in a sheet lay stretched out on a table. His face was the color of worn-out underwear, and tubes and bottles hung down on all sides.

"*This* elevator?"

"You're not at a bus stop," Naomi said. "This is a hospital," and seeing her face—thin, distant, and severe—reflected in the glass-covered bulletin board, the aunt could suddenly imagine Naomi with her white smock, round glasses, and plain hair—perhaps in a bun—bending over a microscope: it was not Naomi she was thinking of at all.

"Did your mother ever tell you about your Great-aunt Masha?" she tried whispering past the sick man's feet. "For a Jewish girl in Russia in *her* generation to become a doctor—you can imagine what that was. She was a very unusual person. It was practically unheard of."

"It couldn't have been that unheard of," Naomi said in a perfectly conversational tone. "In an Isaac Babel story there's a doctor who's a Jewish girl."

"I'm not talking about stories, I'm talking about a person. In the middle of a revolution, completely on her own, she went all the way to Moscow. You never even heard about her? Your mother told you nothing?"

"She told me about her."

"In Palestine she lived in swamps and in deserts and if she ever earned a penny, she immediately gave it away. What did your mother tell you?"

"That she was stubborn," said Naomi, and wheeled out the door to a silent, blank hallway.

"Stubborn?" The aunt had to squeeze with her purse past the man on the stretcher. "What she was was not stubborn. Masha was a nut. She never got married, she worked day and night, she lived for her profession and died all alone."

"Maybe she was good in languages," Naomi said. "Let me get you Toby's present."

"Naomi, why can't you bring it to her yourself? She isn't used to living out of town yet. Every time I talk to her I can tell that she's crying." It was what she could see on the phone: Toby, in whose face people had always seen so much sweetness—*cheyn*—sitting on a beige sofa in Connecticut, her face dark and red, simply from crying.

"As long as she doesn't get her medical advice from newspapers," the stone said, and disappeared with her braid so that there was no point in following her.

Not that there was anywhere to go: the hall was filled up with closed doors and blank spaces. Finally, at the far end of the corridor there was some sunlight which opened itself out from a room marked LOUNGE. Here, plants were on the windowsill, newspapers lay on the chairs, and a television with nobody anywhere near it just kept on going. People, mostly in bathrobes, sat around doing nothing. A woman in a black nightgown was putting polish on her fingernails, a man who hadn't shaved yet was shuffling a deck of cards, and next to the long window, bobbing back and forth in the sun with their bathrobes, two boys were playing Ping-Pong. The aunt looked around for Mrs. Grossbard, a woman who didn't know yet that her life would mean waking up one morning to say, "Oh my God, I don't even know what day this is," and found instead that she couldn't stop herself from staring at a very young girl who looked as if she had just stepped out of a cemetery. That she was wearing a pink quilted bathrobe made no difference—it could not substitute for flesh, which she simply did not have. Bones and sockets stood out in her so far that when she stood or walked, her arms and legs looked like marionette strings, and when she began to open her mouth, it did not seem possible that her voice—which was shrill—had anyplace to come from.

"I gained one pound and I found out what my doctor's first name is," she said to a boy in bedroom slippers whose hair fell into his guitar. "It says *N* on her thing, but I asked her and she said it's Naomi."

"They have to tell you if you ask them," said the boy, who did not either raise his beard or play his guitar.

"If I gain five pounds, she said that she'll take me to the Coffee Shop, and if I gain ten pounds I'll be able to go off the Sustagen."

"The Coffee Shop sucks," the boy said, and began to look out through the room with the small, sour eyes of a definite maniac.

"What would you do if you got stuck in a plane right next to a maniac?" the aunt ran out to ask Naomi, who, it turned out, was sitting inside a glass cage labeled NURSES' STATION. On one side of her was S. Sonnenborn of the glowing tie, on the other, a fat, red-faced boy who was eating a Danish. In their white coats, they sat perched on a desk like children at a soda fountain. Naomi's legs dangled, they could not reach the floor.

The aunt knocked on the glass and Naomi came out carrying a large package beautifully wrapped in blue-and-purple paper, perfectly tied with a dark purple bow. Obviously, she had not done it herself: it was *Toby* who wrapped things with fine, perfect fingers, *Toby* who once painted tiny birds on her old bedroom wall, Toby who even now could weave rugs that people offered money for.

"Naomi, do you remember when Toby made you that scrapbook for a present? She got the leather from her Arts and Crafts Club, and she pasted in for you all the old pictures of your family that you didn't even remember?"

Naomi looked as if she were about to say something, but it was only to smile at the unfortunate skeleton-girl, who had crept down the hall in her pink quilted robe.

"Do you sign *death* certificates?" it suddenly occurred to the aunt.

"On Psychiatry? What do you think I do here?"

"I don't mean *here,* I just mean if somebody happened to die, and you were the one who was there—"

"And it *happened* to be in the middle of the Belt Parkway, and there *happened* to be an off-duty cab—*that's* what you're trying to say to me. *That's* the only reason you're here."

"Naomi!" the aunt said, and felt her face swelling out in a thousand directions, but hanging over the vague and cloudy-eyed stone whom Bluma had named Nechama—comfort, solace— and who was not so vague about languages that she did not know what it meant.

TALES OF MY
GREAT-GRANDFATHERS

———————

One morning in the clamorous early 1970s—that hectic, electric time of flower power, angry demonstrations, saffron-clad gurus, and their chanting, shaven-headed acolytes—one morning, waiting for a New York City bus in that gaudy, psychedelic time, I ran into a woman with whom I had gone to high school and college. The daughter of artists, she had grown up in sophisticated Greenwich Village, while I, a teacher's daughter, had emerged from the subway provinces.

We had never really been friends, Mara and I; still, we knew each other and had many acquaintances in common. So standing there together, waiting for the bus, we fell into an uneasy early morning exchange. All too quickly, though, we exhausted the juiciest gossipy good stuff and an edgy silence overtook us, until suddenly my old schoolmate—who was at that juncture, she had just informed me a member of a women's guerrilla street-theater troupe—said: "You know, I was just thinking about you recently. In my consciousness-raising group . . ." And then, very guardedly, "You were like really always into being Jewish weren't you?"

"I guess so." I said this with reluctance, immediately feeling defensive.

Because in a time of so much ferment and ecstatic disruption, who could believe it? Hear about Johanna? Pathetic, really—still into her same old boring *Jewish* trip. But this, it turned out, was not at all what she had in mind. What I did not know, and would never have guessed, was that Mara herself was even then inching her way toward reclaiming a Jewish inheritance she had been raised to disdain. On that long-ago morning, as she stood peering down the yet-to-be gentrified Upper West Side street for a glimpse of the bus, she carefully avoided my eyes as she finally blurted out, "What did you—I mean, how did you get *into* it?"

But the bus was at long last arriving, and I took incoherent refuge in rummaging for my fare. "Oh well, you know . . . my parents," was all I managed to summon up before we climbed on and became separated by the determined stream of onrushing passengers.

As it happens, Mara would eventually find her way to an unfamiliar and decidedly not home-inspired sense of Jewish belonging by way of klezmer music. You just never know: Jewish destiny is a great mystery, said the illustrious Rav Kook, Israel's first Chief Rabbi. So for Mara, the world at large, or the zeitgeist, filled in the blanks, and she did not need what should have been my answer.

Which might have been what, exactly? Surely, even in that pervid time, I could have offered her at least a few surface details—for instance that my grandfather had been a cantor, that I was raised in a moderately observant but specifically Zionist family, and that my intense adolescent years of membership in the Zionist youth movement Habonim were in my own mind still, precious and formative. But suppose I hadn't left it there? What if I'd done better?

Suppose, for a moment, that I'd let whistle through the stale air of that crosstown bus a shiver of my earliest memories: a child's tentative, barefoot decipherings of only the close-by world. That child (we lived then with my mother's parents in Massachusetts while my father was far from home in the army)— that unkempt, backyard little girl who squints out at me from a scatter of snapshots—was first of all, absolute primary identity, an *eynikel*: a grandchild. So, as my cantor grandfather's *eynikel*, I sat, on Sabbath mornings, within the grandeur of a deep, high-backed, wine-red chair on the bimah, entranced and even dizzied by the lofting space and swaying worshipers to sing, as my first songs, what were in fact prayers. The cadence of my diminutive, combative grandfather's voice—its clean, climbing intensity—can sometimes come back to me still when I hear the yearning penitential High Holiday prayer *Avinu Malkeynu*.

And I was just as much *eynikel* to my grandmother—my murmuring, *tichl*-clad grandmother—whose pantry wall, on late summer afternoons, would become so gorgeously ablaze with row upon row of many-colored sun-dazzled *pushkehs* that often she would find me staring up in baffled delight at this shifting, rush-of-color display. But these radiant rows were no mere design of pretty boxes meant to excite my infant eyes—this my grandmother made sure I learned as she put coins into my hands so I could drop them in with my own fingers. They were charity boxes, money to help poor Jews in faraway places, places where terrible things happened, things so terrible they could make her cry.

What were her tears about? In my parents' new, postwar apartment in the Bronx, I would find out. There, from a leafy, unremarkable New York City neighborhood, I came to rudimentary consciousness at a time of Jewish enormity: a rift moment when awesome events masqueraded as ordinary days. The stunned remnant Jews of Europe were trickling into grief-pierced American freedom; at the same time, in a sun-toughened, orange-fragrant sliver of Palestine (then still usually a long ship's travel away), an independent Jewish nation was flailing to be born. Exactly how distant were those abstract events? In my mother's kitchen, over cups of tea that got cold, newcomer survivor-neighbors—two blondish, small-boned sisters with ugly blue markings on their arms—whispered their horrific accounts. In Polish, so I wouldn't understand.

But as soon as they left, my mother always translated; more than that, she always explained. (After all, it would forever be my born-in-America responsibility to help Jews from foreign countries.) A few steps away, in the living room, my father, still buttoned into his shirt and tie, hunched over a shortwave radio: any minute now, he might—just might—be able to pick up a broadcast straight from the *Yishuv*'s own airwaves. (You could never know beforehand if their signal would get through.) Despite the radio's awful crackling, I sat beside him, and I listened, too: Lake Success, Czech arms, British troops, Jews, for weeks and weeks on boats, now forced back to Cyprus. I was in kindergarten. What did I understand? Like nothing else was this drama of Zion, this all-senses-raw throb of tightrope elation—could it really happen—that after so many long, terrible centuries of danger and suffering our own old-new flag might unfurl to start flying among flags of the nations. How could I understand? How could I miss it?

Still, no matter how much I might have confided to my old schoolmate on that crosstown encounter decades ago, I know I would have been incapable in those years of formulating the deeper, more elusive answer that her poignant, baffled plea— "How did you get *into* it?"—deserved.

I THINK NOW THAT EVERY FAMILY HAS ITS SIGNIFICANT MYTHS, ITS AG- glomerations of told and retold stories, memories, and experiences, and that these myths, even as they may diverge from literal truth or documentable historical facts, lay out a felt but invisible path, a subterranean template that defines and sometimes even determines, if you will, a kind of barely traceable spiritual DNA. Because these myths are the very air we breathe in childhood, we tend to take them for granted, to be a little bored with them— they can seem foolish, even embarrassing—so that it becomes impossible for us to recognize what makes them, after all, our *own,* unique or remarkable. Perhaps it is only later, with life's perplexing turns and middle age's apprehension of the shocking flight of time, that they come back to us in new and sharpened focus.

In my own family, I might have told Mara, the formative myths arose from the very different life stories of two of my great-grandfathers. I call them the Tale of the Great Rabbi and the Tale of the Simple Jew.

THE TALE OF THE GREAT RABBI

USUALLY STORIES ABOUT GREAT RABBIS—AND NEARLY EVERY JEWISH FAMILY has one, somewhere—center on their singular wisdom and prodigious learning. Not so for my mother's grandfather Rabbi Jacob Meir of Minsk: in his case, the family stories were about his austere, remote, otherworldly aspect and character, and his countless (if sometimes highly peculiar) good deeds. This improbable combination—*Twilight Zone* manner and one-man social-service-agency activity—is said to have inspired awe in the surrounding *gubernya,* or district, and to have led some, Jews and Gentiles alike, to attribute to him nearly magical powers, though he was most definitely *not* a "wonder" rabbi, *not* a Hasid. "Reb Jacob Meir of Minsk, a saintly *Mitnaged*" (or anti-Hasid), is how he is characterized by Zalman Shazar, Israel's third president, in his autobiography, *Morning Stars.* How Shazar in particular came to regard him as saintly is something I'll return to, but first let me provide a taste of the stories I grew up on.

Before the Sabbath—every Sabbath—Rabbi Jacob Meir would not only empty out the pockets of his coat in order to give whatever money he had to the needy, but he would actually also give away his coat. When the members of his congregation remonstrated with him about this highly idiosyncratic practice, he would say only, "God will provide." But clearly it was those same congregants who would each time be obliged to provide, and though this exemplary story would always, in childhood, fill me with a terrible frisson—how reckless and unnatural to give away your brand-new coat!—it is apparent to me now that my great-grandfather's famously remote gaze harbored a surprising shrewdness. However his congregation might guiltily begrudge its numerous coatless poor, it could hardly deny its own rabbi.

But here is a more substantial story. Scattered throughout the *gubernya* of Minsk were children known as Rabbi Jacob Meir's *mamzerim,* bastards. Who were they? When a woman had a baby she knew she could not keep—in telling this story, my mother, mindful of my sheltered, childish ears, would always suggest extreme poverty as the reason for the woman's dilemma (though she sometimes darkly murmured, "Or who knows?")—the anguished new mother would bring the baby to my great-grandfather's house. He became godfather to these infants, each of whom he would place with a family in one or another of the surrounding shtetls. The given-away children would bear the last names of the families who raised them, but to each distraught birth mother my great-grandfather pledged that he would personally watch over the education and development of her child, that he would always consider himself to be bonded with that child—to remain forever as a special presence. And these were not mere empty consolatory words: my grandmother grew up knowing some of these children and regarded them as semi-cousins.

In one instance, the dynamic of this special relationship was to take a dramatic twist. In the turbulent early days of the new Bolshevik government, a nephew of my great-grandfather's, a pharmacist, was arrested and thrown in jail for "economic crimes"—I suppose he had his own little store, and as such was regarded as a bourgeois parasite. His prospects looked exceedingly grim until my great-grandfather thought to seek the help of one of his *mamzerim,* who had grown up to become first a fervent revolutionary and then, rising very quickly, a local commissar. The newly minted commissar sprung the hapless pharmacist and hurriedly arranged for him and his young family to get to Warsaw, where they could take up a new life. (But in the twentieth century, too many Jewish stories did not have happy endings. So, lucky once, but only once: the Warsaw pharmacist and his family were to perish during World War II in the Warsaw Ghetto.)

Perhaps the strangest, most legend-like story I heard in childhood about this great-grandfather refers back to czarist times, when an extremely onerous tax on kosher meat was levied against the Jewish community. So burdensome was its effect that my great-grandfather went to the local official to plead that it be rescinded. Denying him even the most minimal courtesy, the official peremptorily refused. The next day, that man's young son fell ill—so ill that it appeared the boy would die. At this, the father became convinced that his harsh dealings with the Jews and specifically with Jacob Meir were the cause of his misfortune. The official rescinded the tax; his child recovered; and from then on, rumors began to spread among the local peasantry about Rabbi Jacob Meir's powers.

But what did my great-grandfather himself regard as the most important undertaking of his life? The curious answer to this question I learned only from reading Shazar's memoir. It was Jacob Meir's firm belief that the Geulah, the long-awaited redemption of the Jews, could never come about as long as there was a chance that the holy name of God might be "trodden underfoot . . . whenever a page of an ordinary siddur [prayer book] or *chumash* [Pentateuch] fell on the floor." What did he do? Writes Shazar: "Very carefully . . . he had [typeset] pages of a siddur where the letters of the Name were scattered and printed on a slant, so that even if the page became loose and dropped out there would be no desecration."

To raise money for the printing of these special volumes, Rabbi Jacob Meir went from shtetl to shtetl, escorted to the homes of the wealthy by local heder (religious primary school) boys who were judged capable of appreciating the significance of his mission. And that is how a very young Zalman Shazar came to encounter my great-grandfather, and ultimately, to offer the only physical description of him that I know: "a tall, thin old man wearing a black velvet hat and a long robe that reached to the top of his shoes; he walked along with me, splashing in the mud, while his lean, yellowish hand shielded his eyes to keep him from looking at that forbidden sight—a woman."

Now, there is no way, today, that you can look over a photocopied page from that bizarrely set siddur, as I did only recently—a giddy, nearly expressionistic swirl of Hebrew letters swooning before your eyes like the guilty, fevered visions of a dying, errant Jew—without immediately acceding to the darkest suspicions about at least one thread in the psychic component of your own genetic makeup. How, then, can a rational contemporary mind make sense of so deeply premodern a preoccupation? For myself, I have reached the conclusion that to my great-grandfather, the world-to-come was at least as real as the muddy roads he splashed through daily. He believed absolutely what he read every Sabbath in the rabbinic treatise *Ethics of the Fathers:* "This world is a vestibule before the world-to-come; prepare yourself in the vestibule so that you may enter the banquet hall."

So totally did he believe this that when his daughter, my great-aunt, decided she wanted to go to medical school in Moscow, it never dawned on him to forbid or discourage her, even though the only way a Jewish girl could get the requisite identity permit to live in Moscow was by allowing herself to be declared a prostitute. What difference could it make to Rabbi Jacob Meir: What was all this anyway but the vestibule? When his outraged *balabatim,* his money men, stormed to his door to protest such a shocking prospect—*their* rabbi's daughter, bearing the papers of a prostitute?—and even threatened to fire him if he did not change his mind, he gave them this reply: "She will go to Moscow; she will become a doctor; she will serve her people." And she did just that, my stern-faced great-aunt. She left Russia for Palestine to become the doctor for a company of pioneers who were draining the swamps of the Huleh Valley.

At his death, the family story had it, Jacob Meir was given a state funeral by the local Soviet government, and was hailed as "the rabbi of the people," ostensibly because of his lifelong devotion to the welfare of the poor. And although this was true—and although it was also true that, contrary to the usual rabbinic practice, he had never accepted money for resolving ritual disputes—the family myth held that the real reason for his state funeral lay in the profound superstition of the local peasant populace and their age-old fear of offending the spirit of the powerful dead.

THE TALE OF THE SIMPLE JEW

THERE ARE NO LITERARY ACCOUNTS OF MY *FATHER'S* GRANDFATHER. IN fact I do not even know his first name, though my guess is that it would have been Joseph—Yosef, Yussl—since that was the name of my own father's eldest brother, my grandfather's firstborn son. What I do know was that his last name, my original family name, was not Kaplan. Was this change in our family name the peremptory doing of some ignorant Ellis Island immigration clerk? Far from it: my great-grandfather never came close to leaving Russia. His story is much darker. His entire life's trajectory was defined by a particularly horrific episode of child persecution in Russian Jewish history that is not particularly well known. My great-grandfather was a cantonist.

This strange-sounding designation—it names a devil's detour from childhood, not a religious or political splinter group—was the brainstorm of Czar Nicholas I, who, like a latter-day Haman, had conceived a specific plan to rid his realm of Jews. This was the so-called Plan of the Thirds, according to which one-third of Russian Jewry would be compelled to emigrate, one-third would die of starvation, and one-third would be forcibly converted to Christianity. It was in brutal pursuit of that last third that my great-grandfather's fate was sealed.

At the age of seven, he was ripped from his family in a Lithuanian shtetl, swooped away from his birthright life among Jews, kidnapped by the dreaded *khapers*—snatchers—and transported, along with other seized, impoverished little heder boys like himself, to a remote, frigid outpost of the Russian empire. Officially, all these captured, terrorized, often ailing small boys, abruptly torn from their mothers' arms and thrust into stiff soldiers' overcoats, were made lifetime conscripts in the czar's army, and in that guise were housed in army barracks called cantonments (hence "cantonists"). In those dismal precincts, they were subjected to the harshest military discipline and relentlessly tortured to give up every vestige of their Jewish lives—robbed of their ritual fringed garments, forbidden to pray, prohibited from speaking Yiddish, and, finally, the true goal, forced to perform the rituals of the Russian Orthodox Church. These were small children, after all. How hard could it have been? Any who resisted were starved till they acquiesced or died.

So, though this was never part of the family myth, to me it is clear, from my reading, that my great-grandfather must at some point have submitted to baptism. What *was* told to me was that from the age of seven, he had spent his entire childhood on a frozen, isolated waste of a farm in Siberia, in servitude to a peasant family that required him to do their foulest, filthiest, most backbreaking work. And here the *Enyclopedia Judaica* confirms the family account: "The cantonists were sometimes sent to Russian farmsteads in remote villages where they performed exhausting labor and were forced to change their faith." In other words, he was a slave—an isolated, forcibly baptized, brutalized child slave.

But maybe, just maybe, that harrowing reality was something he could in some inchoate sense recognize—even hang on to—as a measure of spiritual resistance. After all, it had happened before: *avadim hayinu,* "We were slaves unto Pharaoh in Egypt." Through all those lonely years, did he retain—could he have retained—from some dim corner of another life, the memory of a seder table? Or was it perhaps the hazy echo of a buzzing heder bench where he'd studied the Book of Exodus?

"We were slaves unto Pharaoh in Egypt. And the Lord delivered us from there with a mighty hand and an outstretched arm." Because something, surely, did sustain him. Through years of howling Arctic blasts and blinding blizzards, he remained a stubborn, solitary child Marrano—and one who was denied even the Marrano's small solace of occasionally glimpsed secret brothers somewhere in his environs.

At the age of eighteen, eleven years after his first kidnapping, he began his mandatory twenty-five years of duty in the czar's regular army. He was forty-three, then, when he was finally released, his sole, unlikely possession in the world a plot of land in Siberia, given him in return for his service to the czar. After thirty-six years, at last delivered into freedom, what could he have been by that time but an odd, remote, rough, uncommunicative man? Decades of military rigors, numberless privations, involuntary servitude, and confused, hidden identity had ensured that he had missed just about every ratified stage of normal human development. Yet out of that prolonged nightmare half-life at the ends of the empire, he made his way back to the shtetl of his birth in Kovno Gubernya, there to request a bride.

And who could she have been, my great-grandmother, but a penniless orphan girl, utterly without prospects, to have accepted a match with a strange, hardened old soldier who barely spoke Yiddish, who had had no bar mitzvah, known no calendar of Sabbaths, fast days, and festivals, let alone any ordinary family tenderness or communal nurture? Who else could she have been to find herself under the huppah, tearily bedecked, circling seven times around a groom who would promptly take her off to, of all places, Siberia?

But in Kayinsk, Siberia, there was, as it turned out, a small community of other released cantonists who had retained their Jewishness—enough for a prayer quorum, enough to form a tiny

congregation, the Soldatski Synagog. There, in remote Kayinsk—
a place so cold that a party of determined visiting cousins were
discovered frozen to death in nearby woods en route—my own
grandfather was born and did become bar mitzvah. And when,
as a young man, this grandfather of mine set off on his own long-
planned journey from Kayinsk, Siberia, to New York harbor,
ship's passage clasped hard in hand, he, too, traveled first to his
father's birthplace in Kovno Gubernya, there, hurriedly, to gain
a bride: my grandmother, the undowered orphan daughter of an
itinerant coopersmith.

And the name? Well, in fact, Kaplan was the name of a rich
Jewish boy—a boy whose father's resources had ransomed him
out of the dreaded schoolboy conscription. Was he perhaps the
pink-cheeked pampered son of a grain merchant, the honey-
licking firstborn of a timber dealer? I'll never know. I only know
that shoved in under the name Kaplan in his stead was my luck-
less, destitute great-grandfather.

Still, I had always assumed—it was the family myth—that
Kaplan's bribe had been paid to the czarist officials. Not so: on
this point, the *Enyclopedia Judaica* provides a highly disturbing
correction. It was the Jewish communal authority, the kehillah,
that was compelled to furnish the quota of conscript heder
boys; it was the kehillah that made up the list, and a member
of the kehillah, a Jew, who would have accepted the bribe, and
consigned a helpless, expendable child into the pit of oblivion.
A little uncanny, then, that my great-grandfather should have
been named Joseph. Like that Joseph in the Book of Genesis—
the Joseph whose story is the prelude to the Passover saga of
redemption—he, too, had been bundled into slavery by his own
brothers, his own people.

But they *were* his people still. That he never forgot this, but
clung to it with all his might to survive and prevail as a Jew

against the grimmest of odds—in itself an amazement—is surely the luminous lesson of his haunting, impenetrable life.

THESE DAYS WHEN I THINK ABOUT THE TWO DISPARATE FAMILY MYTHS THAT made up the household hum of my childhood, I am struck by their odd, asymmetric link. I am the great-granddaughter at once of an eccentric, lofty-minded rabbi who rescued abandoned children and of a desolate, kidnapped child conscript whom no one in his community ever made the smallest attempt to save. How could I not, then, as a writer, be drawn to the paradoxes and disruptions that stumble through generations of Jewish families' lives? How could I not be preoccupied, in my fiction, with the terrible deforming power of history's privations when I know that its remnant anachronistic tendrils are still so alive within me?

As a child, I read Jewish history with the rapt reader's out-of-body removal that only in adolescence would I begin wholly to derive from fiction. And this is not surprising. I knew early on (but at best in an inchoate way) from my own family's life and all those curiously instructing undulations of my upbringing that the past, and with it, the force of external events not only shapes the arc of lives, but also infiltrates even the most private spaces of the imagination. Yet I knew and I didn't know at the same time. Both a chapter in a children's Jewish history book about the Mortara case (the nineteenth-century Italian Jewish boy baptized by his Catholic governess and taken away from his family) and equally then, a library-discovered children's story about a girl on the American frontier kidnapped and raised by Indians—each of these drew me in with a sickened lingering fascination. So I was captivated by stories of captives, though I did not even remotely intuit the lurking family source.

A storytelling family, a story-*laden* family, the whole strange whirl of lives I could observe around me—relatives, neighbors, strangers, even, and beneath that surface, the enigmatic trudge of all those oddly clothed antecedents who leaned in so vividly from the past—all that overheard bustle gave me a sense of the phantom quickenings of stories, of characters always already *present,* always already streaming, waiting maybe, somewhere above the TV aerials, in the ether. I wanted to catch hold of these phantom stories, these phantom characters—to write them down. And now when I write fiction, I think of history as an implicit presence—in a way akin to the world of dreams: perhaps not always clearly recognized, yet undeniable, a ground bass in people's ordinary, surprising day-to-day lives.

Still, linked forever to that unquiet sense of history is the hovering imperative I gleaned as a child: the primacy of peoplehood. If, as the Talmud tells us, all Jews are responsible for one another, then isn't this my larger, latent, hidden family—my *nistar* family, call it? And that vast *nistar* family—though at times flying under the radar, and always so far-flung—is at least as generous with its anguish, arguments, exasperations, but also nourishments as the small one I grew up in. So even though I cannot, with my rabbi great-grandfather, negotiate the day-to-day world as if it were a mere waiting room for the Redemption, I am sufficiently inhabited by both family tales to cling, with bemused intensity, and under conditions of American ease my cantonist great-grandfather could never have begun to apprehend, to a complicated, vexing people. Somewhere, among their ancient, unlikely dreams and far-fetched adventures toward fulfillment, lies my own ineluctable walk-on in a drama of catastrophe and renewal any imaginative writer would be hard put to equal.

FAMILY OBLIGATIONS

———

*My great-grandfather, a rabbi in Minsk, was remembered
even many years after his death, for his startling
unwordliness. He had two daughters. One immigrated to the
United States with her husband and children, and was my
grandmother, so her life is familiar to me, not mysterious. But
his younger daughter, my great-aunt whom I didn't know,
became a doctor and ultimately went to Palestine; her first
job in Russia was as a medical officer to the Red Army during
the 1919 to 1920 civil war. This is the same campaign
in which Isaac Babel served as a war correspondent. K. Lyutov
was the name Babel used when he wrote for a Tbilisi
newspaper, and the name he gave to the central character in
"Red Cavalry."*

—FROM *A TRAIN AT THE FRONT* BY K. LYUTOV
(SPECIAL CORRESPONDENT FOR *RED DAWN*)

Do you wonder ever, my comrades, my countrymen, how our revolution still only an infant, a tiny, bright-eyed nursling, has already brought about such an explosion in the hearts of all those who hear its lusty cry? Just now, outside the windows of this train which serves with the campaign of General Budenny, a silent, scouting dawn mist is slipping over ruined Polish towns and blown-up bridges. The dawn itself, blue and ghostly, settles around our carriage like an old peasant granny's shawl, and I decide to put my question to our doctor. I must hurry with my question, I know, for soon when the sun is up, as hard and yellow as these dusty fields of rye and buckwheat, the wagons of the sick and wounded will begin arriving, and our comrade doctor will have no time for the likes of me.

"Comrade doctor, dear comrade doctor," I begin, but I see that in the milky light of dawn she is at last snatching a little sleep. Her hair, always so sternly coiled around her head with net and pins has fallen onto her shoulders in all its deep, brown, satin solemnity. She has the primeval forest hair of so many sturdy provincial Jewish daughters; but her wrists, curling out of the stiff sleeves of her uniform, are tiny, slender as leaf-stems. If she were at home now, so wide-browed and dreaming, she would be a dutiful wife with a wig, for our frowning comrade doctor is the daughter of a rabbi in Byelorussia! So, is her presence on our train an answer to my question, or does it, in the fashion of the swaying Polish Talmudists, whose miserable villages we travel through, merely answer a question with a question?

We pass a narrow, mucky stream, a shrine charred by artillery fire, and now, just as we approach the edge of a small birch woods, here comes one-armed Pawelko who rides with the engineer, to tell the doctor that the first aid wagons have been spotted.

"Comrade doctor! Miss doctor! They're here!" he cries in the hoarse, powerful voice which can summon wild, straying ponies throughout the entire breadth of the steppe.

The startled doctor, her eyes only half-open, foggily takes in the amputee's flushed, sweating face and glittering eyes. "Typhus. Typhus. All of them," she mutters in a parched, despairing whisper. Her face is chalky from sleepiness, but already, tilting her head to the side, she has begun gathering up the hairpins from the dark, downy nape of her neck.

I know where there is still a kettle of weak tea to be had, so I say, "Comrade doctor, dear, I'll bring you some tea while you make your toilette. I know how it is for girls from strict Jewish families. You must have a long time." But she has none of the teasing, graceful languor of our wide-hipped girls of the South.

"Maybe that's how it was done in Odessa," she says, looking past me with distant, rebuking eyes. "But not in my family. Not where I come from."

Once, in the flickering light of Sabbath candles, our comrade doctor learned: "This world is a vestibule before the world-to-come; prepare yourself in the vestibule, so that you may enter the banquet hall." And if those shuddering, golden Sabbath eves seem far away and she no longer believes in the banquet hall, there is one part of the ancient, wine-blessed lesson which has stayed with her. "This world is a vestibule," her distant eyes proclaim, as she bends over caved-in, bloody skulls and limbless torsos in the burning early sun, "only the vestibule." In nearby oaks, birds of prey hover over the summer meadow littered now with maimed bodies and dead horses; and in the distance, as the dust rises in the shimmering heat, a rosy, crenellated castle looms blindly above the carnage like a hallucination of lordly, medieval Europe.

Much later in the day, the doctor and I make our way into the little town that lies huddled at the base of the nobleman's castle. The sun is still blazing above us, enthroned in the harsh, white sky like a maddened, aging pharaoh, but the town itself, with its narrow, curving streets and wretched, muddy houses, is sunk in the sunless depths of gloomy Jewish centuries. Generations of haggard, black-coated rabbis with yellowing beards have raised their voices in phlegmy disputation all along these rutted lanes, but right now, in the crazing midsummer heat, there is no sign of squabbling life. Only a few ragged, emaciated little boys with side curls peer up at us; and at the edge of a small, chewed-up pasture, a tall, gaunt Pole pulls a coppery calf through the dust.

The doctor and I are longing for a glass of tea, so we stop at a house where some of our cavalry troops are billeted. In the bare, stony yard, a burly, bare-chested Cossack is currying the tired horses; his scimitar gleams beside him on the ground. I call out a greeting to our comrade cavalryman, but his splendid, massive frame is bent over a steppe pony's lean, cinnamon-colored flanks, and he doesn't answer. Finally, as we approach the door, his voice rumbles toward us. "You'll get nothing here, Comrade Four-eyes. These lousy Jews are hoarders."

Inside, there is a stench of rotted, moldering onions, and in the sweltering gloom—a blackness as arid and airless as the last night on earth—it is impossible at first to make out more than lifeless, crouching forms. There are only women and children in this room; their clothes are in tatters, and they sit or lie in a sour, stuporous remove amid filthy pots and broken crockery. Fat flies drone about the disorder, and outside, in the yard, the cavalryman begins singing with tuneless vigor about a legendary Cossack horseman who can kill with any weapon. "Now he grabs his saber and lunges at the foe," the cavalryman sings. "The icy winds whip past as he fiercely strikes a blow."

In slow, simple Russian, I attempt to explain who we are, but there is no response. The doctor steps forward and begins speaking in Yiddish. Before she can even finish a sentence, a woman springs out of the dim chaos, and in an enraged howl, assails us with an anguished, rancorous harangue. First the Poles rampaged through the Jewish quarter as soon as they learned the Red Army was about to overtake the town, she says, and now that the Red Army has actually arrived, these Cossack soldiers have forced her to cook their foul meat in her pots, and on the Sabbath. "And today is the Sabbath!" she repeats with such bitter force that a chorus of wailing fills the choking, fetid space. A baby cries, and a small boy with a pinched, scab-marked face approaches us saying, "The Poles cut off my father's beard. They made his face bloody."

"He's had nothing to eat, you see," a sallow, unkempt young woman says as she stumbles toward the boy, and cradles his head. One of her eyes is clouded by a milky, iridescent film, and in a shrill whine she repeats, "We have no food. Nothing. Not even for the children."

The first woman, still loudly complaining about her defiled pots, brings us some tea made of carrot scrapings; she is so inflamed with anger that her reddened cheeks look bruised. The doctor inclines her head and thanks the woman of the household with ceremonious gravity, but she sets the steaming glass down beside her on the earthen floor. In her clinic in Moscow, they have signs in huge letters saying CHILDREN ARE THE FLOWERS OF OUR NEW LIFE, but right now, in a backward Jewish village in eastern Poland, she is standing over a bed where there is a small, starved-looking girl with wild, dark hair and a remote, listless expression. She has clapped her hands and snapped her fingers behind the child's ears several times with no response, and now, turning to the ruddy-faced woman, she asks in a stern, formal tone, "How long has this child been sick? Was she able to hear before her illness?" The woman shrugs. At Passover time, she says, all the children were sick; this girl's twin sister died, and she herself just didn't get better.

Our comrade doctor's sister, whom she hasn't seen for years, lives with her husband and children in a Polish village, perhaps like this one, but in western Poland, between the Vistula and the German border. She has never been to her sister's house, and has not even seen most of her nieces and nephews. Perhaps that's why she makes her way through this squalid, airless room with the dazed, intent gait of a sleepwalker. At the baby's cradle she stops. A brigade of flies is lazily roaming over the infant's sweaty, emaciated body, and above his head, a worn printed sign says LILITH! KEEP AWAY FROM THIS CRADLE! The doctor says nothing, but she stands there staring with such transfixed ferocity that the bewildered young mother finally calls out, "I couldn't *get* the lucky cradle. I tried, but the baker's wife already asked for it before me."

Outside, as we leave the blighted household, the hot, adamant sun is finally waning. Soon, beneath its deepening, dissolute violet glow, the men will return home from synagogue, the Sabbath ended.

"You see how it is," the towheaded Cossack bellows from the yard as we walk off. "These lousy Jews don't want to help the Red Army. It's only the Jews who behave this way."

At night, in our darkened train, the moonlight casts long, white shadows across the scorched Polish fields, they gleam like far-off snowy trails in the sweltering stillness. From the next carriage, we can hear the plaintive nasal strains of a harmonica playing a Cossack lullaby. It is a melancholy tune, a song of evening yearning, and soon in a straggling, mournful chorus the soldiers raise their tired voices.

> *The river flows back to its home in the sea*
> *The wind whistles back to its home in the hills*
> *The sun sinks back to its home 'neath the clouds*
> *Now the first shining star lights a path home for me*

Our comrade doctor has already noticed the first shining star. For the light of this star in the evening sky marks the end of the Sabbath—in her father's household, a time of such sudden, empty sadness that even now, on this train, as the fragrant, billowing Sabbath flies off into the lowering night sky, she feels bereft, immured once again in the dreadful, nerveless desolation of her first remembered grief.

At the close of the day of rest,
O grant relief to thy people;
Send Elijah to the distressed,
That grief and sighs may flee away.

The doctor closes her eyes. In her father's house, in the forlorn dusk of the Sabbath's departure, they sat in the chilly, spice box–scented gloom singing the ancient entreaty to the prophet Elijah. "O swiftly and in our own day," they sang, pleading each week in the clove-traced darkness that he hurry his return. Now, in our rank, airless train, the doctor suddenly seems to smell that quickening aromatic scent of cloves, and pressing her face against the window, she can no longer find the moonlight illusion of gleaming snowy trails. Instead, as the long, luminous shadows sweep across the fields, she sees in them the bare, primitive glow of wild, wasting sands and stony, thin, silver paths stretching toward an olive grove.

"O swiftly and in our own day": the doctor lights her alcohol lamp, and in the pale flickering of its bluish flame, she hurriedly writes a letter in Yiddish.

My dear sister,

I long to see you again, but I don't know when that will be,
or where, even. I cannot describe to you the unbelievable

misery I've seen in just these past few months, and I finally
realize that your husband and his friends were not so foolish
in their ideas. For us, Russia is still a prison, I am now
convinced. There has to be a place where Jews can have a
real future. When my army duty is over, I am determined
to go to Palestine.

"Excuse me, Comrade Correspondent," the doctor says, tapping me on the shoulder. "But perhaps when you send out your dispatches you might find a way to help me post this letter."

In Palestine, in the 1920s, the rabbi's daughter who became a doctor—not in fact a character in an Isaac Babel story, but my grandmother's wide-browed, single-minded sister—lived, with other young Russian Jews, many of them perhaps like her, in a bare, tent-scattered field in the desolate Huleh Valley. When they looked up into the hills around them, they saw the green and stony terraced slopes where the psalmist had found his help; but when they tried to set their spades into the soft black soil, they found that beneath their sandalled feet, it was all swampland. What did it matter? They were all of them rapt with the ardor of self-denial; they knew they were in the vestibule before the world-to-come. Still, the swamp bred diseases. So the rabbi's daughter treated her comrades for malaria and tuberculosis; feverish, they longed to wake up once again in the early morning mists, to set out water jug in hand, hoe and shovel against the shoulder, to fill the spongy, untilled fields with eucalyptus seedlings. They sang:

Dress me, Mother, in a striped shirt of splendor
And at the break of dawn
Lead me to work.

Their mothers were thousands of miles away in the impoverished Jewish villages of Eastern Europe; the splendor of their shirts shone only in the renunciant light of their own eyes. But work! No one had to lead them. The rabbi's daughter got up at dawn to drink one cup of tea, while in the field all around her the small, flapping tents bobbed like toy sailboats on a vast, black, brackish sea. If she ever felt lonely or frightened, what did it matter? After all, it was only the vestibule.

In the late 1940s, the rabbi's daughter, my great-aunt, by then a woman over sixty, came to America on a six-month clinical exchange program. She had spent her entire working life in a medical backwater, but now since her country was hastily absorbing vast numbers of refugee children—orphans from the war in Europe, and large, impoverished families from North Africa and the Middle East, she was suddenly in a hurry to learn what she could from American medical advances. The hospital she was working at was in upper Manhattan, just below the black-grid bridge and rocky outcroppings of Spuyten Duyvil, so she stayed with a niece who lived a bus ride away—across the oily, barge-lined Harlem River, among the humpty-dumpty hills and wandering, oddly angled streets of the leafy northwest Bronx. On scattered empty lots and in the gardens of their private houses, the Italians of the neighborhood grew tomato plants, grapevines, and occasional fig trees; above the high ocher banks of the large municipal reservoir, straying gulls from the rank Harlem River continuously circled and called, as if this trim store of fenced-in city water was merely the rounded placid inlet of a wide, unknown, eventful ocean. So though the sidewalks were alive with shouting, rope-jumping, ball-playing children and the small, grassy parks hummed summer and winter with the merciless energy of their hard-gossiping mothers, it was not in any way a neighborhood of urban blight.

But the doctor's niece was no longer the lively, rushing, intense-eyed working girl who'd come to visit her Upper Galilee clinic in 1936. She was a married woman with an undistinguished husband, a small, thin, sallow daughter, and a cramped apartment, and she could not believe her life had declined to this. What had she to do with a life where women discussed methods for meat browning, as if these were ideas, or declared themselves partisans of a particular nail polish color, as if this could be construed as an issue of passion? By herself, then, the rabbi's granddaughter—the doctor's niece—my mother stood at the living room window of her small apartment in the northwest Bronx, her eyes (of such a distinctly Oriental cast above the Slavic high cheekbones so common in her family, that even now, occasional news photographs of Japanese women in Western dress startle me with a rending, deceptive, primal familiarity)—her Tatar eyes so filled with tears that even the simple, heart-lifting, blue radiance of the reservoir, like a separate sunny country just beyond the glass, yielded nothing. Her life made as little sense to her as the first English verse she had been set to memorize when she first came from Poland as a girl.

> And moving thro' a mirror clear
> That hangs before her all the year,
> Shadows of the world appear.
> There she sees the highway near
> Winding down to Camelot:
> There the river eddy whirls,
> And there the surly village-churls,
> And the red cloaks of market girls,
> Pass onward from Shalott.

The doctor slept on the living room sofa; she was up early and back late, and saw no shadows. She perceived neither that the apartment was small, nor that her niece was unhappy. As her father had ordained, she was serving her people, and happiness or unhappiness as a personal claim did not come into her field of vision. Often when she returned from work, there would be visitors waiting to see her: cousins, distant relatives, landsleit from Minsk who remembered her father, or complete strangers who had recently found they had refugee cousins in Haifa or long-lost schoolfriends in a Jordan Valley kibbutz. They arrived with gifts, messages, and packages for the doctor to take back for them. They came and went in a steady stream; it was novel but boring. Once, though, on a Saturday afternoon, a gray-faced Israeli bringing a bag of grapes came to see my great-aunt because his young daughter was in a hospital in New York. His American cousin and her red-haired little boy accompanied him for moral support, since he was asking the doctor for an important favor. The gray-faced man had lived in Jerusalem with his wife and children for many years before the war, he said, but his wife had always suffered from terrible bouts of homesickness for her mother and sisters in Poland. Above all, she wanted them to see her children. One summer, overcome again—

"Oh, how I love red hair!" my mother cried out, staring past the fidgety, freckle-faced boy who was playing with his Gene Autry gun and holster set. "How I wanted a red-haired child, a red-haired daughter! . . . When I was single and I lived in Manhattan, my bedroom window looked out on that Quaker school all the way downtown—I can't even think of what the name of it is right now. But almost every morning, just before I left for work, I used to take my coffee cup to the window, and stare and stare at all those beautiful little Quaker girls with their lovely, delicate, clear, sweet faces and their long, fine, shining red and gold hair. How much I wanted a red-haired daughter! . . ."

"*He's* the only redhead in the family," the cowboy's mother said, uneasily stirring in her chair. "And who knows *where* he got it from? . . . My daughter, God bless her, is a brunette. She's just regular, my Rosalie. Like me."

My mother looked away. In one simple turn of phrase— "She's just regular"—the woman had revealed herself utterly.

The gray-faced man resumed in an embarrassed rush. One summer when their daughter was only a few months old, his wife was so overcome with a longing for the sight of her mother's face and the sounds of her sisters' voices that she decided she had to go to Poland, just for a short visit. She took the two older boys with her, but the summer was 1939, and the man never saw his wife or sons again.

"Bang-bang! Bang-bang!" the red-haired boy shouted as he went circling through the living room, dashing around furniture, playing with his toy guns.

"Stop it, Gary!" his mother said. "Stop all the noise and the running this minute! Or else I'm telling you right now—when that tooth on top falls out, the only thing you'll find under the pillow is the mattress! No quarters, no box tops, no ray gun, no nothing!" She shook her head, and turning to my mother, said pleasantly, "I don't know . . . With girls it's so different. With Rosalie it always had to be charms for her charm bracelet. That was the big thing . . . What do you give your daughter when a loose tooth comes out?"

Across the street, the setting sun had so inflamed the top-floor fire escape, that it seemed to be moving off by itself—a separate, stately, orange-glowing ship slowly, slowly listing in a sea of its own brilliant hue.

"What did you get when *your* teeth came out?" the rabbi's granddaughter said finally. "Why would you want to bring up your children with such foolishness?"

The Israeli leaned forward stiffly, his eyes narrowed against the sudden, fierce, late-afternoon summer light. When his wife and sons did not come back, he and his infant daughter moved in with his sister's family. During the siege of Jerusalem, the child once emerged too early from a basement shelter and was hit by flying glass. To repair the injuries, particularly to her face and shoulder, she was now undergoing a series of operations in a hospital in Brooklyn. The doctors were hopeful, but the hospital was very strict about visiting hours: what he wanted my great-aunt to get him was a doctor's coat—any kind of hospital uniform, so that he could stay with his daughter as much as possible, especially when she woke up at night frightened or in pain.

"Bang-bang! Bang-bang!" sang out redheaded Gary to himself as he ran up and down the length of the living room, knocking into an end table. "Bang-bang!" the oblivious child still called out intently, and rounding the bookcase, "Bang-bang!" he shattered a lamp.

"Oh my God, the lamp!" My mother clapped her hand to her mouth and ran out of the room. For how could the rabbi's granddaughter cry at a broken lamp when her white-haired aunt still strode so cleanly through the taunting shadows of the vestibule?

"Don't cry. It's only a lamp. Why are you *crying*?" I said, though only a few weeks before I had been caught out crying over a pair of bright red, blue, and yellow sandals in the window of a shoe store.

"A peasant girl's wedding shoes!" My mother turned away, her Oriental eyes suddenly hooded with contempt, as if with smoke or distance. Above us, the Jerome-Woodlawn train rumbled on toward the bucolic, old-fashioned calm of Woodlawn Cemetery, the end of the line. She said, "When I was young and living in Manhattan, I could always have had the most beautiful, unusual shoes. I didn't earn so much money, but my feet were so small that I could always get sample sizes. *You* won't be able to do that—*you've* had the benefit of American nutrition. I, on the other hand, didn't see an orange or a banana till I was fifteen. And when I saw my first banana, how I laughed! I couldn't imagine what anyone would do with it!"

The trains, braking and squealing overhead, emitted leaping white sparks now and then, and each car drew out as it moved uncanny, disappearing shadow-worlds on awnings and storefronts in the sunless streets beneath the elevated tracks. An oblong lake and some long, low cottages appeared on the awning of a bakery; an endless covered-wagon train roaming across the prairies followed a slow, lurching trail on the window of a lingerie store. This was another thing my mother could never have imagined when she was a child in a small, muddy town in Poland. So I pointed to the brightly colored sandals and taking a deep breath, began, "Tina Kantrowitz has them, Stephanie Margolies has them, Enid Gottschalk has them, Shari Abarbanel has them, Lorraine Del Vecchio has them, Jessica Lapidus *and* her cousin Diane from New Rochelle *both* have them, Bonnie Altschuler has them, Claudia Lubin has them, Rhonda Melnikoff has them, Mindy Feierstein has them—*everybody* has them. Why can't I have them? Not just in our building. Not just in my class. Every single girl in every single first-grade class! *Everyone! Everyone!*"

My mother continued walking toward the steep, slanting subway stairs, her face upraised, in distress, to the elevated tracks overhead.

"Elizabeth Derounian has them," I finally cried in crafty desperation. Because my mother believed that you could perceive in small Elizabeth's olive-skinned face, especially in the precocious solemnity of her deep-set, very liquid, dark eyes, all the terrible suffering borne by the Armenian people, which was similar to, though less than, the sufferings of the Jews. People had already forgotten about what had happened to the Armenians, she said;

give them a few years and they would be happy to forget about the Jews, too.

A downtown express train came rushing by overhead. "Oh God, how is it possible?" she called into the dreadful, acrid, trestle-crossed darkness beneath the hooded platform and trembling tracks. "That I should have a child who would cry over a pair of shoes! How is it possible? How? How can I endure it? What can I have done that God would choose to punish me in this way?"

"Ronnie Brandwein has them," I said sobbing. "Sherry Tabachnik has them, Nina Danziger has them, Michelle Piacentino—"

"Bonnies and Ronnies! Sharis and Sherrys! God Almighty, when will you take pity on me? When will you rescue me? A child who doesn't let me live, doesn't let me breathe! Who sucks the life out of me with shoe reports and the one thousand and one nights tales of the *unheard* of riches of Bonnie Brandwein!"

"It's *Ronnie* Brandwein," I said, still crying. "*Bonnie's* last name is Altschuler."

"And you can see a difference between them, is that what you intend to tell me?" my mother suddenly wheeled around at me. "Maybe you'd even like to tell me that you can see a difference between their mothers! Or maybe you'd prefer it if you *had* one of their mothers! A mother who would make the beds and drink coffee—isn't that what you always come back telling me mothers do in other houses? *They make the beds and they drink coffee.* While you, unfortunate child, are forced to suffer, day in and day out, with a mother who leaves beds unmade and drinks tea! . . . Oh God, when I think back to my young self and remember how much I wanted a daughter! How it was the *only* thing I really wanted in the whole world! When I think of how *sure* I was whenever I looked at your face staring up at me in the carriage, from your crib—how *convinced* I was that if I only, only speak to you honestly, if only I explain things to you as they really are, from my heart, that you would understand. That you would really *understand*. I *know* I saw it in your face then, that understanding. I'm sure of it."

A group of nuns approached, their pinched-in pallor as eerie and disquieting as their long, black habits and remote, secretive sweep. One, at the end of the line, had very pink cheeks just like the little Irish parochial schoolgirls in the playground.

"Look," my mother said, quickly taking a wide step backward, because she was afraid of nuns. But she said again, "Look! At that very young, still-pretty one. My God! A young and pretty woman and she's thrown her life away! It will never come back to her. Never. *Never.*"

The nuns climbed up the subway steps, and my mother turned back to me crying out, "How will I ever explain anything to you if you don't *let* me? You don't *let* me! You *don't,* you *don't!* You *know* you don't! *Please,* Adina! *Please!*" She stared into my face pleading, and the echo of her fervor rent the air. "Listen to me! . . . It doesn't *matter* what Bonnie Brandwein has! It doesn't *matter* what Shari Altschuler has! Such things can *never* matter. Not to you. Not to me and not to you. These things are of no importance in life. *None.* Only for the Bonnies and Ronnies of this world. Because all they are is foolishness, silliness. That's all they can ever be. You can't *want* things like that. You *mustn't.* How can you ask life to bring you foolish things? It's *impossible.* Do you understand what I mean? Do you see what I'm telling you? *Do* you? *Do* you?"

"Yes," I said, twisting in her grasp, grateful suddenly for the thundering trains which continued going uptown and downtown, on to Yankee Stadium or Woodlawn Cemetery, oblivious and persevering. So I darted ahead, saying, "Yes," and two weeks later, in the wake of the shattered lamp, I followed my mother into the kitchen, whispering, "It's only a lamp, Ma. Why are you *crying?*"

She raised her head from the kitchen table, still weeping. "Don't you *understand*? Don't you *realize*? It's the one good thing I had in this house. It's the only good thing I had."

The doctor, my mother's aunt, white-haired now but as obstinate as in her youth, did not look at it that way. When her many American relatives pressed her to tell them what she wanted now that she was returning home, at first she looked around at them bewildered. Finally, she pointed to the toweling dispenser above the sink in her niece's kitchen—*that* was what she wanted! If only her clinic could have *paper* towels like those—so that patients would not all have to use the same cloth communal towel. If only her clinic could have a wonderful thing like that! For a minute, the room was silent. These relatives were not rich; they were not generous, nor were they lighthearted, gift-giving people. Still, there was no one sitting around that kitchen table—with its bowls of fruit and cups of tea—no one who would not have immediately rushed out to the nearest hardware store and bought the doctor a toweling dispenser. But paper towels were not available then in Israel. So the rabbi's daughter, just as arrogantly self-denying, as naively self-contained as she'd been as a girl, was merely making it clear that she wanted nothing.

In the 1960s, a popular song in Israel asked:

> *Where are they, those lovely young girls of our pioneering*
> *   days*
> *With their long, single braids and their Russian tunics*
> *Why don't we have girls like them anymore?*

Can it be that the rabbi's daughter—that remote, austere, forbidding-looking woman might once have been one of the girls the song writer had in mind? My mother's stocky, slow-walking aunt whose short, thick, straight white hair was combed directly back from a face so stern, so without playfulness that when she came into a room I slunk away from her? Once, though, not long before she was preparing to go home, she called me over to her. I had just taken a bath, and in the thrall of its odd, high, pure ecstatic energy, I ran into the living room draped in a towel.

"Come here, Adina!" my great-aunt suddenly called out from the sofa, holding out her arms. "Come over here! To me!" I must have had then the flushed, radiant, wild-haired abandon of all small children emerged from a bath. She said, "Come . . . Let me show you how my little Arab patients look when they come to see me." And taking the striped towel that was meant to dry my hair, she wound it around my head so that it made a turban.

"Look, Ma!" I shouted, bounding into the kitchen where my mother was peeling potatoes. "Look what the *Tanteh* did! She fixed up a towel so I look like a girl from the Bible!"

"*Why* must you say such foolish things? *Why?*" my mother cried out, her eyes raised toward the ceiling. "You *know* you can only look like yourself. You're old enough to realize that . . ." She dried her hands on her apron and said, "When I was a girl, whenever I read a book, I would walk around for days—*weeks*— thinking I was a character in the book I'd just finished. I would be just like an actress playing it out in my head constantly. *Constantly.* I would change it according to whatever I was doing in my real life, and then simply because it was in my mind all the time, it made my real life seem different . . . When I read *Uncle Tom's Cabin*—I was hardly older than you, I read it in Polish— when I read that book as a child, I just cried and cried and cried. I couldn't stop myself. And sometimes I felt I was Topsy, and sometimes I thought I was Eva. Then, later, when I read *War and Peace,* for months—*months* I was Natasha . . . Ah, Natasha at her name-day party, Natasha at a ball! . . . Can you imagine? I, who had never been anywhere *near* a life like that—never even *seen* a party, outside of books never even *heard* of a ball, that I, in that backward, little, ignorant town, should have walked around imagining myself a Russian princess?"

"Oh, yes," I said, swept off as always into my mother's stories by the force of her bitter passion. "Like Cinderella."

"No, *not* like Cinderella! Oh my God! How can I endure it?" She turned around to me, saying, "You will *never* be able to read a really worthwhile book. *Never.* Because you'll only get it in English. They don't *teach* foreign languages here. Not really. By the time they start, you're already too old for it to make a difference. And for all I know, they know exactly what they're doing. Who around here ever wants to read anything except the sales pages in the newspaper?"

> She left the web, she left the loom,
> She made three paces thro' the room,
> She saw the water-flower bloom,
> She saw the helmet and the plume,
> She look'd down to Camelot.
> Out flew the web and floated wide;
> The mirror crack'd from side to side;
> "The curse is come upon me!" cried
> The Lady of Shalott.

In the kitchen, my mother, in a teary rage, continued peeling potatoes. I ran back to the living room, and pulling the turban off my head, said to my great-aunt, "Do it again what you did with the towel. Show me how you do it."

She smiled, her wide forehead wrinkling above her rimless glasses, and putting her hand on my shoulder, my great-aunt sat looking up into my face. Abruptly then, withdrawing her hand, she turned me around and rewound the towel. I do not resemble her side of the family at all, so it's certainly true that if she had had a child, it would not have looked like me.

But that may not have been in her mind at all. Maybe she thought of herself as a mother to all the children in the Upper Galilee she had treated and watched grow up; or maybe her early years among families whose lives were so bleak and overburdened had bred in her a distaste for the entire enterprise.

When she died, her pension and small savings were left to several extremely Orthodox charities: from this peculiar list, you could never even have made a guess at the kind of life she had actually led. That whole way of life—with its brusque, earnest, unbending Utopian rigor, had already come to be laughed at by the time she died. But the song that so lovingly recalled the look of girls of her generation—their eager, unadorned, wistful, energetic charm—was at the height of its popularity.

It could be said that when my great-aunt died, her few possessions legitimately carted away by some long-bearded, black-coated charity collector—a total stranger—there was nothing of her remaining on earth. But when I wash my hair and wrap it turban-style in a towel, this everyday routine still retains for me the private aura of ritual. It reminds me each time within the frame of my familiar face that you do not necessarily only look like yourself. But that is not something any of the rabbi's descendants would have wished to teach me.

For on the humid, late August Sunday afternoon before I left for college, when my grandmother, with her prideful indifference to the ordinary things of this world, the vestibule, put a tealess teacup in front of me, and said, "Always remember who you *are*," she meant also: *And who you are not*—the whole tumbling, desiring, heedless, insensate world. But I knew this already. I knew who I was not. And it made me an envious, gullible spy in the world of ordinary desires.